DEFY

DEFY

SARA B. LARSON

SCHOLASTIC PRESS
New York

3/14

Library of Congress Cataloging-in-Publication Data

Larson, Sara B.

Defy / by Sara B. Larson. — 1st ed.

pages cm

Summary: Seventeen-year-old Alexa's parents were killed by a sorcerer during a
raid, so she has disguised herself as a boy, joined Antion's army, and earned a place
on Prince Damian's guard — but Antion is ruled by an evil king, and "Alex" must
find a way to defeat him and protect her prince.

ISBN 978-0-545-59758-6 (jacketed hardcover) 1. Identity (Psychology) —
Juvenile fiction. 2. Magic — Juvenile fiction. 3. Princes — Juvenile fiction.
4. Conspiracies — Juvenile fiction. 5. Adventure stories. [1. Identity — Fiction.
2. Magic — Fiction. 3. Princes — Fiction. 4. Conspiracies — Fiction.
5. Adventure and adventurers — Fiction.] I. Title.

PZ7.L323953Def 2014

813.6 — dc23

2013011011

10 9 8 7 6 5 4 3 2 1   14 15 16 17 18

Printed in the U.S.A.   23

First edition, January 2014

The text type was set in ITC Galliard.

The display type was set in Kennerly HSC.

Book design by Abby Kuperstock

To Trav, who has always believed in the beauty of my dreams

In loving memory of Josh Lloyd — gone from sight,
but never from our hearts

before

THE CRACKLE AND hiss of the flames devouring our house couldn't block out the screaming and wailing of those who were still alive. My friends, the children, and babies. Orphans. Most of the men were dead. For how few of us there were, scattered around what used to be our village, the noise was almost deafening. I stood in the damp mud in front of our home, pressing my hands to my ears, trying to shut out the sounds. My jaw was clenched, but I couldn't stop the tears from welling up and slipping down my cheeks.

"Alexa, hurry!" Marcel grabbed my arm, trying to pull me away. But I yanked out of his grip.

"I can't leave them," I said, still staring at what remained of my mother and father. I did not look at my brother. Nor at the flames engulfing our home. Nor at the backs of the retreating enemy. Not even at the king's army, which had become visible on the horizon. It had materialized too late from the depths of the jungle that wrapped around our village, finally scaring off the Blevonese soldiers, but not before their sorcerer had done *this*.

"Alexa." Marcel's voice was more urgent as he reached up and turned my face to his, forcing my eyes away from the two bodies. But I couldn't see him, not really. The image of my parents lying broken, charred on the ground in front of us, was burned onto my retinas. Onto my memory. The sorcerer had been no match for Papa's fighting skills — but no one was a match for the unholy fire the sorcerer had used against him and Mama.

I shuddered as I remembered the feel of magic in the air when the sorcerer killed them both, a stream of fire bursting from his hands.

The smell of burned flesh and the sight of them lying there were too much. I dropped to my knees and vomited into the thick undergrowth that never stopped trying to reclaim the ground we'd built our home on.

Papa made us promise to hide when we saw the soldiers from Blevon heading for our village. But then he and Mama were slain — and I had done nothing to stop it.

"The army's coming, Alexa. We have to do it now." Marcel knelt down and held my hair back for me as I wiped my mouth on my sleeve, my stomach still heaving. "If they see me cutting your hair, they'll take you . . . they'll force you into the breeding house."

I looked up at him, fear hitting me square in the chest. His hazel eyes, mirror images of my own, were bleak.

I glanced toward the winding trail that led to the jungle, which would take us to Tubatse, to King Hector's palace. And his breeding house. The army was getting closer. Too close.

"Maybe if I show them how well I fight, they'll let me join the army instead?" The panic in my voice was matched by the desperate pounding of my heart.

Marcel shook his head. The wind turned, and the smoke blew into our faces for a moment, burning my nose and obscuring

Marcel from view. His hand tightened around my hair, which he still held back from my face.

"Fine," I said. "Let's do it. Hurry," I added, spitting into the dirt one last time, trying to get rid of the bitter taste in my mouth. My knees were still weak when I stood up. Marcel grabbed the shears he'd managed to save before the fire grew too large, and moved to stand behind me.

When the blades bit through my hair and the first long, dark strands landed on the ground at my feet, I had to choke back a sob. It was stupid and vain, but my hair was the one feature that had truly been *mine*. Looking so similar to my twin brother had been fun as a child, but as we grew older, it became irritating. My jaw was too square, I was too tall, I hadn't even managed to grow breasts yet. Other than my hair, I could have passed for a boy.

But now the very traits that I'd always been frustrated with would hopefully save me.

When the last lock of hair fell, my head felt lighter, colder, naked. I reached up with trembling fingers, but couldn't make myself touch it.

"How do I look?" My voice wobbled, but I refused to let myself cry again. The army would be here any minute.

"Like me," Marcel said.

Together, we hurried to pick up all the hair and threw it into the flames that were consuming what was left of our cottage. The long strands, years' worth of growth, curled up and burned away in moments. Gone. Like my parents. Like my home. All taken, burned, hewn down, and turned to ash.

⊰ ONE ⊱

now

MARCEL LUNGED AT me, his movement lightning fast. But my block was even faster. Our practice swords collided, sending a jolt up my arm. We'd been sparring for quite a while, but neither of us was ready to back down. I jabbed at him again, but missed a beat when I noticed Prince Damian standing behind the other members of his guard, outside the practice ring, watching us. Marcel took full advantage of my momentary distraction and landed a blow on my shoulder. I grunted, aggravated with myself, but quickly recovered, spinning away from him and Prince Damian's unwavering gaze. The gloating expression on Marcel's face wasn't going to last long. I twisted around in the opposite direction and before he could parry my blow, I hit him in the rib cage.

A killing strike.

Marcel threw his weapon on the dirt, rubbing his ribs with a grimace. My wooden sword would probably give him a bruise, despite the padding we both wore.

"I never should have taught you to hit me," Marcel grumbled as most of our audience whooped and hollered from outside the practice ring.

"I'd hit you again, except I know you aren't serious." I bent down and picked up his sword, daring a peek to see if the prince was still there. He'd come to watch me spar before, but he always seemed to slip away just as I finished a match. Not this time. He still stood there, the sunlight bright on his dark hair. I could have sworn there was admiration on his face — admiration and something else I couldn't name — but when I blinked, it was gone, replaced by his usual sardonic expression.

Prince Damian clapped slowly twice, making a couple of the guards in front of him jump. They spun around quickly, and upon seeing the prince, they immediately straightened to stand at attention.

"An impressive display, Alex, but next time, keep your guard up at all times. It never pays to get distracted," Prince Damian observed. I had to clench my jaw to keep from blushing at the condescension in his voice. Part of me longed to challenge him, to tell him to take a turn and see how long he lasted. Instead, I stiffly tipped my head to him. He looked at me for a moment longer, his gaze inscrutable, and then turned on his heel and strode away.

I stood in the ring, clutching both my and Marcel's swords, my heart pounding with anger.

"Give that to me." Marcel swiped his sword back with a furtive glance at the other members of the prince's personal guard. But they were all still watching the prince, their backs to us. "I don't need you to carry my sword for me."

I blinked as he stormed away. I knew he wasn't really mad. Death was once nothing more than a game to us, back at home, when we were children and we practiced for hours every day with sticks instead of swords. Back when I was still Alexa, instead of Alex, Marcel's twin *brother* and member of Prince Damian's personal guard. He used to get so mad at me for beating him, he wouldn't talk to me for the rest of the day.

Before our parents were killed and death suddenly became so very, very real.

Marcel didn't get angry when I beat him anymore.

"Nice job, Alex. Don't listen to the prince. We all know he couldn't use a sword if his life depended on it." Rylan nodded at me with an approving smile when I walked over to him and the other men who'd been watching.

I laughed, modulating my tone to keep the sound of my amusement low and as unfeminine as possible. I'd been doing it for so long, I didn't even have to think about it anymore. Trying to sound like a boy was natural to me now. "When have I ever cared what the prince thinks? The day I start taking advice about fighting from him will be the day Marcel can finally beat me."

Rylan laughed. "True. I think Marcel's going to be feeling that hit for a few days."

"Well," I replied, "it's always good to give him a reminder of why I'm going to beat him out for the captainship someday." I chucked my sword through the air and Asher grabbed it at the last second, just before it hit him in the chest. He and Deron were up next in the practice ring.

"Which won't be anytime soon," Deron, the current captain, said as he passed by us.

I watched Asher enter the ring as I peeled off my padding. The oppressive heat held the promise of a storm, a damp weight to the air, as if the very earth were sweating almost as profusely as I was. My shirt stuck to my body, but luckily the leather vest hid the binding I'd wrapped around my breasts earlier that morning. I glanced up at the cloudless blue sky, stretching across the palace and the jungle that surrounded us, and wondered how long it would take before the humidity worked itself up into a mass of dark, threatening thunderheads.

"Come on, *Captain*, let's do this," Asher called from within the ring. The sun made his red hair practically glow — or possibly, it was the reflection off his skin. I'd never seen someone so white before in my life until I'd met him. Most of the people of Antion had at least a hint of olive or darker tones to their skin, to varying degrees. But Asher was originally from Dansii, the nation north of us, where almost everyone's skin was that white — or so he'd said. But King Hector was also from Dansii, and though he was pale, he wasn't *that* white.

In comparison, Deron's dark skin seemed to absorb the light. I'd known Deron for so long now, he didn't frighten me anymore, but I still shivered as he lifted his sword and walked into the arena to face Asher, who was ten years younger than him and at least fifty pounds lighter. Deron was the biggest man in the guard, and at thirty-six, also the oldest. But that wasn't why he was captain — no one had ever beaten him in a challenge. Well, no one except me.

But when I fought him to earn my position on the guard a year ago, I was too new and too young to be made captain, so it didn't matter.

Marcel came back with two tall cups, one in each hand.

"Water?" I asked, eagerly reaching out.

"Yep," he said, but he pulled back, keeping the cups out of my reach. Then he lifted one of them to his mouth and drank deeply.

"Are you planning on sharing that, or am I supposed to apologize for beating you first?"

"Nope. No apology necessary. I fully intend to give you what you deserve."

Before I had a chance to react, Marcel tossed the entire contents of the second cup into my face, drenching me. At first, I was too shocked to do anything except stare at him. Then I burst out laughing. The cool water actually felt good as it ran down my nose and chin, dripped off my short hair onto my shirt.

"Well, that's one way to admit you're a sore loser." I ran a hand through my wet hair, shaking the excess water off.

"You two never stop, do you?" Rylan shook his head, a wry grin revealing his straight, white teeth. His skin was the color of cream with a hint of melted chocolate stirred in.

"I need to go check on things inside the palace," I said, forcing myself to look away from Rylan's warm brown eyes. I had no business noticing his smile or his teeth or what shade of chocolate his skin and irises resembled. "Try not to lose any more sparring matches." I pointed at Marcel. "I don't think too many would-be assassins are deterred by cups of water in the face."

"Yes, sir." Marcel saluted me with the empty cup.

With a sigh and a suppressed smile, I turned away from my brother and strode across the courtyard, purposely making my stride as long as possible.

⇥ TWO ⇤

HE DINING ROOM was lit by hundreds of candles. The scent of hot wax and too much perfume made my head hurt. I stood at attention a discreet distance from where Prince Damian sat, eating his dinner with his customary bored expression. The women on both sides of him vied for his attention, one more blatantly than the other, bending too close to the table, pushing her very visible breasts even higher out of her dress. But the prince only raised one dark eyebrow and lifted a spoonful of chilled pear soup to his mouth.

I wanted to tell the women to quit bothering. Prince Damian never took anyone to his rooms, and as one of his personal guards, I was certain he never visited anyone else's, either. I believed it was because engaging in *that* activity would require too much effort — and if there was one thing the prince excelled at, it was laziness.

I looked away from the long table filled with lavishly dressed men and women, and scanned the room. Marcel stood a few feet away from me on Prince Damian's other side. Across the room, Rylan and his brother, Jude, stood near the door.

As the next course was brought out, the conversation turned, as it nearly always did, to the war. After a few minutes of discussion, Prince Damian sighed.

"Must we always converse about this dreary topic?" He lifted his wineglass to his lips. King Hector had wine and champagne shipped in from Dansii, but only the royal family and their most esteemed guests were allowed to drink it on a regular basis. The rest of the dinner party had goblets full of native juices from Antion — mango and papaya.

"But surely *you* don't find it dreary, Your Highness?" A young woman I hadn't noticed before tonight asked, her expression one of surprise. "This war comes at a steep cost, of course. But I would think that *you* of all people would be thrilled at the recent success the army has had in stopping those Blevonese sorcerers."

Oh, here we go, I groaned internally.

"I should?" the prince asked, his voice deceptively inviting. "Why do you suppose that would excite me, in particular?"

The young woman — who couldn't have been more than fifteen or sixteen, most likely newly presented at court — leaned forward eagerly, exhilarated to have garnered the prince's notice.

"Well, because of what happened to the queen. I'm sure you're just as eager to avenge her murder as the king is. Aren't you?"

The entire room seemed to freeze, silence descending swiftly as the prince pinned her with his gaze. I couldn't see his eyes from my vantage point, but I knew Prince Damian well. I could easily imagine the icy glare he'd turned on her, his shockingly blue eyes cold. The girl's color drained slightly, to be quickly replaced by a flush creeping up her neck.

"I find that this . . . meal . . . has become unappetizing," Prince Damian finally said, rising from his chair. Everyone else rushed to stand as well. "Please, remain and enjoy the food. Celebrate the army's victories with as much exuberance as possible."

The girl stared down at her plate in humiliation, her former excitement completely gone. She looked like she was about to vomit the food she'd been eating all over the table.

"Guards." Prince Damian flicked a wrist, signaling us. We fell into line, Rylan and Jude in front of the prince, Marcel and myself in the rear, as he exited the room. Once the dining table and the awkward conversation were far behind us, Prince Damian stopped. "Alex," he said, turning to face me.

"Yes, Your Highness?" I stood at attention.

"I haven't received word of this supposed victory." He glared at me like it was my fault. "I do *not* like to be ill informed at my own dinner parties. You will find Nolen at once and tell him that I require news of the war efforts brought to me personally from now on."

From behind me, Marcel said, "My lord, Nolen has taken the evening off to visit his sister in Tubatse."

Prince Damian looked past me to my brother. "Ah yes." He pressed his lips together in irritation. "Then go find Iker instead. Give him the same message. He's probably better informed than Nolen anyway."

I nodded. Iker — the king's most trusted advisor — probably *did* know more than Nolen, Prince Damian's "handler," as we dubbed him. But I hated dealing with Iker and wished Nolen hadn't picked tonight of all nights to be gone. "Would you like me or Marcel to go, my lord?"

"Your shifts are ending soon, I believe?" he asked.

"Yes, my lord," Marcel confirmed.

"Both of you go and bring me word of his response before you retire for the night." He waved us off as Marcel and I pressed our right fists to our opposite shoulders and bowed.

The king's chambers were in a completely different wing of the sprawling, massive palace, and Marcel and I had to turn around and head back the way we'd come to find Iker's room, next to King Hector's private quarters.

Once we were out of earshot of Prince Damian, Marcel and I both began to walk more slowly. He seemed to dread talking to Iker as much as I did.

"Did you hear about any victories recently?" Marcel asked as we climbed the staircase to the second floor.

I shook my head. "No. And I've never seen that girl before. I wonder if she's really that stupid, or if someone put her up to it to try and get a reaction from the prince."

"If so, she's an excellent actress. I was sure she was about to throw up when Damian stood to leave."

I had to agree with Marcel; she'd been very convincing. Maybe there'd been a report of a victory we hadn't heard yet. But even if there was, I couldn't believe she'd had the audacity to bring up the murder of Prince Damian's mother at dinner. It didn't matter if that was why King Hector had declared war on Blevon; it was not something to discuss over chilled soup and poached whitefish.

When we reached Iker's door, it wasn't completely shut. Marcel tapped lightly on it. We waited, but there was no response.

"Should we go in?"

For some reason, I had to suppress a shiver. I didn't like Iker. He was a narrow man — everything about him was angular and sharp: his beaked nose, his chin, the point of his head, which was ill concealed by his greasy black hair. I did not wish to go into his room, yet we had no choice but to try and find him. "I guess so. Prince Damian will throw a fit if we come back without a document signed in blood, swearing to bring him news of any and all victories as soon as Iker has them."

Marcel went first, pushing the door open a bit wider. The room was encased in darkness, all except for the back corner, where a tall figure stood hunched over a table. The meager glow of a low fire in the hearth next to him revealed the bony outline of Iker's body. There was a slight haze in the room, and an acrid, coppery scent turned my stomach.

The moment we walked in, Iker straightened and whirled to face us, blocking our view of what was on the table. "What are you doing, barging into my personal room without permission?" he demanded, his expression furious. He clutched a small knife in one hand.

"Prince Damian sent us and your door was open. . . ." Marcel gestured behind us.

"Leave my chamber at once." Iker glowered at us, the faint light of the fire behind him barely illuminating his features, giving him a dark, wild look. The air felt thick, heavy, entrapping. Something was wrong in here and I was more than willing to comply with his command. I spun on my heel and strode out. But Marcel lingered. I turned to see him still standing in the doorway, meeting Iker's glare.

"Iker, was there word of a victory today that Prince Damian was kept unaware of?" Marcel crossed his arms over his chest and I groaned. I knew that position well. He wasn't going to back down or let Iker intimidate him. Normally, I wouldn't have either, but it wasn't just Iker I was eager to escape. It was his room; the smell; the little knife in his hand, which was stained with something all too similar to blood; and the darkness that felt thicker than normal, somehow. I couldn't imagine what he was doing in there, and I was surprised Marcel wasn't as eager to leave as I was.

"I said, leave my room," Iker's voice was low and threatening now as he marched toward us. Marcel had the good sense to back away. Either of us could have taken down the greasy-haired, older man in a fight without even breaking a sweat. But he was our superior — almost as powerful as the king himself. It wasn't a good idea to infuriate him.

Iker pulled the door shut behind him and pointed at us with the knife. "You may tell your prince that I will inform him of any and all victories over Blevon at the king's discretion. As for the both of you, since you obviously have nothing better to do than barge into people's private chambers, I now require your services."

Even with the door shut, the smell still lingered in my nose. I looked down at his knife and tried to keep my expression neutral, despite the uneasiness in my gut.

"We have a new batch of orphans to place," Iker said, "and the king's guard is down a few men right now because of illness. I believe they should be arriving through the west gate shortly. No one seems to like the job of taking the girls to the breeding house, but I'm sure the both of you won't mind." His fingers tightened on the hilt of the knife. "Am I correct?"

Revulsion made my stomach turn. I'd only been forced to enter the breeding house once before. Even though I'd been inside for just a few minutes, I still had nightmares about the place. The stench of unkempt bodies and overused sheets. The echoes of screams, the desperate sobbing behind closed doors. The heat and fear that coated the air like smoke. The empty eyes of the girls. The swollen mounds of their bellies. Bile rose in my throat and panic seized me. I couldn't go back there — I couldn't lead other girls to that fate at sword point.

Iker looked directly at me with a cruel smile on his thin lips and repeated, "Am I correct?"

"Yes, sir," Marcel finally answered for us both. "We'll go right away."

"Maybe next time, you will think twice before disturbing me." Iker gave me one last dark look before going back into his room, shutting the door firmly behind him this time.

⊰ THREE ⊱

𝒯HE HEAT-DRENCHED NIGHT made my uniform stick to my damp skin as Marcel and I walked silently across the palace grounds. Farther away from the main entrance to the palace, we could see a large group of people being herded through the side gate by some of the king's guards. I had to employ every bit of training to keep my expression passive, to keep control over the panic racing through me when I got close enough to make out their faces, to see the terror in the girls' eyes. I counted eight boys and twelve girls. The youngest girl looked no older than five. She gripped an older boy's hand tightly, her face ghostly pale in the meager light of the crescent moon hanging above us.

Don't think about it, don't think about it, I commanded myself, swallowing the thick lump in my throat and clenching my teeth together.

"What do you two think you're doing?" one of the king's guard asked when we were only a few feet away.

"Don't tell me you've come to help," another sneered. "The prince's guards aren't man enough for this type of work."

A trickle of sweat ran between my breasts, sliding down my belly. I reached down and grasped the hilt of my sword. For some reason, it helped calm me down. "Do you want help or not?" I asked. "Because we'll leave if you're going to be pigs about it." I was grateful when my voice came out biting and hard. My stomach churned and my heart pounded as I forced myself to stare at the guard, refusing to look at the orphans.

"We'll take the help," the first guard replied grudgingly. He began to shout orders, telling the other three men to separate the boys from the girls. "You two can help me escort the girls to their new home," he said to us with a nod of his chin toward the breeding house. "You three" — he lifted his voice at the other guards as they worked on getting the boys and girls into separate lines — "take the boys to the barracks, get them assigned to separate battalions."

I watched helplessly as the girls followed the guards' nudges and shouts, most of their faces resigned. This could have been me, forced into a life of rape, attempting to breed as many new soldiers for the king's army as possible before my body gave out.

"Breathe," Marcel murmured from next to me.

I realized that I was gripping my sword so tightly that my knuckles were white, and my chest was heaving. I had to get myself under control. There was nothing I could do to stop this — there was nothing I could do to keep these girls from their fate. No matter how badly I wished I could.

When the guards reached the littlest girl and her brother, the brother wouldn't release her hand.

"You can't take her," he said, stepping in front of her. He couldn't have been more than ten.

"Step away, boy." The guard's voice was hard.

"No. You can't have her!" he repeated more vehemently, turning and wrapping his arms around the little girl, whose whole body shook violently as tears ran silently down her face. She clung to her brother, her small fingers clutched in his tunic.

"You take the girl, I've got the boy," the guard said, gesturing to one of his companions.

The first man grabbed the girl's arms and pulled, while the second guard took the boy, yanking him away from his sister. She screamed, a desperate sob, reaching, grasping for her brother as they were torn apart by the guards.

"*Kalen!* No! Leave her alone!" The boy shouted and thrashed, but it was no use.

I hadn't even realized I'd started to move forward until Marcel grabbed my arm, forcing me to stop. My chest was on fire, my whole body thrummed with horror, with fury.

"Come on, let's get these girls out of here before they draw too much attention to themselves. We don't want to disturb the king," the guard in charge said, marching forward to the first girl in line. "You two take the rear, and keep an eye on that one; she tried to escape once already." He pointed at a tall girl in the middle of the line, who glared back defiantly.

The other guards herded the boys in the opposite direction, leaving us alone with the girls.

"Follow me," the guard shouted at the frightened line of girls, "and don't even think about trying to run away. You'll be shot down before you make it ten feet." With one last look, he turned on his heel and began to march across the grounds to the breeding house. The girls hesitantly followed, even Kalen, who was still sobbing quietly. An older girl held her hand now and was speaking softly to her.

"I can't do this," I whispered to Marcel, my breath coming in spurts.

"We have to," he said, meeting my panicked gaze with a bleak one of his own. "I'll go first. You follow me."

He turned and marched across the grounds behind the row of girls. I made myself follow, and forced my mind to go blank. I concentrated on staring up at the building in front of us instead of the row of girls, until the guard in front stopped and pounded on a wooden door.

A few moments later, it swung open to reveal an older man with thinning hair and small, watery eyes. "Brought me some new girls, eh? We're almost full, until they finish building the new addition, but I've got a few rooms open. Doesn't hurt to make 'em share, either." His jowls were ruddy, and a sheen of sweat glistened on his fat upper lip.

"That's fine, Horace," the guard said.

Horace opened the door wider and gestured for the girls to go in. "Come on, then. I haven't got all night. There's still work to be done." He winked at the guard and I had to swallow the bile that rose in my throat.

The guard went in first and the girls slowly followed. Some of them walked in tall and proud, others went in with their shoulders trembling. When Kalen entered, still holding the other girl's hand, Horace whistled. "My, aren't you a pretty young thing? Don't worry, you can stay with your friend for a while. You're no good to us yet. Not for a few years anyway." He chuckled.

My hands clenched into fists at my side, but Marcel threw me a warning glance over his shoulder, as if he could read my thoughts. Or maybe he was having the same ones but knew we were helpless to stop this. It was the king's orders and no one could defy them, least of all Marcel and me.

When the last girl had filed through the door, into the dim interior of the breeding house, Horace shouted, "Marie, we got new ones again. Get down here and help me find 'em rooms!"

I stood a little bit behind Marcel on the threshold, hoping our part was done. I had to breathe shallowly to keep from wincing at the smell that wafted out of the entryway, a mixture of sweat and fear and something else foul.

The guard noticed when I started to back away and motioned at us. "Get in here and help me make sure they all get locked up in a room. Then you can go."

The small foyer was lit by a couple of oil lamps, sitting on two small tables on either side of the doorway. The unsteady light revealed a run-down interior, with dust gathered in the corners and on the tables. Grime coated the stones beneath our boots. The girls were lined up along a wall to the left of the door, and straight in front of us was a narrow staircase. A painfully thin girl who looked like she was my age slowly made her way down the steps, cupping the swollen mass of her pregnant belly with one hand and holding a lantern in her other. Her cheeks were sunken, making her already large eyes appear huge in her gaunt face.

"Ah, there you are, Marie," Horace said, motioning for her to come all the way down. "Help me get these new ones situated, will you? I've got to hurry and get back upstairs." A look of hunger crossed his sweaty face.

"We've only got four rooms left, if you include the attic," Marie said, her voice chillingly empty.

Horace looked over the row of girls. "How many of you have already started your monthly bleedings?"

I flinched at the awful question, but slowly five girls raised their hands.

"Not you, eh? You can't fool me, you know." Horace stepped in front of one girl who obviously had firm, rounded breasts beneath her tunic but who hadn't raised her hand. "It'll be worse for you if you try to hide it from me. We'll have to make up for lost time, my men and me." He leered at the girl and she began to visibly shake, her eyes filling with tears.

Slowly, she lifted her hand, and Horace grinned, revealing stained, uneven teeth.

"Take all the girls who are too young up to share the attic. Put the rest in the other rooms."

A door opened down the hallway and another man walked out, buttoning up his pants. Before the door shut behind him, I caught a glimpse of a girl lying motionless on an unmade bed, her head turned toward a small window above her where a sliver of the moon was just barely visible in the dark sky.

I took a step back and bumped into the door behind me. My hands shook and my heart pounded. I couldn't stay here one minute longer. Not without killing Horace or the man striding toward us, still tucking his tunic back into his pants after doing his "work."

I grabbed the door handle and yanked it open.

"Where does he think he's going?" I heard someone ask, but then I was running, tripping, fleeing from that place. From the disgust and horror and fury that had almost made me do something that would have ended my own life.

"Marcel!" I heard my twin call after me but I didn't turn back, not even for him. Not even to see why he'd yelled his own name at me, instead of mine. I ran and ran, all the way across the grounds, through the palace, dodging servants and furniture, up the stairs, and to my room. When the door was finally shut behind me, I slid to the ground, buried my head in my arms, and sobbed.

Marcel came into our room about twenty minutes later, when I'd finally regained control of myself. But before he could cross the room to me, a king's guard opened the door after him. I turned away, trying to hide my tear-stained face.

"Marcel?" he barked out.

"Yes," my twin responded.

"You will come with me," the guard said.

Before I had a chance to ask what was going on, Marcel had rushed out after the guard, shutting the door firmly behind him. I stared at the door in concern.

He didn't return to our room for over an hour. While I waited, I realized how stupid I'd been. How much trouble I had probably gotten us into. I'd run away from my duty — disobeyed a superior. I had never made such a big mistake before. I'd always been able to maintain control. To keep calm — stoic, even — no matter what. But the breeding house had been too much — *Horace* had been too much. I still wanted nothing more than to take my sword and embed it in his fat gut.

When Marcel finally came in, looking haggard, I was standing by the fire, my arms wrapped around my body, holding myself together.

"Marcel — I'm so sorry," I began but he shook his head and walked very slowly over to his bed.

"You don't need to apologize. I wanted to run away, too. I'm sure it was worse for you."

I sat down next to him on the bed and he took one of my hands in his, gripping it tightly. I stared down at our intertwined fingers, grateful that at least when I was alone with my twin in our room, I could be myself. That I could admit my weakness, my fear. "How much trouble did I get us into?"

"None. I took care of it." He sighed and grimaced suddenly.

"They weren't mad?"

"Oh no, they were mad. But I told you, I took care of it."

"Marcel, what did you do?" I asked quietly, fearing that I already knew.

He tried to turn away from me, but winced suddenly. That's when I noticed the blood seeping through the back of his tunic.

"*Marcel — no!* You took my punishment!"

He didn't deny it and my heart constricted.

"What did they do?"

"Ten lashes," he muttered, his voice tight with pain.

My eyes burned with tears as I gently helped him out of his ruined tunic and tried not to gasp when I saw the crisscrossing lines on his once-smooth back. "You shouldn't have done this," I whispered. "It was my mistake. I deserved to be punished."

"And be exposed as a girl? They don't whip you with your shirt on, you know." He turned to face me, his face contorted with pain, but his eyes were tender when he met my ashamed gaze. "The king's guards don't know us well enough to tell us apart. I had to take your place. I had to protect you."

I shook my head, unable to say anything.

He took my hand again and squeezed it. "I'm glad it was me and not you. Now help me get bandaged up and let's get to bed. It's been a long night."

I was quiet as I did what he asked, cleaning the wounds, then winding the extra bandages I kept to bind my breasts carefully around his torso. When it was done and I'd helped him pull on a clean tunic, I finally said, "I can't believe you thought so quickly to call out your own name."

He shrugged, then winced in pain. "You might be the better fighter, but I was always the smarter one."

I couldn't bring myself to laugh, because it was true. His quick thinking had saved me from discovery and the breeding house twice now.

"Do you want me to get you anything?"

"No," he said. "But I *will* let you be the one to deal with Prince Damian in the morning."

I grimaced. "Of course."

He carefully lowered himself to lie down on his bed with a smirk on his face. "I'd take ten lashes over one of Prince Damian's temper tantrums any day."

I shook my head with a rueful smile. "Thank you, Marcel."

"I'll never forget that little boy, trying to protect his sister," Marcel said suddenly, his voice quiet. "I did what I had to do."

I waited until his breathing was deep and steady before I finally crawled under my own covers. Even then, it was hours before I was able to go to sleep. I couldn't stop thinking about what Marcel had done and the horrors of the breeding house. Of Kalen, lying down in the attic, probably still crying with the other girls. Of the girl I'd glimpsed on the bed, her face turned toward the moon.

And just before I drifted off, I thought of Iker, hunched over a table in his room, doing something with a knife that smelled of

⊰ FOUR ⊱

HE NEXT NIGHT, the air was still damp from a passing storm, and would most likely stay that way for hours. The darkness was so complete, it felt alive, as though it sucked at me, pulling my eyelids lower and making my limbs heavy. Because of King Hector's dinner party, the normal perimeter squadron had been called inside the ballroom, and Prince Damian's guard was assigned to patrol the outer doors to the main palace until the party ended.

"I'm going to go walk the perimeter," I announced, pushing away from the wall. Walking would help me stay alert. The drenched heat of the jungle was too much for me tonight; I'd never stay awake if I continued to stand in place.

Marcel glanced over at me from his position on the other side of the doorway. "Would you like me to come with you?"

"It's been a quiet night. Stay here and rest," I said, noticing the sheen of perspiration on his forehead and the pain in his eyes. "I'll take the whistle just in case."

The palace grounds were mostly peaceful, although inside, the royal dinner party was still going strong, and had apparently turned into an impromptu dance. Strains of music began to waft through the air as I neared the dining hall windows. I caught a

27

glimpse of Prince Damian waltzing with a pretty young woman across the dance floor. In his evening attire, with the warm candlelight painting his features so softly, his customary sneer absent from his face, he was almost painfully beautiful. His dark hair, olive skin — so much like mine, since we were both half Blevonese — and his pale blue eyes were a striking combination. I couldn't deny that he was attractive. Too attractive.

There had been a moment when I'd first met him when I wished I didn't have to hide that I was a girl. But then he'd opened his mouth to speak, and it didn't take long for me to come to dislike him.

Realizing I was staring at the prince, I squared my shoulders and scowled at myself. The heat was getting to me. That was all. I nodded at another guard, one of the king's men, as I continued forward. Echoes of laughter and voices slurred by drink were clearly audible as I crossed in front of the open windows, scanning the courtyard.

I'd nearly passed the length of the dining hall when I heard the thud of a body. Instinct took over, and I dropped to the ground, whirling at the same time. An arrow pinged as it hit the wall, right where my head had been moments before. One of the king's guard lay on the ground across from me, an arrow protruding from his eye socket.

Sliding my sword from its scabbard, I turned my back to the wall, and spun to face the unknown enemy. My heart beat erratically. How many were there? At least one of them was obviously an excellent shot. If they had breached the outer wall without a racket, there couldn't be too many of them. No, this was a small group — possibly even a single assassin.

Straining my ears, I barely heard the whistle of another arrow before I spun again, raising my sword up to the level of my face. It bounced off the wall inches from my cheek.

I was blind, sitting like a target in the spilling light of the party, staring out into the black night. Raising the whistle to my lips and simultaneously leaping through the open window, I blew on it hard, three times. It was a special whistle that emitted an earsplitting sound, so loud, not only would Marcel hear it and repeat the call, but so would the rest of the guard who were above us in their beds or on duty in the hallways.

The people nearest me gasped and screamed in horror when I vaulted through the window, the echo of my whistle blows still ringing in my ears. I got a glimpse of the king sitting on his throne, watching the party with his pale, cold eyes, before a servant bearing a tray of wine collided with me, dumping the tray on the floor with a crash as flutes filled with the scarlet liquid shattered.

"Attack! Guards, clear the room!" I shouted into the sudden silence as the music stumbled to a halt.

Immediately, those of the outer guard, the king's guard, and Rylan — who was guarding Prince Damian at the party — jumped into action, herding the royals and their court out of the room. Prince Damian glanced at me, his expression inscrutable before turning and guiding his companion, resplendent in diamonds and silk, out the door in front of him. Iker ushered the king behind the throne to a special passage hidden there.

"Rylan, come with me!" I shouted before turning away from the flashing jewels and bright silks to plunge back outside into the darkness and the aim of the unknown shooter.

Marcel was already there, holding his bow. "I shot down the one who killed the king's man." He nodded behind him, where the guard's body lay prone, a puddle of blood surrounding his head. "But there was someone else. He scaled the wall before I could get off another shot."

"There could be more outside the walls as well. Let's go." I took off at a run, sheathing my sword and pulling my bow over my head, drawing an arrow from the quiver on my back. The outer squadron for the west gate was nowhere to be seen. Most likely shot as well. We had to waste precious seconds locating the key ring hidden behind a loose stone and heaving the door open. By the time the jungle was in full view, the rest of the prince's guard had arrived.

"Not a single king's man showed up to help, huh?" Asher noted, glancing behind us.

"Typical," muttered Jerrod, his extremely pale blue eyes ghost-like in the darkness. "They're probably all too busy waiting in line for their turns at the breeding house."

"Fan out," Deron whispered harshly, ignoring them and pointing into the jungle. "They won't have gone into the city; they must be out there. If they're assassins from Blevon, they won't be comfortable in the jungle. Use your senses, track them."

The men nodded and we began to slip away silently in pairs. Shouldering the bow so I could move more easily through the trees, I headed straight forward, straining for any sign of the men who attacked the palace. The leaves and vines of the jungle were still coated with drops of moisture, and the ground sucked at my feet as I moved ahead without a sound. My heart thudded in my chest, but I gritted my teeth and kept going. There was no time to waste on being afraid of the jungle.

I motioned at the ground, and Marcel nodded. His hairline was damp and his eyes bright with pain, but he gamely followed me into the jungle without a word of complaint. Directly ahead of us were a broken leaf and a fresh boot print. We were on someone's trail.

The darkness was so complete, the shadows seemed to take form around me as we plunged deeper into the belly of the rain forest. My mind made enemies from the mist. As I stalked through the jungle, stealthy as a predator, I had to sort what was real from what was imagined. Trees, vines, rocks — all were menacing in the steamy night. But my prey was cunning and far more intelligent than any jaguar's quarry — and a better shot. The pungent scent of moist soil filled my nose. Heavily laden leaves, swollen with water, brushed against my face. A hanging mist coated the air. Not true rain, but enough to make my skin wet.

I caught sight of a shadow ahead of me. Not one of our own. He tried to blend in, but he wasn't at home here. Not like we were. Though I was afraid of the jungle, I understood it — I *knew* it, and how to blend into it. I halted, lifting a fist silently. My eyes narrowed, and I squinted to make out the details as the assassin melted from tree to tree, trying to conceal himself. I silently lifted the arrow I'd been holding the whole time, felt the smooth wood, the tickle of feathers against my fingers.

He froze. Possibly felt the weight of my stare. Time was short now before he realized he'd been caught. Would he turn to fight or try to flee?

In one smooth movement, so fast there were few, if any, who could match me for speed, I swung the bow off my shoulder, notched the arrow, and let it fly. Only the smallest twang from the string sounded as the arrow whistled through the damp air toward the enemy.

There was a cry of pain and the shadow dropped to the ground. My arrow hit true. I never missed.

Someone drew up next to me on my right. Without looking, I could sense my brother. Marcel was always close by — always trying to protect me.

"Is there only —?"

I jerked my head to silence him, but it was too late. I heard the returning whistle right before the arrow embedded with a wet thunk in Marcel's chest. He cried out, sucked in a shocked gasp of air. Just as before, the aim was perfect. Marcel fell to his knees, his eyes wide as he stared up at me. I could see my name form on his lips, my true name.

Alexa.

But the word was nothing more than a gurgle as his mouth filled with blood and he collapsed to the ground.

The blackness of night was like a living thing, breathing in hope and expelling terror. As I stood next to his body, the darkness took the shape of death, reaching, grasping for him. I was helpless to stop him from leaving me.

The night was painted red now, red with my fury, red with his blood. There was a small snap from a twig, near the first assassin I shot down. I grabbed an arrow and let it fly, barely even looking. The second attacker — the one Marcel didn't see, the one who killed him — dropped next to my first victim. But it wasn't enough. I wasn't fast enough.

Sure now that there were no more assassins hiding in wait, I dropped to my knees beside Marcel. My fingers clenched the blood-soaked folds of his tunic. A prayer to beg God to somehow save my brother formed but didn't leave my lips before his chest fell and did not rise again. A tear slipped off my chin and splashed on his motionless face. Already he looked different, now that he was really gone. Was this how I'd look when I died? His olive skin was beginning to turn ashen. Once-full lips were bloodless. I gently closed his eyelids, hiding his sightless hazel eyes. Stroking the thick, raven hair back, I pressed a kiss to his still-warm forehead. Tears ran down my cheeks now, hot and urgent on my skin.

Marcel couldn't be gone. He was my twin, my other half.

"No, Marcel, no," I sobbed, bending over and pressing my forehead to his, my fingers still clutching his bloody tunic. "Don't leave me, don't leave me here alone. . . ."

"Alex! Where are you?"

"Here." I forced myself to call out, belatedly remembering to lower my voice. Hopefully in the turmoil of the chase, no one noticed the higher pitch. Or maybe they'd attribute it to grief. "Over here," I tried again, swallowing my tears. A member of Prince Damian's guard didn't cry. Not even for his own brother. "Marcel is dead."

We were a somber group as we walked back through the gate, carrying Marcel's body. The regular perimeter squadron parted for Prince Damian's elite personal guard — the squadron that hadn't been here at its normal post because of the king's infernal party, and hadn't joined us in pursuit of the men who'd done this. I forced my face to be blank, to hide the pain that was tearing through me, shredding me, threatening to pull me apart inside. Marcel was the one who'd kept me together when our parents were killed, convinced me to pretend I was his twin brother when the army came for us. He was the one who'd saved me again last night, taking my beating for me. He had saved me over and over, and now he was gone.

I had failed him.

With the loss of Marcel, there were only eight of us left. I looked into the familiar faces as we gently laid Marcel down on one of the many funeral pyres that always stood ready, awaiting their fuel. Another one was already in use — probably the king's guard. There was never a shortage of bodies to burn, not for long. King Hector's war on King Osgand's kingdom ensured that. Our captain, Deron, met my gaze, his dark eyes sorrowful. Jerrod, next to him, stared forward, stone-faced.

Someone handed Rylan a torch. He stood on my left, so close that the fire burned hot by my face. He cleared his throat. "Marcel was one of the best of us. Brave, strong, loyal." His voice broke and he paused, trying to regain control. Finally, he whispered, "Go in peace, brother."

"Go in peace," the others murmured.

I couldn't speak. The words stuck to the tears in my throat, the sobs I desperately swallowed back down.

Rylan looked to me, and I realized they were waiting. Waiting for me to give the signal. As his brother, I was to either light the pyre or give Rylan the go-ahead. I couldn't bring myself to do it, so I gave the barest of nods and Rylan slowly lowered the torch. The dry wood of the pyre ignited instantly, spreading to encompass Marcel's body in a bright orange grave of heat and smoke.

The firelight played across the faces of the other guards. Deron's skin was so dark, he almost blended into the night, but the firelight revealed the grief on his face. Jerrod, Asher, Jude, Kai, Antonio, and Rylan next to me, all stared into the flames, watching as my brother was consumed.

Finally, I couldn't bear it any longer. I turned and strode away from the last member of my family.

⇥ FIVE ⇤

*C*HE NEXT MORNING, I woke up in the same clothes I was wearing the night before. I'd collapsed onto my bed and cried for hours, smothering the sounds in my pillow until I finally fell asleep. I rolled over to see Marcel's empty bed and the pain hit me all over again. I bent over double and clutched at my stomach, tried to push the agony away.

The smell of the fire was still in my hair, in my shirt, on my skin. The scent of Marcel's death.

I tore the clothes from my body and threw them in the still-hot coals in the fireplace, then scoured my body with water and soap, trying to scrub away the smoke, the sweat, the tears, the guilt.

I was supposed to be the best. I was the fastest, the most skilled at archery, unparalleled at swordsmanship. And yet I let my brother get shot down right next to me. All my training, everything I'd learned and become were for naught.

My clothes finally caught fire. Thick, black billows of smoke chugged into the air, then were swallowed up into the chimney.

I heard noises from the other side of the wall, muted and indistinguishable from the rest of the palace sounds. My room was next door to Prince Damian's. All of the guards' rooms except

Deron's flanked the prince's. Two guards per room, two rooms on either side of his chambers to keep us close, even in sleep. I knew I'd be summoned any moment if he was up. He'd want an accounting of our pursuit of the attackers last night — and he'd most likely want it from me, since I'd shot down the enemies. And since my brother had died.

I raked my hands through my short hair. Already, it was almost dry. That was one benefit of wearing it short. I'd mourned the loss of my hair for a year after Marcel cut it off. Now, after three years, I was used to it. But I still wished things could be different. I wished I could be a member of the guard *and* a girl.

Instead, I stood in front of the mirror, staring at my traitorous body. We'd lied about our age when we joined the army, claiming we were seventeen, afraid of what would happen to us if they knew we were only fourteen. Now everyone on the guard believed me to be twenty, when I was actually only seventeen. But my body had really begun to change in the past year, since I'd won the position on the guard and left the regular army behind. Rather than feeling joy — planning a party with my mother and friends to celebrate my coming into womanhood — I glared at the breasts that had doubled in size in the last few months. They were still small by anyone's standards, but *anything* was too big for a boy.

I took a long strip of cloth and bound it around myself, as tightly as I possibly could. It hurt, but there was no other choice. Now, more than ever, I couldn't risk discovery.

I'd barely pulled a tunic over my head when there was a knock at the door, and it opened after a pause.

"Prince Damian wants to see you," Rylan said.

I finished tucking the tunic into my long pants and turned to face him. I was tall for a girl, thankfully, but Rylan was taller. Almost everyone in the guard was taller than me. That often worked to my advantage, though; no one worried about the small guard taking him down — until it was too late.

I nodded and bent to quickly pull on my boots.

"Alex, are you okay?"

I stood up, grateful my tears had dried and the red blotches that would have given me away were gone. "I'm fine," I answered, making my voice gruff. It had taken me a long time to gain the respect of these men. I couldn't afford to show weakness, not even for my brother. I moved to storm out of the room, but Rylan grabbed my arm. I immediately tensed, jerked away.

"You know that no one would blame you for being upset. He was your brother. We get that." I met his gaze, just long enough to notice again how much the color of his eyes resembled melted chocolate, with little flecks of gold in the morning light. *That* was something none of the other men would ever notice.

I clenched my jaw, keeping my expression severe. "I told you, I'm fine." I crossed my arms, taking a wide stance.

"Okay." He held up his hands. "Then do you still want to spar this morning?"

"Of course." I nodded curtly as I exited the room.

"I'll go make sure everything is ready," he said.

I lifted one hand to acknowledge him without looking back. Prince Damian didn't like to be kept waiting. And I was too vulnerable to be standing alone in my room with Rylan right then — Marcel's death had made me feel all too much like a girl again.

Squaring my shoulders, I took a deep breath, and opened the door to the outer room of Prince Damian's chambers.

"There he is," Nolen grumbled. "Alex, get over here before —"

"Alex!" I recognized the bellow from the inner room, Damian's bedroom. The prince was on the verge of having another temper tantrum. I'd already endured one yesterday, when he demanded to know why Marcel and I hadn't come to report Iker's response to him as he'd commanded us. It was hard to believe that had been less than twenty-four hours ago.

"His Highness is rather unhappy this morning." Nolen pursed his thin lips together. He was a small man, an inch shorter than me, with scrawny limbs that seemed too long for his body. He almost made me look burly.

"I gathered that." I grimaced.

"Alex!"

"You'd better go. Good luck." Nolen sat back down at the desk where he went through all of the prince's correspondences, picking out only the most urgent and important missives with which to bother His Royal Highness.

I stood as tall as I could possibly lift my five-foot-ten-inch frame and marched into Damian's room.

"Finally." The prince stood by his window, watching me enter. Thick, velvet curtains the color of blood framed the enormous glass panes. His room was luxuriously appointed, full of furs, velvet, silk, and every other expensive fabric known to man. An enormous four-poster bed dominated the far side of the room, but he stood near his mahogany desk today. He was tall, with broad shoulders and a narrow waist. Even though his posture was perfect, he somehow exuded an air of indolence. His dark hair was perfectly pomaded into the current fashion, swooping back from his broad forehead, emphasizing his aquiline nose — his father's nose. But his olive skin was a gift from his Blevonese mother.

Sometimes it seemed like those with the most rotten interiors were blessed with the most exquisite exteriors.

"Your Highness." I pressed my fist to my heart and bowed to him.

"Yes, yes, get up already." The entitled boredom of his voice grated on my nerves. He seemed to think it created loyalty to him, to act like the niceties of court were a nuisance, but in reality, it was one more thing that annoyed me. He knew I *had* to bow, to posture to his demands and acquiesce to his every whim — even though, at twenty-three, he was only six years older than me. To pretend like it was all for show, and one he didn't enjoy, was ludicrous. I'd seen the gloating expression on his noble face too many times to believe that he didn't relish everyone's subservience.

I stood up straight again, at attention. The one thing I disliked most was when he looked at me as he was right then, his blue eyes cold and calculating. His lashes were dark, and the corners of his eyes tilted slightly, giving him an exotic look. But his irises were such a clear, crystal blue, it was a shock the first time I'd met him. For all of his whining and tantrums and other spoiled behavior, there was true intelligence and cunning in his eyes. Usually hidden, but sometimes, as was the case now, the sharpness of his gaze cut me through. There was a part of me that wondered what he really thought. What did he see when he looked at me as he was now?

I'd had years of practice at hiding emotion, of staying calm under pressure. Even the unwavering eyes of the prince couldn't shake me. Not visibly anyway. But no amount of control could keep my pulse from quickening.

"I hear there was a death during last night's pursuit." Prince Damian tilted his head.

"Yes, Your Highness."

"One of my personal guard?"

"Yes, sir."

"Someone important to you, Alex?" He lifted a hand, examined his perfectly trimmed nails. Hands that had never seen work, never gripped a sword or loosed an arrow. He had the perfect build for fighting, tall and lean, but it was wasted on him.

"My brother, sir." I clenched my jaw, looking down at the ground in an effort to maintain my composure.

"Your twin, if I recall?"

"Yes, sir." Was he trying to drive the pain deeper? "The attackers were all taken down, Your Highness." Keeping my voice low had become second nature to me, but I always had to work harder to make it sound natural when I was under stress.

"Very good." He paused. "Always duty first with you, right, Alex?"

"Sir?" I couldn't keep myself from glancing at him briefly. He looked up from his hand at the same time, so that our gazes met. There was something in the depths of his eyes, an echo of my own grief — an unexpected empathy — that made my breath catch in my throat. The intensity of his gaze — this wasn't the way a prince looked at just another member of his guard.

"I had a brother, too," he said, his eyes never leaving mine, his voice strangely soft. A flash of unmasked pain crossed his face. "I kept a stiff upper lip when he died as well. I'm . . . I'm impressed with your dedication to me and my safety."

"It's my duty, Your Highness." My voice came out unsteadily and I hurriedly clamped my jaw shut. In the year since I'd won a position on his guard, I'd never heard him speak of his brother. His unexpected admission brought my own grief far too close to the surface. It took all of my willpower to force the emotion back down, to keep control.

Prince Damian watched my battle silently. "Alex." He took a halting step toward me. "Must you always pretend — even with me?"

Despite all my training, I could feel the shock on my face, the sudden fear, and he froze with his hand partially outstretched to me. My heart pounded so loudly in my ears, I wondered how he couldn't hear it as well. What did he mean? There was no way he knew my secret — it wasn't possible. Was it? Panic made my throat constrict. He had to be referring to trying to hide my grief about Marcel's death. That was all. I had to remain calm. Breathe. In and out.

With a sudden shake of his head, Prince Damian waved his hand in the air and in the space of a heartbeat, his normal, apathetic expression slid back into place. "Well, as you said, it is your duty to attend to my safety. I'm fortunate indeed to have such a dedicated soldier in my guard." He paused and the knot of terror in my chest slowly ebbed away. He wasn't going to accuse me of being a girl — I wasn't going to be thrown into the breeding house. Prince Damian raised one eyebrow. "However" — his normal, condescending tone of voice returned as well — "I really wish you hadn't killed the attackers. They could have proven informative. Next time, just maim them."

My blood pulsed hot through my veins as I forced myself to give him a curt nod. The strange conversation, the look he'd given me, they had to have been because of Marcel's death. I had no idea what had just happened — had it even been real? The prince showing empathy, acting like he cared? Maybe it had been a grief-induced hallucination. For one brief moment, I'd wondered if he might be playing a part, too. It had never occurred to me that he might be as trapped as I was. The thought sent a shiver down my spine. I couldn't afford to entertain ridiculous thoughts like that. Not about him.

"Nolen." Prince Damian suddenly raised his voice.

"You called, Your Highness?" Nolen appeared at the door within moments, holding a parchment in his right hand.

"I am afraid these attackers' failed efforts won't be the last attempt to break in to the palace. We must be more vigilant than ever. The next few weeks are crucial to the war on King Osgand's kingdom. *Apparently*, there have been some recent victories I was unaware of, turning the tide of the war in our favor." His lip curled in irritation. I wondered who had finally delivered the news to him. It hadn't been me. "Blevonese assassins will most likely be trying harder than ever to breach the palace. If people must work double shifts, so be it. Alex, let the captain know I expect at least half of my personal guard to be alert at all times, even at night. Is that understood?"

"As you wish, Your Highness." I bowed again.

"That is all. You may go." He turned to the window, dismissing us both.

I stalked out of the room, seething at his insinuation that we weren't doing enough. That he was in some sort of danger. Mad at myself for thinking that maybe there was more to him than an arrogant, spoiled prince seeking attention, digging for reactions. I hoped Rylan had our sparring equipment set to go, because I was ready to fight.

⊰ SIX ⊱

SWEAT DRIPPED BETWEEN my shoulder blades and ran beneath the binding on my chest. The air was heavy, sticky with humidity; the sun's glare was nearly unbearable. My lungs ached, but I ignored the pain, the heat, the burn of calluses on my hands as I swung my sword to parry Rylan's attempts to strike me. It was too easy to let myself remember that I'd been sparring with Marcel two days ago, in this same ring.

Rylan had left himself unprotected on the right side. I struck out hard and fast. My wooden blade hit him in the ribs with a dull thud, knocking him to the ground. If it had been a real sword, he would have been dead.

A light round of applause greeted my victory.

"Remind me never to spar with Alex when he's upset," I heard Asher say.

"No kidding. *I* try to avoid sparring with him when he's *happy*," Jude commented back.

I stood over Rylan, my chest heaving, loosely holding the sword. Extending my free hand, I helped him back up. "Good fight."

"Not from my end," he grumbled, rubbing his chest.

Swiping at the sweat on my brow, I whirled to face the others, who stood outside the ring, watching. "Anyone else?"

Jerrod, Kai, and Antonio were on duty, guarding the prince. That left Deron, Jude, and Asher. They all shook their heads.

"You need to take a break, Alex. And we all need lunch," Deron said.

"I'm not that hungry, but you go ahead. I'll catch up." I gestured for them to go.

Jude, Asher, and Rylan left, but Deron hung back.

"What is it?" I recognized the pensive look on his face.

"You know how upset we all are about losing Marcel."

I remained silent, my jaw clenched. I didn't want to talk about it, but he was my captain.

He shifted his weight and looked down at me. "It's just that we have to fill his position soon. We can't afford to be down one man."

"You think I'm not aware of that? Can't I have at least one day to grieve the loss of my brother before we pretend like he never existed?"

"That's not what I meant, and you know it." Deron's voice held a note of warning.

I lifted my practice sword back up and slashed it through the air. "Either stay to spar or go away."

Deron's dark eyes narrowed at me. "Losing your brother was a horrible blow, but that doesn't give you an excuse to take it out on the other members of the guard. Watch your tone with me and try not to hit your sparring partners so hard."

I clamped my teeth together, ignoring the uncomfortable squirm of guilt in my stomach.

"I will give you the day to grieve Marcel. But I must post notices that the competition to fill his position will take place tomorrow afternoon." Deron paused, and his expression softened. "You know how sorry we all are."

Deron turned without another word and walked away.

Even though my muscles burned with exhaustion, I forced myself to lift the sword and work through my forms one more time. Thrust, jab, parry, spin, and attack. The reason I was the best was because I was relentless with my training. That, and if Marcel was to be believed, I had been blessed with a gift. I'd always teased him, saying that was just his excuse for why I always beat him.

But the villagers had believed him. The fact that we were half Blevonese didn't make us many friends once the war started. I'd heard whispers that we were enemy-lovers. But I didn't love Blevon — I just loved my family. It didn't matter to me where my parents were born. After a Blevonese sorcerer took them away from me, though, any love I had for my heritage had turned to hatred as strong as anyone else's.

The memories flooded up as I spun through the ring, lunging, crouching, fighting a whole horde of imaginary foes and ghosts of my past. I thought of the night when I was five and overheard my parents talking about the king and his war. We lived close to the border between Antion, King Hector's kingdom, and Blevon, King Osgand's, and the threat of attack was always likely. Papa began teaching Marcel how to fight, and I asked if I could watch. I studied them, memorized the moves. Watching Papa spar thrilled me in a way I couldn't understand at that age. I only knew I *had* to do it, too — I had to learn to move like that, to spin and twist

47

and lunge, to make my sword become an extension of my body. Beautiful and deadly, the most intoxicating dance I'd ever seen.

When I turned six, I asked if I could join them. Mama protested, but Papa thought it was just for fun. He was amused by my interest — at first. I held back for the first few months, nervous that they would be mad if I was any good.

Now, as I continued through my practice, the ghosts of my family seemed to surround me. I imagined sparring with Papa while Mama watched us, her expression hooded. I never knew if she was proud of how good I became or ashamed.

Papa had called me his *zhànshì nánwū*. Though I'd begged him to tell me what it meant, he never did. It was the language of Blevon, not Antion. His parents had been from Blevon; they'd moved to Antion when there was still peace between our nations. Before Hector came with his Dansiian army and won control of Antion, making himself king. Before he tore apart the alliance that had once existed between the two nations by declaring war after the queen's death. I didn't dare ask anyone else what *zhànshì nánwū* meant. Having ties to Blevon wasn't a good thing in Antion — especially not inside King Hector's palace.

I licked my lips and tasted the salt of my own sweat and tears. I hoped that if anyone still watched me, the extra moisture on my face would be indistinguishable from the perspiration dripping down my neck. My muscles were on fire, my whole body cried out from the exertion, but it wasn't enough to drive the pain from my heart.

I'd just grabbed a towel and wiped down my face when there was a shout from across the courtyard.

"Alex! Come, quick!"

I turned to see Asher running toward me. The sunlight shining on his red hair gave the illusion of his head being on fire. I picked up my real sword, shoving it into the scabbard hooked around my waist.

"What is it?"

He stopped halfway to where I stood, my hand instinctively going to the hilt of my sword again. "The guard has been summoned immediately. There's been an attempt on the prince's life."

⊰ SEVEN ⊱

PRINCE DAMIAN'S CHAMBERS were in an uproar when I rounded the corner and rushed through the door, sword drawn and ready — just in case.

"Alex, go assist Nolen. Asher, come over here," Deron shouted the moment I rushed through the door.

The entire guard stood around the outer room, swords drawn. There were also some of King Hector's men standing near Prince Damian's door — which was shut. I hurried across the room to where Nolen stood behind his desk.

Asher had filled me in on the way back, telling me that the would-be assassin had been a girl masquerading as a maid delivering the luncheon service to Prince Damian's rooms. It was unusual that he had been in his room for lunch. He usually joined his father and the rest of court for luncheon and dinner. When the girl had pushed the cart into his room, she'd drawn a knife from her waist and lunged at the prince. Antonio had stopped her in time and supposedly she was now being detained for questioning before being executed.

"Where is the prince?" I asked when I was close enough to speak quietly to Nolen.

"In his room. It was quite a shock to him, I'm sure. He's not used to women attempting to murder him." Perspiration dotted Nolen's forehead, which he wiped with an already limp handkerchief. It looked like Nolen was suffering from quite a bit of shock himself.

"Where is the girl now?"

"Over there." Nolen pointed to the other side of the room, and I realized the king's men were not hovering near the door, as I first thought, but surrounding a chair just to the side of it.

Nolen continued to chatter in my ear, but I stopped listening the moment one of the largest men shifted his weight, moving aside so I had a clear view of the would-be assassin. She was tied to the chair and gagged. But when our eyes met across the room, hers widened.

"Asheshka!"

She struggled in the chair, trying to speak around the gag. Panic burned hot in my veins. What was *Tanoori* doing here? When had she left our village and become an *assassin*?

"Why hasn't someone taken her to the dungeons yet?" I yelled over her attempts to speak my name. "Remove her from the prince's rooms immediately! Keep her tied up and gagged."

The other guards looked to Deron. His dark eyes met mine questioningly, but then he nodded. "Do as Alex says. One of us will be down to interrogate her as soon as possible. No one else speaks to her until then, is that understood?"

"Yes, sir," the tallest man said. "You heard 'im, let's get her down in the dark where she belongs."

I watched as the other men took her from the room, still

51

struggling, her neck straining as she tried to speak through the gag. With what I hoped was an imperceptible shudder, I forced myself to turn away, to remain in control. Calm, collected.

"Asher, take Jerrod and Kai out in the hall," Deron barked out. "No one enters or leaves these chambers without being searched — do you understand? No one!"

"Yes, sir!" Kai responded first. Jerrod and Asher both nodded as they all trooped out the door.

"Alex, you, Rylan, and Jude stay here with me outside the prince's bedroom door. The rest of you may leave. We have this under control."

"I'm not sure we should leave. Maybe you aren't capable of handling this job. The king will want a report of how something like this happened," the largest of the king's men said.

"I am the one in charge of the prince's safety," Deron said. "If you have a problem, you are welcome to make it known, but not right now. Right now we need to make sure he is secure." Deron met the man glare for glare. "Alex," he continued, without turning to look at me, "go to the prince and check on him."

"Yes, sir," I said. My heart skipped a beat as I turned, heading to the door of Prince Damian's bedroom. Hopefully this time, he would be his normal, petulant self. I didn't think I could handle any more surprises today.

I knocked once and when there was no response, I slowly opened the door. "Your Highness?"

The room was darkened, the curtains drawn. At first, I couldn't see anything, until my eyes adjusted to the thickness of the gloom. The prince sat in his large armchair, his head between his hands, elbows propped up on his desk. His perfectly pomaded hair was actually in disarray. There was a feeling of heaviness in the room, as though the air had taken on the weight of something unseen, something pressing in, pressing *down*.

"Your Highness?" I repeated, my stomach twisting nervously when he didn't respond.

Prince Damian lifted his head, his piercing blue eyes meeting mine. There was a look of such unguarded unhappiness on his face that my heart lurched unwittingly beneath my ribs.

"Alex," he said, his voice low, in a tone I'd never heard before.

"Sir?" I took a half step toward him.

The prince stood up abruptly, turning his back to me, and I froze. A strange, unaccustomed silence settled upon the room.

"Sir, are you . . . all right?" My heart beat harder in my chest.

He drew in a sharp breath and I flinched. Had that been too womanly a thing to say? Would a man have asked after his well-being? I was a member of his personal guard — shouldn't it be normal to be concerned if he seemed . . . out of sorts? This was twice now that I'd seen a side to him I never had before. I felt unbalanced, as though the ground I stood on were suddenly shifting beneath me.

"The girl — where is she?"

"She's in the dungeon awaiting questioning, sir."

"Very good." When he faced me again, the unhappiness, the *something* that was in his eyes, was gone. Here was the prince I knew. He reached up to smooth his hair back into place, his motions practiced, memorized, almost lazy. One eyebrow lifted while a small smirk slowly pulled at his mouth. "You will make sure she receives the full punishment of the law, I assume? You, who always puts duty first, right, Alex?"

I wasn't sure I understood what he was asking of me. It felt like there was an underlying question, a hidden meaning beneath his drawling voice. Sentencing Tanoori to death while practically yawning.

"She will undoubtedly be punished to the full extent of the law, Your Highness. Your safety is of the utmost importance."

"As it should be. As it should be." He lifted something from his desk, and rubbed it between his thumb and forefinger. It looked like a trinket of some sort. He suddenly closed his fist over it, and I barely heard it clink against the signet ring on his finger. "I'm quite all right. It was a shock, of course, to have the servant come at me with a knife. But my men are good and stopped her in time, obviously." A strange look crossed his face when he looked down at the object in his hand — that same hint of grief I'd seen earlier this morning when he briefly spoke of his brother. "If she had succeeded, though, do you suppose anyone would mourn my loss?"

I stiffened. "Sir?"

Prince Damian looked up at me, his expression hooded. "My mother is gone. My brother is gone. My father hardly realizes I'm alive. If I had died today, do you think anyone would have cried at my funeral?"

I stared at the prince, at a complete loss for words. My hands were clammy at my side. "Sir, I . . . I believe there would be many —"

"Would *you* have cared?" He cut me off abruptly. "If you had come back from the practice ring to find me lying here dead, would you have cried for me, Alex?"

"Y-your Highness, how can you ask me such a thing?" I realized too late that my voice had come out too high, too feminine, but he didn't even blink.

"I suppose that's my answer, then." Damian set the trinket down hard on the desk and waved his fingers at me. "You may go."

I nodded, backing toward the door. "Yes, sir."

I had failed him somehow, but I didn't know how to fix it. Or why I would even care to try. I was glad to be dismissed, grateful to leave behind the unexpected pang of concern for a prince I'd long ago convinced myself was as corrupt as his father.

The door swung open without a sound — the hinges were well oiled. But voices lifted in anger greeted me. Deron, Rylan, and Jude stood in front of the doorway, their stances tense. Facing them were three of the king's guard and Iker.

"Captain, I require a word with you and Prince Damian," Iker was saying. His greasy hair looked even shinier than normal and his robes were stained and wrinkled, as though he'd slept in them. I couldn't imagine how he'd managed to garner such favor from the king as to become his chief advisor.

"The prince is indisposed and needs some time to collect himself." Deron glanced at me as I walked over to where they stood.

Iker's lips pursed. "The king is concerned for his son's well-being and I have come to make sure proper measures are put into place to ensure his safety."

"I assure you that we have things well under control and that the prince will be more closely guarded than —"

"That is not enough." Iker cut Deron off. "By order of King Hector, one of you will personally stay here at night, guarding the prince's door at all hours. He must have someone by his side at all times. We can take no chances with the life of the heir to the throne."

Deron was silent for a moment; a muscle stood out on his jaw. Finally, he barely inclined his head. "It will be as the king wishes. Alex is the best man we have. I will assign him to guard the prince's door."

I stared at Deron for a moment too long. "You wish me to sleep *here*?"

"What is the meaning of this?" Prince Damian's voice made me jump.

Iker bowed to the prince, then smiled — a smile as oily as his hair. "Your father is concerned for your safety. We are putting greater measures of protection in place to ensure your continued well-being."

"By making me a prisoner to my own guard?"

I stepped aside as Prince Damian strode up to Iker. Damian's expression was sardonic, his voice insolent. But tension hung around him like a palpable shroud.

"Not a *prisoner* — imagine the thought." Iker tittered. "Always, you've had such a lively imagination. No, you may continue your life as you see fit, but Captain D'agnen or members of his guard will always be with you to make sure no one can get close enough to threaten you ever again."

"I see." The insolence was gone from Prince Damian's voice, replaced instead by a coldness that made me shiver.

"Captain D'agnen has assigned Alex to sleep here, in the outer chamber, to protect your door from intruders."

"*Alex* is going to be sleeping right here — outside my door?" There was a strange hint of bemusement in Prince Damian's voice.

He glanced at me with his eyebrows lifted. For some odd reason, I had to fight to keep from blushing. Men on the prince's guard did *not* blush.

"As the captain pointed out" — Iker looked back at me with a mysterious glint in his eyes — "your men are good, but Alex is the best. Surprisingly."

My mouth felt dry, but I forced myself to lower my head in acknowledgment of his somewhat backhanded compliment.

Iker turned back to Prince Damian. "This ensures the king's peace of mind for his son's safety."

"As my safety is the king's greatest concern." Prince Damian's voice was biting.

"Indeed, Your Highness," Iker said. "You are his heir."

"You will have to thank him for his concern on my behalf." Prince Damian turned on his heel, heading back into his room, until he paused. "I wish to lie down and rest, maybe even use my chamber pot. Does Captain D'agnen or Alex need to come hold my hand? Make sure no one sneezes near me while I relieve myself?"

It took every bit of control I possessed to keep my face impassive in that moment. I was torn between letting my jaw drop and bursting out in laughter. I could see the other men struggling as well.

Iker flushed an ugly shade of puce. "Do you make *light* of the attempt on your life?" There was a strange note to his voice, but I couldn't place it. Almost sarcasm.

"Absolutely not," the prince replied. "I only seek to know just how involved you — I mean, *Father* — intends to have Captain D'agnen be in keeping guard over me."

Iker met Prince Damian's icy glare. "As involved as necessary to keep you from coming to harm."

"Well, as I see no one hiding in my bed with a sword or standing over my chamber pot with an ax, I believe I shall retire to my room. This has been an exhausting morning, to say the least." Prince Damian yawned deeply as if to prove his point, walked into his room, and slammed the door shut.

"You will do as the king wishes, won't you, Captain D'agnen?" Iker's glance paused on me before pinning Deron with a pointed stare. Iker's eyes were such a dark gray, they almost looked black, and his skin was sickly pale. I'd never liked being around him, but after seeing him in his room the other night and after what he'd made us do to those girls, looking at him made my skin crawl.

"Yes, we will do everything required of us to protect our prince."

I pressed my fist to my chest along with the rest of the guard and we all bowed to Iker. Even though I was completely panicked inside, I had to appear calm. There was no reason Alex Hollen, second only to the captain of the prince's personal guard, would have a problem sleeping near his liege. Alex had nothing to hide. But *Alexa* did, and I had no idea what this would mean for keeping up my disguise.

"Excellent. That is all." Iker swept the other men with his dark gaze, then turned on his heel and exited the room, the king's guards behind him.

I stared after them, shifting my face into a mask to conceal the dread coiling in my belly. I had to get down to the dungeons right away, before Tanoori undid Marcel's sacrifices to protect me by revealing my secret.

⇥ EIGHT ⇤

Y FOOTSTEPS ECHOED on the stone stairs leading down to the dungeons. The outfit I wore was intended to intimidate: tall, heavy boots; thick gloves with metal knuckles; my sword at my side. That was what I intended to do — what I *had* to do. Intimidate Tanoori to keep her from revealing who I was. I'd managed to convince Deron to let me be the one to interrogate her, thankfully. My secret depended on keeping her silent.

The dungeons were dank, the air hot and wet and stale as I descended into the depths of the palace. I'd always thought it would be cooler down there, but the dungeons were built above the forge and the heat of the constant fires seeped through the ground into the dark cells. It would be a kindness on our part to fulfill Tanoori's sentence quickly. To die fast was better than to rot down here, slowly losing who you were to the dark, the filth, the stench and madness that claimed all long-term tenants of the cells eventually.

"Where is the prisoner?" I asked Jaerom, the keeper of the keys. He was Deron's cousin. Deron was taller, but Jaerom was bigger; his arms were the size of small tree trunks. His skin was slightly lighter than Deron's, closer to the color of coffee, rather than the darkness of the nighttime sky.

"She's over here," Jaerom said, picking up his keys and a torch, which he handed to me. I followed him to one of the cells and took a deep breath. "The cap'n asked you to do the questioning, huh, Little Boss?"

"Yes." I stared at the door that stood between me and possible discovery. Jaerom thought it was hilarious that I'd beaten his huge cousin in the fight to join the guard. Even though Deron had kept the captainship, Jaerom had called me Little Boss ever since. "I'd like to question her alone. Make sure no one comes or goes until I say so."

"Going to lull her into security and then go for the throat, eh?" Jaerom shot me a wry grin as he flipped through his key chain.

"You know me too well," I replied, watching as he selected the right key and pushed it into the lock. The dead bolt scraped back with the screech of metal on metal.

"She's all yours. Enjoy." Jaerom opened the door with a flourish and I marched past him.

I waited until the door shut behind me and his footsteps receded before I placed the torch in a bracket on the wall and turned to face Tanoori.

She was still tied to a chair, the gag as tight in her mouth as it had been an hour before, but the fight seemed to have gone out of her. She stared up at me, motionless.

"You are going to be tried and found guilty for the attempted murder of our prince." I walked over to her, my hand resting on the hilt of my sword. "Do you know what the penalty is for would-be assassins?"

She glared up at me.

"Answer me!" I bellowed, pulling out my sword and leveling it at her throat in one swift movement.

She gasped, pulling back instinctively.

"Do you know what the penalty is?" I repeated, enunciating each word slowly.

Finally, Tanoori nodded, and tears filled her eyes. She spoke, but the word was garbled by her gag. I lifted my sword to her face and her eyes widened in terror. But instead of cutting her face or fulfilling her sentence prematurely as she surely feared I was about to do, I used the sharp tip to pull the gag out of her mouth.

"What was that?" I let the sword rest against her cheek.

"Death," she whispered, visibly trembling.

"Yes, death."

"What's *happened* to you, Ale —"

"Why did you try to kill the prince?" I snarled at her, cutting her off.

"It's the only way."

I stared at Tanoori incredulously. How had a girl who was afraid of her own shadow when I'd last seen her found her way into such a position? I hadn't known her well, but I had not pegged her for the assassin type. "The only way to what? Ensure your own death sentence?"

"I know you recognize me. We all wondered what happened to you after your parents died. Someone said they saw Marcel and another boy being taken by the army. That boy was you, wasn't it?"

Hearing Marcel's name felt like the red-hot tip of the farrier's iron tunneling into my gut. I pressed the edge of my sword into her cheek, not hard enough to cut her, but enough to stop her from talking. "I have no idea what you're talking about, and if you know what's best for you, the only words out of your mouth from now on will be a confession and an explanation of why you tried to kill Prince Damian." The fear in Tanoori's eyes turned my stomach. Self-loathing filled my throat with acid. But my life depended on silencing her — and as much as I wished I could change things, Tanoori's life was already forfeit. "Why did you do it?"

"His death would end the war, bring down King Hector. His death would mean a chance at a normal life for the rest of us." A dark shadow crossed her face as Tanoori lifted her chin, scraping her cheek on the edge of my sword, showing the first bit of backbone that led me to believe she really could be the one who had raced toward the prince with a dagger.

"How could the death of the prince bring down the king? All it would mean is that an inferior relative would inherit the throne and his war."

"I wouldn't expect you to understand, since you're apparently one of the prince's right-hand *men*." Tanoori's eyes flashed in the dim light, her tone snide.

"What you're talking about is treason. And for that alone, the punishment is death. Who convinced you that killing the prince would end the war?"

"Why, are you interested in finishing the job?" She grinned at me, growing bolder by the second.

"Silence!" I roared, pressing the sword against her throat again. The hot, rank air pressed in around me, slippery and stifling. The putrid smell of unwashed bodies and unemptied chamber pots was enough to make me gag.

Tanoori leaned forward, as far as her bindings allowed. "I

watched you practice with your brother. If pretending to be a boy is what you had to do to save yourself, it obviously worked well."

My hand trembled on my sword and I glanced wildly over my shoulder, terrified Jaerom could be eavesdropping.

"I won't reveal your secret, even though you sentenced me to death. I knew the risk I took and you're only doing your duty. It's the way of the world. But if you wish to help change the course of events, if you wish to do something meaningful, all you have to do is follow the river. The answer lies in the Heart of the Rivers for those who want to find it."

"I said, *silence*!" I yelled again, trying to cover up the unsteady beating of my heart, the pulse of fear and fascination that surged through my blood.

Tanoori sat back in her chair and closed her eyes. I shoved my sword into its scabbard and pulled the gag back up to her mouth. Just before I got it into place, her eyes opened again and she whispered, "Please make it fast."

My fingers shook as I forced the gag back into place, but then I paused. "You won't tell anyone who I am?" I breathed into her ear.

She shook her head once and I saw truth in her eyes.

I yanked the gag back out and threw it on the ground. "I'll do what I can."

"Thank you, Alexa," Tanoori said softly.

I turned and grabbed the torch, leaving her in darkness, then rushed out of the cell as fast as I could. I had to get out of there. Away from the heat, the sweat, the smell, the fear that filled my mouth with the bitter taste of copper. The door slammed shut behind me and I shouted for Jaerom.

"All done?" he drawled as he sauntered down the corridor.

"Got what I could out of her." I twisted my head, making my neck crack. "How do you stand this heat?"

"Get used to it eventually, I guess, just like all the others stuck down here in hell." The lock ground back into place, sealing Tanoori in to await her fate, and me out to try and erase what she'd said to me.

"Right." I strode back toward the stairs, desperate to get away, though I tried to look as nonchalant as possible, hoping Jaerom didn't notice how flushed I was, how my pulse raced against the skin of my neck. I doused the torch in a bucket near his desk and set it back on the pile.

"See you soon, Little Boss." Jaerom called after me as I rushed back up the stairs, away from the fear of discovery, from the tantalizing thought of finishing what Tanoori started — of finishing this war. How many times had I dreamed of that very thing? But after two years in the army and one in the prince's guard, I didn't think anyone had that power anymore.

It was impossible. She was deranged. Killing the prince would only infuriate King Hector even more. He'd already lost his elder son; Prince Damian was his sole direct heir. And Tanoori's hint made no sense. Follow the river? The key could be found in the Heart of the Rivers? There were rivers all over the place. We lived in a *jungle*. No, I wouldn't even consider it. My duty was to my prince, whether I liked him or not. Whether I believed in his father's war or not.

Finally, I emerged onto the main floor of the palace. A window was open nearby, carrying the scent of the jungle. The smell of green things and flowers and soil and rain. Thick clouds, bruised the color of dark wine, rushed across the sky toward us, carrying

64

lightning and rain. The growl of thunder was a distant threat, menacing but still soft.

Some said that Blevon, King Osgand's kingdom, was dry and filled with peaks and canyons because he was cursed. They said a powerful sorcerer made the water sink deep into the earth, so they had to dig for it, just to stay alive. Papa had always said that wasn't true, and I secretly agreed with him. Off to my right was the breeding house, which I avoided walking past at all costs. As I watched two of the king's guards come out the door, laughing raucously, I had a hard time believing anyone could be more deserving of a curse than King Hector, and our land was verdant and full of water.

I had to stop, turn away, and press my fist to my belly to keep at bay the nausea that welled up into my throat, threatening to make me vomit as I thought of little Kalen in there somewhere, dreading the time when her monthly courses came and the attic was no longer safe for her. Across the courtyard, boys barely old enough to lift a sword were sparring, forced to join the army and die for a war that had no end in sight.

Avenging his wife's death had sounded like a noble cause in the beginning, but after so much death, so much rape and horror and atrocity enacted in the name of helping Antion win the war, I couldn't help but hate my own king as much as the enemy's. No matter the outcome, there would be no true victors.

Tanoori's words echoed in my mind and I squeezed my eyes shut. If there *was* a way to end this war — to stop King Hector — did I have the courage to try?

⊰ NINE ⊱

*T*HAT NIGHT, RYLAN carried a cot into Damian's outer chamber for me. Thunder rumbled through the palace as rain pelted the stone walls, echoing off the roof above us. The air was taut with the charged heat of the storm.

"Where do you want it, Alex?"

I pointed. "Just set it down next to his door. Hopefully, that will be close enough to appease Iker." I couldn't quite keep the irritation from my voice. I'd stood at attention outside Prince Damian's door for hours, with no sound from within to give me any hint as to his activities, lightning and thunder my only companions.

The long silence had given me far too much time to think about Marcel and Tanoori. About my life before the army came into our village and took Marcel and me away. About the difference between *training* to fight and the reality of actually killing someone.

Or watching someone you love die.

The pain of Marcel's loss washed over me and I stared at the cot, willing myself not to lose control. I balled my hands into fists, tried to hold back the sudden, consuming grief.

And soon Tanoori would die as well.

"Alex?" Rylan's voice was concerned.

I clenched my jaw and, through sheer willpower, forced the emotion away. The tightness beneath the cage of my ribs receded enough to allow me to breathe without gasping and I looked up at him. "I can't talk about it."

He nodded and turned away, allowing me to pull myself together. "Do you need anything else?"

Taking a deep breath, I glanced around. The room was bare of anything I needed to wash with or prepare for bed. But that brought up the question of how I was to accomplish my toiletries without revealing myself. If anyone walked in while I was bathing — or if Prince Damian came out of his room . . .

"No," I finally replied. I'd ring for a maid to bring me a bowl of water and a cloth. That would have to suffice.

He started to walk away, but I called out. "Rylan?"

Pausing, he looked back.

"The prisoner I questioned earlier . . . I haven't been told. When have they scheduled her execution?"

"I haven't heard, either. I'll find out and let you know."

"Thank you."

Rylan looked at me for a moment longer, as though he wanted to say something more. Our eyes met and locked. For a moment, I wondered what would happen if he knew. If he stood across from me right now, knowing that I was a *girl* who had just lost her brother and been forced to move into the prince's chambers — would he take me in his arms and wipe away the tears I'd been choking back all day?

My neck growing hot, I barked out, "That's all, Rylan. What are you standing around staring at me for?"

"Sorry." He shook his head slightly, a strange look crossing his face. Before I could try to guess his thoughts, he turned and walked out.

I exhaled sharply when the door shut and I sat down heavily on the cot. Marcel's death was too much to handle. It was making me vulnerable, revealing the secret I'd spent years trying to cover up. I had to pull it together. I couldn't allow myself to stare at Rylan like that ever again. My only hope was that he'd chalk it up to exhaustion and grief. He seemed concerned. He obviously knew I was more upset than I let on.

"Ah, my favorite guard, ready to do my every bidding."

The prince's voice startled me and I jumped up to attention again. "Your Highness, I apologize for my inattentiveness." I bowed deeply, hoping he didn't notice the wetness on my cheeks. How did he get the door open without a sound? And what did he mean by his "favorite guard"?

"Alex, rise and quit apologizing. As this is now your bedroom, I understand that you won't be standing at attention at all times. Unless your strength and training extend even to the ability to resist sleep?"

I stood up and pressed my fist to my heart. Prince Damian was dressed only in pants, boots, and a loose-fitting white tunic, unlaced so that the top of his chest was exposed. A chest that was more muscular than I would have expected, considering the depths of his laziness. I'd never once seen him exercise or train with any sort of weapon. He did ride fairly often, but that wouldn't have made a difference in his upper body. The analytical side of my mind wondered what he could possibly be doing — and when — to create muscle like that. As a member of his personal guard, I was unsettled to think that I didn't know. But the other side of me — the feminine side — had to crush a sudden rush of butterflies in my stomach.

"Do you need anything, Your Highness?"

"Alex, I believe I've told you before that you need not address me so formally all the time. Especially now that we're practically bedmates." He gave me a sardonic look, one eyebrow lifted. I could have sworn he was suppressing a smirk.

My cheeks felt flushed, and I prayed that my olive skin hid my blush. A boy wouldn't blush at that comment, would he? "Sir, I would never presume to treat you with any disrespect."

Prince Damian sighed and passed a hand over his face. "Of course not. One must always treat the prince with the utmost deference." He sounded frustrated — almost disappointed. After the last two days, I wasn't sure it was just an act anymore, as I'd always believed.

Trying to hide my confusion, I asked, "What might I assist you with, sir?"

He turned and narrowed his gaze at me. "You seem like someone I can trust. Second only to the captain of my guard, a dedicated person, completely entrenched in duty."

"Yes, sir," I said. My heart beat faster beneath my ribs at the look on his face.

"If someone should happen to bring me a letter, I wish you to bring it straight to me. Do not open it or alert Nolen to its existence. Can I trust you with this?"

"Yes, sir," I said again, more confused than ever. A secret letter? That's why he came out to talk to me?

"Excellent." The prince paused. "I *want* to trust you, Alex. I hope that I am making a good decision by asking this of you." His eyes were piercing on mine, sending a sudden rush of heat through my limbs. "I've been told my whole life to trust no one. As a prince and heir to the throne, I'm to assume that everyone is an enemy. Do you think that is wise counsel? Do you think it foolish of me to put my trust in you?"

Why did he insist on asking me such questions? He'd never made an effort to win me over before. Was this some sort of new game? To play on the emotions of the guard who just lost her — *his* — brother?

"I hope that you will find your trust to be well placed in me, sir," I finally replied, the back of my neck hot.

"That's not a very firm answer." He took a step closer to me.

I had to tilt my head back a tiny bit to look up into his face. It made me feel far too much like a girl. "Yes, sir. You can trust me."

"Do you have many friends, Alex?"

"Friends, sir?"

"Someone to talk to or laugh with. Perhaps someone you can confide all your secrets in." He lifted one eyebrow. Though he sounded flippant, there was a serious glint in his eyes that made my throat go dry.

"I had my brother, sir."

"But now he's gone."

"Yes," I said, barely above a whisper.

"So you're friendless. Alone."

A strange, panicky feeling overcame me. I didn't understand what he was doing — what he wanted. "I have the other members of the guard, Your Highness."

Prince Damian was silent for a long moment. "Of course you do. I apologize for prying into your personal business."

Our eyes met and held and suddenly I wondered the same thing — did he have any friends? Or was he, too, all alone? I'd been guarding him for a year, and I'd never even thought about it before. My cheeks grew warm with shame.

Damian took a step back, his expression unreadable. "I should let you rest. But first, would you please ring the maid for some clotted cream and berries? I find myself craving something sweet tonight after all the stress of this day."

"Of course, sir."

He nodded, then turned on his heel, strode into the inner chamber of his rooms, and shut the door. I stared at it for a long time, my mind racing my heart.

When the maid brought up the requested food, she also brought me a bowl of water, a cloth, and a clean tunic. I set the supplies for myself on the floor next to the cot and picked up the bowl of cream and fruit for the prince. Acai berries, such a deep blue they were almost purple, and sliced papaya and mango filled the bowl. Their juices ran down over the cream, staining it and making my mouth water. When I knocked softly, he called out, "Enter."

I pushed open the door and entered his room. The fireplace was dark and empty; it was too hot for a fire. Candles flickered from multiple candelabras around the room, making the shadows stretch and sway, chasing the orange light of the flames.

"You may set it on the desk. Thank you, Alex."

I walked quickly across the room and did as the prince asked. When I turned, he stood by his bed, shirtless, his chest and arms coated with a fine sheen of sweat. His extremely well-muscled chest and arms. His stomach was flat and chiseled. He was as strong as any of the men on his guard, perhaps even more so than most. In the warm light of the candles, Prince Damian was almost painfully handsome. I suddenly felt too hot. Like all the heat in the room had surged into my body, coalescing deep in my belly. Lightning flashed, filling the room with bright white light, making me flinch.

"Was there anything else?"

My eyes widened when I realized I'd been staring at his body. My cheeks flamed, making me grateful for the low light of the candles. "Sir, you're covered in sweat. Are you taking ill?" I asked, keeping my voice low and gruff. Manly. It was as good a cover as I could come up with. No one looked like that unless they exercised — a *lot*.

"I'm in perfect health." He shot me a wicked grin. "As you may have noticed."

My mouth went dry and my face burned even hotter. But before I could think of any other ways to dig myself into a deeper hole of humiliation, he continued, "You may go, Alex."

I bowed briefly and strode out of the room, my body on fire with embarrassment — and curiosity. There was definitely more to Prince Damian than I'd realized. But I was beginning to worry that he had realized there was more to me, as well.

⇥ TEN ⇤

I'D BARELY FALLEN into a restless sleep on the cot when I heard someone creeping across the room. I stayed frozen but opened my eyes, my fingers going to the dagger I kept strapped to my thigh, even at night.

The person was small, and clutched in one hand was a rectangle of paper.

I let go of the dagger, leaving it in its sheath, and sat up in bed. The intruder stepped toward me, holding out an envelope. In the darkness, I was pretty sure it was a young boy, maybe nine or ten at most. Silently, I took the letter. As soon as I held it, he turned and dashed toward a tapestry hanging behind Nolen's desk, his bare feet soundless on the stone floor. He lifted it up, there was a slight creak, and then he was gone, the tapestry swinging back into place.

That explained why the guards outside hadn't been alerted to his presence. A secret passageway was hidden in this room. One I didn't know about. I stood up and crossed the floor as silently as the boy. When I lifted the tapestry, there was no sign of a door. The wall was paneled in wood. I slid my hands along the beams, searching for a knot or button, a lever, something to indicate how the boy had come and gone so easily. I couldn't find anything.

Frustrated and angry, I sat down on the chair behind Nolen's desk. How was I supposed to protect the prince if I didn't even know all the ways an attacker could have access to him? Why had I never been told of this before?

I looked down at the letter. There was no writing on the outside, and it wasn't very thick. What could it possibly contain that warranted being delivered in the dead of night so secretively? I clutched the sealed parchment tightly, wondering if there were any way for me to open it without the prince knowing.

No. I gave him my word. I hadn't lied when I said I was trustworthy.

Standing up with a sigh, I crossed the room and knocked softly on Prince Damian's door. There was no response. I knocked again, slightly louder this time. Still nothing. Would I risk his wrath if I entered without permission? He seemed pretty intent on no one else finding out about the letter.

The door opened silently and I slipped into the darkened room. The storm had passed on, leaving the smell of rain and the sticky heat of humidity in its wake.

I hadn't thought to put on boots before entering. In fact, all I wore was a long white nightshirt over the pants I'd had on the day before. I didn't dare sleep without pants anymore, and I'd left my breasts bound beneath the shirt. Still, without my usual vest, someone might notice the cloth wrapped around my chest — if he looked closely. I halted, trying to decide what to do.

Then Prince Damian cried out.

My first instinct was to protect him. Yanking my dagger from my thigh, I sprang forward, rushing to his side. The bedclothes were twisted around his body and legs, and his forehead had a sheen of sweat across it, his dark hair in complete disarray. He grimaced and his head jerked to the side, but he was still asleep. He mumbled something, so quietly I couldn't quite make out what — possibly a name. His voice sounded . . . pained.

Prince Damian was having a nightmare. A bad one, from the way he looked and how he continued to jerk and thrash in his bed. I held my dagger in one hand, the letter in the other, and stared at him. Should I wake him up? Or put the letter on his table and leave? I had the sudden urge to reach out and brush his hair from his forehead, to let my hand trail down his cheek. To calm his thrashing with my touch.

He was still shirtless, and I wasn't able to resist drinking in the sight of his body unabashedly now that he couldn't catch me staring. I'd seen plenty of men shirtless after living in the army and then earning a position on the guard. But this was different for some reason. He was so beautiful, even in the midst of a nightmare. I'd reasoned away my original attraction to him when I joined his guard, told myself that he was arrogant, spoiled, rotten. But what if he wasn't as bad as I thought — what if it was some sort of strange act?

He thrashed on the bed again, his head turning toward me. My breath caught in my lungs, my heart raced beneath my ribs as I stared down at him. His dark hair fell across his forehead, and his lips parted. In sleep, he didn't look arrogant or spoiled. He almost looked . . . lost. For one brief moment of insanity, I wondered what it would be like to lie next to him, to comfort him from the demons that apparently chased him at night. To be held against his body in the circle of his strong arms. To have his lips touch mine.

What is wrong with you? I shook my head violently, horrified at the turn in my thoughts. Fantasizing about the prince would have been bad enough if I were a normal girl, but as his guard — whom he thought was a *boy*? It was absolutely inexcusable.

My cheeks burning, I hurried to set the letter down on the table closest to him and turned to go. When I was halfway to the door, the floor creaked loudly beneath my foot and I froze, cursing under my breath.

The labored breathing of Prince Damian's nightmare-ridden sleep halted abruptly. I stayed completely motionless, hoping he'd roll over and go back to sleep. Instead, the bed quietly groaned in protest as he sat up.

"Who goes there? Reveal yourself at once."

I turned around, lifting my hands in the air, belatedly realizing I still clutched my dagger in one hand. Though the storm had passed, clouds lingered behind, blocking the moon. The window was behind me, but without the moonlight, I could only hope he wouldn't see the outline of my binding — or my body.

"Alex, is that you?"

"Your Highness, I apologize for disturbing you." My voice was strained from the effort of hiding my embarrassment. "But the letter you spoke of earlier . . ." I gestured at his table, where the letter sat unopened.

He glanced at it, then back at me, his expression inscrutable in the darkness. Even though my sight had adjusted, I could barely see his eyes.

"And why, I wonder, did you feel it necessary to deliver the letter with a knife in hand?" The prince's tone hinged somewhere between curiosity and accusation. I could have sworn I caught him glancing down at my body before quickly looking up at my eyes again.

In one fluid movement, I lowered my hands and slipped the knife back into the sheath on my leg. Would it embarrass or anger him to mention the obvious nightmare he'd been having? I couldn't come up with a different excuse fast enough, and already the silence had stretched too long. "You cried out in your sleep, sir. I was afraid that you had been attacked again."

"That would imply a deplorable lack of awareness on your part, if someone had managed to slip past you and get into my room." He ignored the mention of his crying out in his sleep entirely.

"Sir, the child who brought the letter did so by way of a secret passage — one I was not aware of before this night. I was concerned that another such passageway might exist in your inner chamber."

"Do I detect a hint of irritation in your voice, almost-captain of mine?"

I cleared my throat, and attempted to rein in what was apparently my obvious frustration. "Sir, my only concern is your safety. If there are passages that allow someone access to you that I'm unaware of, it could lead to a failure to protect you from harm."

"Ah, I see."

I tried not to stare at him as silence fell, stretching out to fill the space between us with a strange tension. He sat in his bed, halfway undressed, while I stood in the middle of his room with only a shirt, a binding, and some pants to hide my secret. If I really were a boy, it wouldn't matter how dressed or undressed either of us were. I wouldn't have felt breathless from the force of his gaze on me in the darkness. But I *wasn't* a boy and I needed to get out of this room before he realized it.

Finally, he lay back down in bed without another word, pulling the sheets over his shoulder and shutting his eyes. When he didn't say anything else, appearing to have decided to ignore me and go back to sleep, I turned on my heel and rushed for the door.

If he refused to answer my questions, there was obviously something he was hiding. I only hoped it wouldn't lead to a successful assassination, because if he died, I would, too — for failing in my job to protect him. I grumbled under my breath as I yanked open the door.

"Stupid, stubborn —"

"Good night, Alex." His voice made me jump and I nearly gasped out loud.

"Good night, sir." Cheeks flaming, praying I hadn't spoken loud enough for him to hear, I shut his door.

⇥ ELEVEN ⇤

AFTER A BRIEF sponge bath before the sun rose, hoping no one else would be up so early, I hurried to switch my tunic. I didn't dare change the binding on my chest; it would take too long. I couldn't risk someone walking in on me — especially Prince Damian. Not that I would expect him to be up so early, but then again, he seemed to be full of surprises recently.

Voices outside the door to the prince's chambers alerted me moments before it opened and just as I predicted, Nolen strode in with Deron and Jerrod on his heels.

"The night was uneventful, I take it?" Deron stood in the middle of the room, arms folded across his wide chest. He wore the traditional uniform of Prince Damian's guard: white tunic, thick vest dyed a deep blue with the emblem of the Antion nation on the right breast — a jaguar crouched on a branch, prepared to attack.

"Yes, sir," I responded, choosing not to mention the letter or the secret passageway. Or the midnight conversation with the prince. I trusted Deron far more than I trusted Prince Damian, but I had promised not to tell anyone. And there was a part of me that wanted to find out what was really going on before alerting anyone else to the prince's strange nighttime activities.

"Excellent. Hopefully, you are good and rested, then. The competition will be held starting at noon today."

"Why would I need to be rested for the competition?" I noticed Jerrod scowling behind Deron. His pale eyes met mine for a moment before he looked away.

"Because the candidates will fight you, of course."

"The tradition is to fight the captain."

Deron nodded. "True. However, you beat me. Everyone knows the position technically should have been yours. If you'd been just a few years older, it would have been. The men will fight you, and whoever lasts the longest will join the guard."

"And the prince?"

"I've assigned Jerrod and Asher to stay with him at all times during the tryouts."

Jerrod's scowl made more sense now. Everyone knew that he wanted the position of captain someday, and before I came, it had looked like he might be the man to beat for the position — if something happened to Deron. But then I beat Deron. While Deron had taken his loss with grace (although having still retained his position as captain probably helped), Jerrod had treated me with thinly veiled contempt ever since.

And now he was relegated to being a babysitter while I was given the task he probably felt he deserved. Of all the men on the guard, he was the only one who refused to spar with me unless forced. He didn't like to lose.

"Kai and Jude will spar first, weed out the men, and then we'll have you fight the best of the bunch. Go grab something to eat and head outside to help Rylan set up the ring and get the gear together."

I nodded at Deron's dismissal. After retrieving my own vest and donning it, along with my scabbard and sword, I started to head out.

"Oh, Alex, one more thing."

I paused and looked back at Deron.

"The girl — the one who attacked Prince Damian yesterday — is sentenced to hang tomorrow morning just after dawn. Rylan said you asked."

"The prince wanted to make sure she was punished to the full extent of the law," I said, hoping the sudden nausea in my gut wasn't apparent in my expression. "I told him I would find out."

"I'll be sure to let him know." Deron waved me off. I turned away once again and this time he didn't call me back.

I easily dispatched the first two prospective guards, barely even breaking a sweat, even though it was another sweltering day. Clouds sluggishly passed overhead, offering occasional reprieve from the relentless glare of the sun, but the air was thick with humidity. As the afternoon wore on, the sky grew increasingly somber and the line of men standing outside the ring grew smaller.

Finally, only two remained.

"There will be a fifteen-minute break, and then the final two will fight for the position of personal guard to the prince," Deron called out when I beat the tenth man in under three minutes, knocking him to the ground with a hit to the back and then finishing him off with my wooden sword pressed to his exposed throat.

"Whoah, you're good," he muttered as he lumbered back up, stepping away from me warily.

I nodded in acknowledgment and then turned and walked over to where Deron stood talking to Rylan and Kai.

Rylan handed me a rag and a cup of water. I downed the water in one long draft while Kai continued regaling them with a tale of some lady's maid he'd apparently seduced the night before.

"I'm out there working while you're over here gossiping about the latest skirt you've been chasing?"

"Or undoing, as the case may be." Kai grinned, unrepentant. "You shouldn't work so hard all the time, Alex. You'd be surprised how impressive women find it when a member of the prince's guard pays attention to them."

I just shook my head, using the rag to wipe away the sweat dripping down my hairline. Kai and his women. I liked him well enough, but I was glad he didn't know I was a girl. He was attractive, I supposed, taller, with his light brown hair pulled back in a ponytail and his green eyes always crinkled at the corners from a constant smile. But if I had to pick the most handsome man on the guard, I definitely preferred Rylan's warm brown eyes. His more subdued, quiet humor. The surprising gentleness he had with children and animals.

But then my thoughts strayed to the night before. Heat rose in my body as I remembered a different pair of eyes. Shockingly blue and —

"Alex?"

I jerked and blinked. "What?" Luckily, I'd been staring at nothing, instead of at someone. But I still had to fight not to blush.

"Are you tired? Do you need a longer break?" Rylan asked. I met his concerned gaze and quickly looked away. What was wrong with me? I had to stop thinking about Rylan and the prince or any other male like that.

"I'm fine."

"We can wait longer if you need," Deron agreed.

"What he needs is a good —"

"Kai, shut it," Rylan cut him off.

"I said, I'm fine. Let's get this over with." I stormed back into the ring.

Rylan could read me better than I wanted to admit, because he was right, I was tired. The sleepless night was wearing on me. But I couldn't afford to let it show. These last two men were the best from the previous rounds with the other guards. So far, the longest fight had lasted six minutes. One of them had to go longer than that, and the position would be his.

I took a deep breath and then nodded my signal.

The second-to-last man was only about an inch taller than me. He was thin, wiry, and he held the wooden sword loosely in his left hand. He obviously hadn't made it this far on brute strength like many of the previous men. He must be more like me — fast, skilled.

A single raindrop splatted on my cheek, taking me by surprise as we lifted our swords up to our faces, acknowledging each other. I glanced up and noticed that the clouds had solidified into a gray tumult above us. Another drop hit my forehead and slipped down my nose as I looked back at my opponent. He wore a piece of fabric over his nose and mouth, hiding half his face from view. Above the covering, he had thick, ebony hair, eyes so dark they were nearly black, and olive skin. An unusual combination for the Antion nation. He must have been like me — someone with Blevonese heritage. The air felt charged as I stared at him, and a sudden chill ran down my spine. Something different — something I couldn't put my finger on — hovered around him.

"Does the dust bother you?" I asked as we began to circle.

He didn't answer.

I tightened my grip on my sword. So that's how it was going to be. I didn't want someone with an attitude on the guard with us, and I was more determined than ever to dispatch him in fewer than six minutes.

He finally lunged first, a quick jab that I easily deflected. Slowly at first, then faster and faster, he attacked and I parried, learning his movements, his method. He was good, but not remarkable. Not what I'd expected. I had a strange suspicion he was toying with me. It irked me that I couldn't see his mouth; I couldn't ascertain his expression other than from his dark, disconcerting eyes.

Raindrops continued to fall sporadically as the minutes wore on. A quick glance at Rylan confirmed what I was afraid of: He held up four fingers. Only two minutes remained to beat the masked opponent. Annoyed and unsettled, I began to attack him, rather than waiting, hitting him with a sudden frenzy of lunges and jabs. I spun and twisted and hit and hit and hit. More than once, I made contact, but he parried more of my blows than I expected, and the ones I did manage to get past his defenses didn't knock him down. But the attack revealed a weakness on his right side; he wasn't as fast at defending it. I faked to his left, and he took the bait. Before he could react, I twisted around and swung with all my might at his right side.

A killing hit. His eyes widened. He couldn't get his arm around fast enough to block me. But just before my sword should have hit him, it collided with a barrier — as though I'd hit a wall instead of soft human flesh and bone. My arm vibrated from the impact and I very nearly lost my grip on the sword. Then, as though I'd imagined it, the barrier disappeared and the wooden blade hit his ribs. He groaned and fell to the ground as though nothing unusual had happened — as though I actually had knocked him to the dirt. I stood over him in confusion and shock, my grip loose on my weapon. It had all happened so fast, those watching probably didn't even notice. But I knew he'd done something — something to stop my hit from hurting him. And then he'd pretended to lose.

He stood up and brushed himself off.

"Five minutes and twenty seconds," Deron called out.

"Pity," my opponent murmured and walked away as I stared after him. Despite the heat and the muggy humidity of the impending storm, an icy chill rushed over me, making goose bumps rise on my skin. Ignoring the final contender, who had stepped into the ring, I went over to where Deron stood watching. He tried to conceal the concern on his face.

"Is everything okay, Alex?"

"Who was that man?"

Deron glanced across the ring. When I followed his gaze, the masked contender was already striding away, not bothering to watch the final fight.

"He said his name was Eljin."

"Is he a member of another palace guard? Does anyone know anything about him?"

Deron gave me a piercing look. "He's supposedly in the army. You beat him, so why all the questions?"

I didn't know if I dared mention my suspicions — that he was some sort of sorcerer. "I wondered why he wore the mask," I finally answered, deciding to keep my thoughts to myself. If I had somehow imagined it and accused an innocent man of using sorcery, it would mean his death. "It was disconcerting and he wouldn't answer me."

I looked over to where the final opponent stood in the ring, waiting for me. Eljin had disappeared from sight.

"I'm not sure. He didn't say."

I shrugged and turned away, just as the clouds burst open above us. Rain, so warm it felt like sweat, poured down on me, coating my face, drenching my short hair.

"Alex, are you sure that's all?" Deron called after me.

I glanced back and nodded, ignoring the obvious worry on his face.

The last opponent shook my hand when I finally entered the ring, introduced himself as Mateo before taking a few steps back and lifting his sword to his face. Polite. He was good, too. Despite the driving rain and the slippery mud beneath our feet, he was quick and strong. It took me just under seven minutes to beat him, by knocking his sword from his hand and leveling mine at his chest. Instead of looking frustrated or tired, he smiled happily through the rain pouring off his brown hair, after peering at Rylan to confirm that he'd lasted the longest.

"It was an honor to fight you for this position. We've heard all about how good you are," he said as he came forward to shake my hand again.

"You're very good as well. Welcome to the guard, Mateo." I shook his hand, but I couldn't quite bring myself to smile back. I was still cold from my encounter with Eljin. There were too many unanswered questions piling up — secret passageways, cryptic messages from Tanoori, assassination attempts, the prince himself, and now Eljin, who I was sure blocked my hit with sorcery. What had been his goal — why did he even try if he didn't want to win? Why reveal his ability when he must know it could mean his death?

I didn't like unanswered questions.

⊰ TWELVE ⊱

HE REST OF the prince's guard was in a boisterous mood; those not on duty later were well on their way to getting flat-out drunk. Kai had two different women sitting on his lap, one on each leg. Even Jerrod was smiling as he listened to Asher tell a story. But I could barely make myself eat. Mateo fit into the guard well, but his presence served only to remind me that he was here because Marcel was dead.

And tomorrow, Tanoori would die as well.

It was all too much. My stomach roiled, threatening to heave up what little I'd managed to choke down.

"Going seven minutes against Alex is pretty impressive." Jude pointed at Mateo. "Well, unless you're my brother. He's the only one who can last longer than ten minutes."

Marcel could, too, I thought. But I remained silent.

"I'm still trying to learn everyone's names," Mateo admitted. "Which one is your brother again?"

"Rylan, over there next to Alex." Jude gestured with his fork, splatting Jerrod with mashed sweet potatoes in the process. "He's a master swordsman."

"Watch where you're throwing that fork," Jerrod muttered.

Suddenly Prince Damian strode in, with Antonio right behind him.

We all rose to our feet simultaneously. My stomach lurched into my rib cage as he strode past me without even a glance in my direction. I hadn't seen the prince since the night before, and the memory of everything that had passed between us made my neck grow hot and my cheeks flush. Hopefully, anyone who noticed would blame it on the sweltering night.

"I hear I am to meet the newest member of my guard tonight." He circled around the table and took his chair at the head of the table. Once he was seated, we all sat back down, except for Mateo.

"My prince, it is an honor to join your esteemed guard." Mateo bowed his head, his right fist pressed to his left shoulder.

"Yes, yes, you can sit down." Prince Damian gestured at him before grabbing a drumstick from the plate in front of him. "What is your name?"

"Mateo, my liege," he said as he took his seat once more.

"Well, then, Mateo, welcome. Now let's enjoy this feast before it grows any colder."

And with that, everyone returned to eating. Conversations rose again, building into a cacophony of noise, hammering through my brain. My skull ached, the pain growing worse every time I looked at Prince Damian. He didn't meet my gaze once. Had he really treated me any differently last night or had I imagined it? I forced myself to take a bite of the macaw roasted in mint leaves, but the freshly flavored meat was greasy and cold in my mouth. I could barely swallow it. I longed for the quiet and solitude of my room — until I remembered I didn't have my own room anymore.

I didn't know how much time passed, only that the pounding in my head was nearly unbearable, when the prince suddenly pushed his chair away from the table and stood up. We all jumped out of our seats as well, standing at attention.

"I have business to attend to, so I must reluctantly leave the celebration."

"Ahem." Nolen cleared his throat from the corner of the room. He'd been so silent, I'd almost forgotten he was there. "Don't forget your father's, ah, desires."

Prince Damian's face darkened, but he nodded curtly. "Of course not. We wouldn't wish to anger my father." He looked around the table before his gaze landed on me for the first time all night. "Alex, you will accompany me. The rest of you may enjoy the remainder of your meal. Welcome once more, Mateo. May you serve me well." The prince inclined his head at Mateo, who bowed in return. Then Damian marched past the length of the table and swept out of the room. I hurried to follow him, my scabbard hitting my leg with each step as I tried to ignore the way my heart suddenly began to pound.

He strode down the hallway without looking back, or acknowledging any of the servants or guests he passed. I practically had to jog to keep up with his longer stride. He walked by the ballroom, then the stairs to his wing, but kept going without even pausing.

The palace was a massive conglomerate of hundreds of years of additions, constructed by kings and queens each trying to outdo the previous monarchs. The newer wings were more open, more opulent. But for some reason, Prince Damian marched right on through them all, on and on, twisting and turning through the palace until we were in the southwest wing, where the oldest monarchs lived long ago. I wasn't very familiar with this wing. It was almost always empty, practically abandoned. As we walked through the much darker hallways, I couldn't quite suppress a shudder.

He finally stopped before a nondescript door. "Stay here, Alex. I'll only be a moment."

"My lord, not to question you, but the king's orders were to —"

"Are you working for the king or for me, Alex?" Prince Damian's expression was cold, almost frightening in the dimness of the barren hallway.

"You, my prince, of course."

"Then stay here."

He reached out, opened the door, and slipped into the room before I could make out anything beyond an empty bed.

For once, it wasn't sweltering in the palace as I stood waiting for Prince Damian. In fact, a light breeze wafted down the hallway, gently lifting the hair on the back of my neck. Despite the cooler temperature, sweat still beaded on my skin, making my hands damp. What was he doing in there? If something happened to him, I would be as good as dead. What was I supposed to say to King Hector if Prince Damian got himself killed? *He wouldn't let me come in the room with him* probably would not be enough to save my skin.

Blasted prince and his blasted secrets. I began to pace, stomping harder with every turn past the door, which remained firmly shut. What little light had been shining through the one stained-glass window in the hallway had long since disappeared, leaving the wing in almost total darkness.

I wasn't fond of the dark. In fact, according to Marcel, it was my biggest fear. Well, that and snakes. I tried to control my fear, but as I continued my vigil in front of the door, I suddenly had the feeling I was being watched. I forced myself to continue walking back and forth a couple of more times, but I slowed my pace, made less noise. I glanced left and right, straining against the shadows to try and make out who might be hiding in the gloom. A friend or foe?

For some reason, I thought back to my fight against Eljin earlier that day. I was suddenly afraid it had been the wrong decision not to report my suspicions immediately. I let my hand drop down to rest on the hilt of my sword, making it a casual gesture, even though my whole body hummed with tension. I needed to rectify my mistake as soon as possible and let Deron know. Unless Eljin was the one at the other end of this hallway, preparing to attack. I could beat anyone — any *natural* man or woman. But I was no match for magic. No one was.

Not even Papa had been, and he was the best fighter I'd ever seen. Swords were useless against the fire that sorcerers wielded.

My blood pulsed hot through my body, and I tensed, waiting for the strike that I sensed was coming.

When the door flung open beside me, I nearly jumped out of my skin. Prince Damian emerged, holding a lit torch. Light spilled into the hallway, scattering the shadows nearest us into oblivion. I spun to face the unknown assailant, my grip tight on the hilt of my sword, but the hallway was empty.

"Let's go," Prince Damian said, brushing past me. The door to the room was already shut. In my attempt to see if someone had really been hiding in the corridor, I'd missed the chance to try to look into the room he'd been in for so long.

Frustrated and still on edge, I followed him. There was no sign of anyone else anywhere in the southwest wing. But I trusted my instincts. We hadn't been alone.

⊰ THIRTEEN ⊱

ESPITE HOW EXHAUSTED I was, I couldn't sleep as I lay on the cot outside Prince Damian's room. Now that Mateo had officially joined the guard and taken Marcel's empty bed, I was grateful for my assignment guarding Prince Damian's door. I lay under the blanket, still wearing the same binding and tunic, having only dared do a quick wash with a wet cloth again.

The skylight above me glowed with the white light of the nearly full moon as I stared up at the ceiling. Though I kept my body still, my mind spun around and around mercilessly. When Damian and I returned, it had been so late, Deron was already in his room for the night. I hadn't been able to warn him about Eljin.

What was Eljin's goal — why was he here? Why had he fought me and purposely lost? And what was the prince involved in? Why was he including me now?

I needed Marcel. As he'd said only a couple of nights ago, I was the better fighter, but he'd been smarter. He would have been able to tell me what to do. He would have been able to figure out what was going on. My eyes burned and I shut them, pressing the heels of my hands against them to push the emotion away. I tried to force myself not to think about Marcel's death, not to long for him, because there was nothing I could do to change what had happened. I couldn't bring him back. Death was final. I knew it all too well.

And now Tanoori, who had once been a weaver's innocent daughter, would die as well.

My stomach twisted and I had to jump out of bed and rush over to the corner of the room. I barely made it in time to heave the contents of my stomach into the dark belly of the chamber pot. Over and over, I wretched, until there was nothing left but bile, burning as it came up. Finally, tears running down my cheeks and my stomach aching, I was done. I shakily put the lid on the chamber pot to smother the smell until I could gather enough strength to do something with it.

I heard the door behind me slip open right before the prince asked, "Alex? What in the name of Antion are you doing on the floor?"

I jumped up, stepping in front of the chamber pot, pressing my fist to my chest. "My prince, why are you up? Do you need something?"

We locked gazes across the room, the pale moonlight washing over him, transforming him into a specter come to haunt me.

"I need to speak with you," Prince Damian said. "And unfortunately, the only time I dared broach this subject with you was the middle of the night, when I knew there would be no listening ears. However, since it would appear that you are not having a very good night, perhaps I should wait for another time."

"Of course not, Your Highness. I am at your service, always."

"You're sick, Alex."

"No, my lord. I was indisposed by . . . emotional upset. I'm fine now." I prayed he couldn't see the way my hands trembled in the indistinct light of the moon.

" 'Indisposed by emotional upset'?" Prince Damian echoed, one eyebrow lifting. "Are you so ill at ease with me that you feel you have to hide being upset over your brother's death?"

I didn't respond, staring at his chin rather than meeting his eyes.

He gestured to the cot. "Alex, come, sit down. You don't need to stand at attention right now."

I haltingly stepped forward but couldn't bring myself to sit down on the bed while my prince stood before me.

"Please sit down. We don't need to always stand on such ceremony, especially when you aren't feeling your best and it's the middle of the night."

We stood there in silence as I battled with myself. I couldn't stop thinking about his nightmare, how I'd stared at him and even let myself dream of him holding me in his arms. How I'd imagined kissing him. We were treading on dangerous water. The closer I allowed us to become, the harder it would be to keep the truth from him. And no matter what, I could never let him find out my secret.

Before I decided what to do, he did as he'd asked me to do, and sat down on the cot with a sigh. He propped his elbows on his knees and dropped his head into his hands. "I know I told you that I kept a stiff upper lip when my brother died, but that wasn't exactly the truth."

I stared down at his bowed head, my heart picking up speed. Whatever it was I'd been expecting him to talk to me about, a confession about his own brother's death wasn't it.

96

"When did you come to the palace — three, maybe four, years ago?"

I nodded, but he didn't look up. "A little over three years ago, in the army barracks, my lord."

"Then you never knew Victor. He was older than me and he was the rightful heir."

So slowly my knee actually creaked in protest, I gingerly lowered myself down to sit beside him on the cot.

Damian turned to look at me. There was an expression of such undisguised anguish on his face, it took my breath away. "I loved my brother. He was killed by an assassin — a hired sorcerer. I was with him before he died, but when we heard the sounds of fighting, he made me leave. There was a passageway from his room to mine. No one else knew of it. He told me to leave and I never saw him alive again."

I fought valiantly to maintain my composure, but it was a losing battle. "Why are you telling me this, my lord?"

"Because you, of all people, understand. Because, for a while now, I've known that of anyone on my guard, you're the one I can trust. I wish that you wouldn't continue to pretend with me, Alex. I'm telling you this so that you may know that you're not the only one who puts on a show for everyone around him. You're not the only one playing a part."

My heart jumped into my throat. I blinked rapidly to clear my eyes, meeting Damian's pointed gaze with a feeling like a hand had reached beneath my ribs and was squeezing the air out of my lungs. My suspicions of him were true, then — he wasn't the man he portrayed himself to be. But was he trying to say he knew *my* secret?

"The fact that you've continued on, acting as though nothing can shake you, even though losing your brother was obviously a horrible blow, proves how alike we are."

I slowly exhaled, the vise on my lungs releasing. He believed the part I played was that of a dedicated guard, unaffected by the loss of his brother. Did Damian suspect that I was hiding far more than that? "Why did you have to pretend your brother's death didn't affect you?" I asked to cover up how flustered I was.

"Because a prince of Antion can't afford to have emotions like love or sorrow or grief. Not unless he wants them used against him."

An uncomfortable silence fell upon us and I looked away from Prince Damian to stare at my bare feet on the floor. It hit me again, how very little I really knew about the prince I'd served day and night for the last year. Before these last couple of days, it had never occurred to me that the haughty, spoiled person I disliked might be nothing more than an act. But I still didn't understand *why*. Why go to such lengths to make your own people despise you? The man sitting next to me on the bed, talking about the loss of his brother, was someone I could grow to respect, even like.

"I need someone I can trust right now, Alex. And I hope I have chosen correctly in thinking that person is you."

"Of course, my lord."

"You may call me Damian when we're alone. I get tired of all the *my lord*s and *Your Highness*es all the time." He sighed, and I glanced over at him. There was nothing of the mocking royal heir I was used to in his expression. Instead, there was only a great weariness that lined his face beyond his years. Sitting this close, looking at him in the moonlight, I was struck by how young he really was — and yet, how old at the same time.

"My lo — um, Damian." I haltingly spoke his name, my heart skidding a bit beneath my rib cage. "I don't understand what you need me for. If you want me to trust you, I need to understand what you're doing at night. The secret passageways and letters and everything else."

Damian's expression was unreadable in the darkness, but his pale eyes pierced me. "If you prove *your* trustworthiness, in time, I hope to be able to answer your questions. But for now I need to ask you to do something for me."

"I am at your bidding, my lord."

"Ah," he said, "so we're back to *my lord*, are we? I didn't mean to offend you." Damian paused and shook his head. "I don't like being so secretive, but I have no choice. Half of my family has already been murdered. And though I believe I've chosen wisely in trusting you, I have to make absolutely certain before I reveal any more. I hope you can understand."

I was silent for several seconds. He was right to be so cautious. It was presumptuous of me even to have asked him to explain himself. I was lucky he didn't punish me for my audacity. My exhaustion, my emotional state, the moonlight on his face, the low timbre of his voice had encouraged me to become too lax.

But he was correct; we were more alike than I thought. Except *both* of my parents had been murdered by the enemy, not just one.

"I understand," I said and I felt him relax slightly next to me, as if the possibility that I might remain upset with him had made him worried.

"I do hope to be able to tell you more someday soon. It would be a . . . relief to have someone to confide in." Damian glanced over at me. "Don't you agree?"

Now it was my turn to stiffen. "What is it that you would like me to do?" I asked, ignoring his question. My heartbeat was probably visible in my neck, it was pounding so hard.

Damian looked at me for a long moment, his expression inscrutable in the moonlight. "The girl who attacked me," he finally said, "the one who is to hang tomorrow, belongs to the group that was also responsible for killing my brother. It's a rebel group that seems to believe killing us both will break my father and end this war. They are unfortunately wrong, if they think losing his last son will stop the king. I believe I have discovered where their headquarters are and I need you to deliver a message for me."

"You wish to send a message to the people who want you dead, and you want me to deliver it?"

"Yes. Does that frighten you?" He pursed his lips, attempting to suppress a small smile.

"Of course not. I just don't understand what you hope to accomplish."

"If you prove faithful to me, I will try to explain it all. But not yet. If they question you, it would be better if you can honestly say you don't know why I sent you. I will give you the message on parchment, closed with my official seal."

I contemplated him silently for a moment. He couldn't know that Tanoori had already told me about this group, that she'd tried to convince me to finish the job for her. Now here Prince Damian was, asking me to go to them on his behalf. "Where is it I'm supposed to go?"

"I will procure a small map for you with exact directions. It's a network of caves about half a day's travel from here to the northeast. It's a place they call the Heart of the Rivers because three different rivers all converge near the entrance to their lair."

"You wish me to go alone into the jungle?"

Damian cocked his head slightly to the side, appraising me. "You *are* afraid. But that's a good thing," he continued when I tried to protest. "People who are too cocky in the jungle end up dead." He tapped one slender finger against his lips. "Is there anyone else on the guard whom you trust without reservation? Someone you could take with you who wouldn't ask questions? You couldn't tell him about this" — he gestured between us — "or the letters or anything else."

Rylan immediately came to mind. "There is someone whom I trust as though he were my brother. But what *would* I say?"

"You may tell him that I demanded you deliver a message for me. That you don't know who the people are or why or what the message is, only that I said you had to do it. Everyone believes me to be a petulant, spoiled prince who forces others to bend to his will, even if it's some crazy whim. He'll easily believe it."

I looked at Damian, surprised to feel a reluctant new respect, even regret, for the life he lived. He spoke of others' opinions of him without self-pity, his tone matter-of-fact. But though his voice and expression were devoid of emotion, his eyes held unhappiness when they met mine.

He must feel so alone. I'd never thought someone who had

servants and guards at his beck and call, parties every night, and women throwing themselves at him all the time could be lonely.

"Rylan won't ask questions," I said quickly, to cover my confusion. "And I would feel better if he came with me."

"Then you have my permission to ask him." Damian looked away, and the window into who he really was snapped shut.

"But what about the king's orders that someone be with you at all times — and Captain D'agnen's order for me to guard your room at night?"

"If you leave at first light, you should be able to make it there and back by nightfall. I will tell the captain that I ordered you and Rylan to go."

I didn't like it. Even if I was back by night, that left an entire day with me gone, and Deron didn't know about Eljin yet. I didn't like leaving Prince Damian here without anyone knowing that a sorcerer might be in the palace. Especially now that I knew a sorcerer had killed Damian's brother. What if Eljin was here for the same reason?

But if so, why wait? And why fight for a position on the personal guard, letting everyone find out who he was first?

"Alex, can you do this for me?"

I only hesitated for a moment. "Yes. Of course."

"There's one more thing. Are you familiar with bloodroot?"

"The plant?"

Damian nodded.

"I know what it looks like. There was a patch of it that grew by my old home. Why?"

"I need you to collect some while you are in the jungle."

"Don't you have servants for that kind of thing?" I immediately snapped my mouth shut, shocked at myself for speaking so boldly. But Damian just lifted one eyebrow.

"I'd rather not ask the servants. I would also appreciate it if you didn't mention the bloodroot to anyone else, either. Including Rylan."

"Why?"

He remained silent, looking at me.

"Fine, I can get the bloodroot, too." I finally agreed, confused by his odd request. Bloodroot wasn't common, but I was sure I'd be able to find it for him. The question was why he would want it — and why the secrecy. As far as I knew, its only use was to be crushed up into a poultice to help slow bleeding.

"Thank you." Damian let out a sigh, then stood up. "I should go, then, and let you get some rest before you leave."

I glanced up at the darkening skylight above us. The moon had traveled out of sight and soon the sky would lighten with the coming dawn. I realized that if I made this journey, I wouldn't be here for Tanoori's hanging. Maybe it was better that way. There was nothing I could do to stop it, and I couldn't bear to watch her die.

"And don't worry about Captain D'agnen," Damian added. "I will speak to him after you go."

I nodded and rose as well, so that we faced each other. Damian lifted his hand, holding it in the air between us. I hesitated to put my hand in his, strangely nervous to touch him when my emotions were in such an upheaval. But when he silently lifted an eyebrow at me in question, I quickly reached up to shake it firmly. A wave of warmth flowed up my arm and into my belly from the feel of his strong hand clasped around mine. I cleared my throat and tightened my grip. *Act like a boy, act like a boy.*

"Good night, Alex. I hope you can get some rest." He let go and stepped back.

"Thank you. Good night . . . Damian."

He smiled at me, a brief, sad smile, and then turned and went back into his room, shutting the door silently.

I stared after him for a long while, my heart beating unevenly in my chest. He'd proven my theory wrong. His interior might be more in line with his exterior than I thought. I almost wished I could go back to when I'd thought he was a blindingly attractive man with a rotten heart. Then I'd done my duty out of necessity, because I'd worked hard to get where I was, and my safety, virtue, and even life depended on it.

Yesterday, I had been in danger of actually letting myself care about him, but tonight, I was in danger of far worse.

⇥ FOURTEEN ⇤

*T*HE JUNGLE SEETHED with life — the whisper of leaves moving in the breeze, the buzz of insects, the call of birds singing and chatting above us in the trees. I suppressed a shudder. Though I'd lived my whole life near the rain forest, I didn't trust it. The dense foliage hid too many dangers. My bow and arrows were strapped to my back, my sword secured around my waist, but I still felt vulnerable. I knew there were creatures hidden in the heart of the jungle that were too sly and too fast for me to have any hope of stopping should one decide to stalk us and turn us into dinner.

The screech of a monkey overhead made me jump, knocking into Rylan, who was walking next to me.

"You're on edge," he commented, glancing up at the trees above us. My hands were slick with sweat as we moved forward, pushing ferns and vines out of our way, consulting the map and compass Damian had provided for me.

"I'd rather not talk about it," I said.

Rylan gave me a look but didn't comment any further.

"We should be there soon. According to the map, there will be a river up ahead, and if we follow that for about a mile, we should reach the Heart of the Rivers."

Rylan nodded and we lapsed back into silence. The sun had risen hours ago, and I'd spent most of the morning trying not to think about Tanoori and the hanging I'd missed. Yet another person I hadn't been able to help — another failure to add to my list.

Would they burn her body or just throw it outside the wall for scavenging animals to drag off and desecrate?

"I know I'm not supposed to ask questions, but don't you find it odd that Prince Damian sent us to do this?"

"You know the prince," I said, forcing myself to stop thinking about Tanoori. "He's always coming up with some sort of crazy demand."

"Yes, but this is taking it to a whole new level. Making us wander through the jungle to try and find a secret group to deliver a message?" Rylan glanced sideways at me and I shrugged, keeping my face impassive.

"You're right, this is beyond crazy, even for him." Even though I knew more about our job than Rylan, I still agreed with him. I didn't understand what Prince Damian expected to accomplish by having us deliver a message from him. These people wanted him dead. What made him think they'd listen to anything he had to say? I only hoped that they didn't believe in killing the messenger.

To our right, the sound of rushing water became audible and steadily grew louder. Soon, we broke through the trees to stand on the bank of a river. Our arrival startled some small creature that had been getting a drink. All I saw was a long tail rushing beneath the cover of a bush before it disappeared entirely.

"I hate the jungle," I muttered.

"Why do you hate it so much?" Rylan asked.

I shrugged, not realizing I'd spoken loud enough for him to hear. "Do you remember that first march to Tubatse?"

"Of course."

The banks of the river sucked at our boots as we walked along, skirting the edge of the trees, staying close to the water, looking for the landmarks that would guide us to the Heart of the Rivers. "Growing up, I'd always thought the jungles of Antion were beautiful, but after that march, I came to *hate* the jungle."

"I don't remember anything that bad happening," Rylan said.

"Well, that's because Marcel was kind and didn't tell anyone. Let's just say I had a run-in with a snake and without Marcel's help, it would not have ended well."

Rylan laughed. "So you *do* have a weakness after all! I have to admit, I'd never have guessed it would be snakes."

I shoved him hard enough that he had to check his balance so he didn't topple into the river. "If you tell anyone, I will shoot you in the mouth without hesitation."

"Whoa." He held up his hands in mock surrender. "You have my word. I'll never mention your mortal fear of snakes to anyone."

"Good."

The river grew as we walked, spreading its liquid arms wider and wider, and soon we could see a large body of water ahead of us through the trees.

"I miss him, too," Rylan spoke hesitantly. "I know you don't want to talk about it, but you have both been my closest friends since we first joined the army."

"But you still have *your* brother," I snapped and picked up my pace, leaving him behind me. When I glanced back to make sure he hadn't stopped entirely, he was right behind me, his expression clouded. Guilt gnawed at my belly. He was right; of course he missed Marcel. And he was my only friend now. Then I thought of the strange conversation with Prince Damian in the middle of the night. It almost didn't seem real that he'd truly sat beside me on my cot, telling me of his own grief. Even after that — even though it seemed like Damian *wanted* me to — I couldn't count him as a friend. He was my prince. I could never let myself forget it.

With a sigh, I stopped and turned, ready to apologize to Rylan, but no one was there. My heart leaped into my throat, and I whipped out my sword. Too late, I felt the sting of something pricking my neck. Cursing my inattention, I tried to fight the spiraling darkness, but my knees buckled of their own accord, and as I fell toward the ground, everything went black.

⊰ FIFTEEN ⊱

THE FIRST THING I noticed was the sound of water. It was everywhere, echoing, a dull roar humming through my head. I tried to open my eyes, but they were so *heavy*, I felt as though I had been drugged. Clenching my teeth, I forced my lids to open. I was lying on my back in a cavern of some sort. The ceiling looked damp and the air I breathed was fetid with the smell of soil and water and humans.

"He's up," someone remarked from nearby.

"That was fast."

I turned to see two men standing over me, swords pointed at my throat and belly. The world spun when I laboriously sat up, unable to use my hands to aid me, since they were tied behind my back.

"I wouldn't try that yet, if I were you."

Ignoring them, I fought the spinning in my head and remained sitting.

"Okay, have it your way." The first man, holding the sword now pressed against my clavicle, shouted over his shoulder, "He's ready to talk!"

"First, tell me where my companion is." My voice came out wrong, like I'd been drinking and couldn't form my consonants and vowels sharply enough.

"He's alive. That's all you need to know."

A third man walked over to me, a woman trailing him. He was short, shorter than me, but his arms were thickly muscled. The woman in his wake was taller than he was, and painfully thin, almost birdlike with a hooked nose and narrow-set eyes. "If you want to live, you'll answer all of my questions truthfully. When your partner wakes, we'll ask him the same questions and see if your stories match," the man said without preamble. "First of all, tell me where you got that map."

"I'm second-in-command in the prince's personal guard. We were sent here by order of Prince Damian. He gave me the map and asked me to deliver a message to your leader."

The man's eyes widened, and the woman behind him stiffened. "You ask me to believe that the prince would dare communicate with us?"

"It would seem so."

The pair shared a glance, then he held out his hand. "Let me see this message."

"First, you'll have to ask your henchmen to untie my hands."

He nodded and the closer of the two guards knelt behind me and, using his sword, cut the ties from around my wrists. "One wrong move, and we'll dart you again. I have three men out of sight, waiting for my signal. If they all hit you at once, you won't wake up until Friday. If you wake up at all."

I lifted an eyebrow at him and, without responding, reached into my vest and pulled out the vellum parchment containing the message held shut by the prince's personal wax seal. He snatched it from my hand and moved to tear it open.

"Stop! Borracio will want to see the seal himself. He'll know if it's authentic." The woman reached out and grabbed the letter. I watched as the pair turned and walked away, apparently forgetting about me for the moment. The effects of the drug they'd put on their dart were wearing off quickly, and I could have easily disarmed the two men standing guard over me. But I didn't move, choosing to wait and see what happened.

While I waited, I surreptitiously took account of my surroundings. We were definitely in some sort of network of caves. There were tunnels heading off in three different directions. Where was Rylan? How big was this place? How large was this group of would-be assassins?

Minutes passed in silence, with no sign of either the man or woman. I wondered what time it was, how long I'd been out. Prince Damian expected me back tonight — and so did Deron. What would they do if we didn't return?

Finally, just as my back had begun to ache from sitting on the hard ground for so long, another man strode out of one of the tunnels, heading straight for me. He was olive skinned, with dark hair and eyes, and he moved with an animal-like grace. I recognized a fighter in him immediately.

"You are the one who brought me the letter from Prince Damian?" His voice was accented; it sounded like he was from Blevon.

"Yes." I kept my face and voice impassive. "Are you Borracio?"

He ignored me. "Were you aware of its contents?"

"Unfortunately not. We are not at liberty to ask the prince any questions when he gives us orders."

He stared into my face, his eyes like flint, hard and cold. There was a strange feeling around him, something . . . unnatural. As he continued to hold my gaze, my stomach tightened into knots. His expression changed suddenly, and he lifted one eyebrow. "This . . . guard . . . speaks the truth." The way he slid over the word *guard* put me on edge. And how could he know if I had spoken the truth so definitively?

"You may give your prince a message. Tell him we are not to be trifled with and expect him to stay true to his word." He stepped closer to me and bent down, until his mouth was next to my ear. I stiffened. "I know your secret," he whispered in my ear. An icy tremor of shock skittered down my spine.

He straightened, his eyes piercing when they met mine. I lifted my chin, refusing to let him see how scared I really was. Who was this man and how did he know my secret? I clenched my fists in my lap to keep my hands from shaking. Then he nodded at the two men standing over me. "You may escort both of the *men* out. I have nothing further to discuss with them. Make sure to take them the back way."

He turned on his heel and strode away as the man on my right reached down and yanked me up. I pulled out of his grasp and barely suppressed the urge to knock him out cold. "I'm perfectly capable of moving on my own." My voice was like ice and the man shrugged. He was obviously someone who underestimated my ability to fight based on my stature. How I would have loved to wipe the smug expression from his face.

But I held my temper in check as the other henchman took a lit torch from a sconce and headed across the cavern. It was more important to get out of here, retrieve my weapons, find Rylan, and return to the palace before nightfall. I wanted to put as much distance between Borracio and myself as possible.

"Where are my sword and my bow?" I asked as I followed the men down one of the tunnels.

"You'll find them where we found you. If someone else didn't claim them already." The man snorted, and his companion couldn't quite hide a bark of laughter, either.

There was no way I was going back into the jungle unarmed. I glanced at them out of the corner of my eye. No bows, but both carried decent swords. That was better than nothing. I docilely followed them on a winding path through various tunnels, the light of the torch the only thing beating back the darkness. At times, we sloshed through water, or it dripped on our heads. I tried not to think about what could be in the tunnels with us. Rats. Bats. Snakes.

I shuddered.

At last, I saw daylight ahead. My sigh of relief was so audible, one of the men snorted again. I didn't care. They wouldn't be laughing anymore soon enough. We had to climb over a huge boulder to exit the tunnel. When we were finally standing on the dry ground with nothing over our heads except sky — a much darker sky than I'd hoped for — there was no one else there.

"Where's Rylan?" I turned to ask gruffly.

"How would we know? We were in charge of you. I'm sure he's around here somewhere." The shorter one smirked. He outweighed me by at least thirty pounds. I'd been watching him walk and noticed that he favored his right leg infinitesimally, most likely from a recently healed injury.

Without any warning, I kicked him in the knee. With a cry, he dropped to the ground, his leg giving out entirely, just as I'd figured it would. Before he even had a chance to realize he was on the ground, I'd already grabbed his wrist, twisting it in a movement so hard and fast, I could hear the bone snap and his sword fell into my free hand just in time for me to spin and parry the blow heading in my direction as his partner charged me. Within less than a minute, I had disarmed him as well, and they were both on the ground. I let the guy with the broken wrist be, since he made no move to attack me again. But his partner tried to get back up, so I hit him in the back of the head with the hilt of one of the swords hard enough to knock him out. Aside from a pounding headache and wounded pride, he'd be fine when he woke up.

"Tell Borracio that I got his message loud and clear," I said as I unhooked the unconscious man's scabbard and tightened it around my own waist. I sheathed the nicer of the two swords, and chucked the other one into the river flowing next to the opening we'd climbed through.

"What *are* you?" the man who was still conscious asked.

"A very good fighter," I said as I stormed away into the darkening jungle.

⊰ SIXTEEN ⊱

HE SMALL FIRE hissed and popped in front of me, like a glowing beacon, announcing my presence to any creature — human or otherwise — that might be lurking nearby in the dark trees. I felt exposed with the bright flames illuminating me, filling the air with light and smoke. But it would have been even worse to huddle in the damp, dark night without them.

My belly ached with hunger and fear. There was still no sign of Rylan. I'd half hoped he'd notice my fire and find me. If Deron and the rest of the guard could see me now, it wouldn't have mattered how many fights I'd won. My fear of the dark and snakes would defeat me in the end. A completely ignominious way to go. My body battled between the adrenaline of fear and the exhaustion and need for sleep that made my limbs heavy and my eyelids slow to open after each blink.

Until I heard a snap in the bushes behind me.

Instantly awake, I held my breath, my fingers inching toward the sword that lay across my lap. I don't think a jaguar or snake would make a noise like that, not if it were stalking me. Could it be Rylan?

I turned to glance behind me and just as I did, I saw a blur of motion out of the corner of my eye. I swung back around to see a massive black body lunging out of the bushes toward me. I only had time to open my mouth to scream and swing my sword up to block my neck before the creature was on me, claws and teeth flashing in the firelight, diving for my jugular. I threw my weight backward and tried to lift the sword up into the jaguar's belly, as its claws tore through my tunic, pressing me into the ground. I felt fire on my ribs and arm, and distantly realized it was pain. But there was no time to assimilate any damage, not while the beast was still trying to get past the blade. The edge of my sword cut into my jaw, but I didn't care. It was the only thing keeping the huge cat from tearing out my throat.

It tried again, biting down hard, and got a mouthful of blade. It growled in pain and swiped the side of my head with one massive paw. More fire exploded across my skull and stars popped in front of my eyes. My grip on my sword weakened.

Suddenly, the jaguar let out a howl of such pain and fury that it almost deafened me. A sword protruded from its chest. Hot, red blood poured from the wound onto me. The cat's eyes rolled into its head and it collapsed on top of me, pushing all the air from my lungs. And then, just when my vision began to go dark from lack of oxygen, it was gone and Rylan stood over me, his chest heaving, holding a sword coated in blood.

"Alex! Are you okay?" He dropped to his knees beside me. The fire was gone now and in its place was a pain so intense, so excruciating, I didn't dare move, afraid I'd make it worse.

I was soaked with blood, my own and the jaguar's. My ribs, my left arm, and the side of my head all throbbed. I was afraid to look down and see how bad it really was.

"We need to get you cleaned up and we have to sew up these wounds. None of them look too deep, luckily, but I can't tell for sure. There's too much blood, and it's too dark." Rylan kept up a steady stream of commentary as he pulled his tunic over his head and began to tear it into strips. "I didn't bring any needles or thread, though, so we're going to have to bind them as best we can and get back to the palace as quickly as possible."

"I can't," I finally said, my voice barely above a whisper. I sounded like a girl — I couldn't get my tone gruff enough, but I didn't care. I was probably going to die in this jungle tonight anyway.

"Yes, you can. You're the toughest fighter in the palace, and you aren't going to let one little jaguar finish you off, are you?" Rylan had bent over me and was tugging on my tunic now. I realized what he was trying to do all at once and I reached up with my right hand and grabbed his wrist.

"Stop." It was hard to speak past the pain, the breathlessness that still plagued me. I wondered if the jaguar had punctured my lung. "Don't. Don't tear it."

"Alex, you're hurt and bleeding. I need to clean the wounds first of all and then —"

"No." I tightened my grip on his wrist, trying to pull his hand away from my tunic. "Please."

He stared down at me, his face shadowed in the firelight. The light undulated in the breeze, briefly illuminating his face, and I realized his eyes were full of remorse. My stomach clenched. He thought I was going to die, too.

With a deep sigh, he covered my right hand with his left. "Alexa, I know."

"You know wh —" I cut myself off with a horrified gasp as I realized what he'd said. *Alexa.* Not *Alex.* A name I never thought

117

I'd hear spoken to me again. I shook my head, my eyes filling with tears. My mouth opened, but nothing came out.

His grip tightened on my hand as my whole body began to tremble. From pain, from blood loss, from shock.

Finally, I managed to whisper, *"How?"*

"I've known since the first day I met you." He stared at my mouth, at my chin, anywhere but my eyes.

The pain that encompassed my body was eclipsed by the shock pulsing through me with each beat of my heart. He *knew*? He'd *always* known?

"You and Marcel slipped up in front of me; he called you Alexa, and you responded. He realized I'd heard and later swore me to secrecy. I'm sorry I never told you. He made me promise."

The tears that had gathered in my eyes leaked out, slipping down both of my temples as I lay there on the ground, broken inside and out. "You knew," I repeated, my voice hoarse.

Rylan nodded, reaching with one hand to brush the tears from my face. "Now, please, let me clean your wounds and figure out how we're going to help you." His fingers lingered on my temple.

"I think you'd better let us help you, or else the girl will most likely die from her injuries."

The voice came from just outside the light of my fire. I forced myself to lift my head, but when I did, the pain became unbearable. Strange, bright lights popped in front of my eyes and then everything began to tunnel into darkness. I saw Borracio step into the circle of the firelight.

And then I was gone.

⊰ SEVENTEEN ⊱

WHEN I WOKE, I was lying on a bed of furs and the pain was gone.

Above me was the same damp stone ceiling I'd seen the last time I'd woken in these caves, but it was a different cavern. Someone's bedroom, from what I could gather, as I turned to glance around. I was alone, with only two torches to light the small cavern. I hardly dared look down at myself, afraid of what I'd see.

"Alex, you're awake." I heard Rylan's voice and turned to see him rushing through the opening toward me. "How do you feel?" There was a tenderness in his voice I'd never heard before, and I remembered that last night when I lay dying on the ground in front of him, he'd admitted knowing I was a girl all these years. Simultaneous relief and anger surged up.

"I don't know," I answered gruffly when he dropped to his knees next to me.

"A healer was with you all night. She only came out an hour ago, but she said you would be fit for travel when you woke." Rylan reached to touch my head, but I jerked out of his grasp. He pulled his hand back and looked down at his lap, but not before I saw the hurt flash through his usually warm chocolate-brown eyes.

119

The eyes I'd taken far too much notice of recently. "You're mad," he said quietly.

"Of course I'm mad!" I burst out. "How could you let me go on for the last three years without any idea that you knew?"

"Marcel made me swear. He was afraid you'd act different around me, accidentally reveal yourself to the others. I cared too much about you to risk that."

His words wormed past my anger, brushing my heart with warmth. I could feel myself softening.

"You look . . . really good. She worked some sort of miracle on you. Are you in any pain?"

I reached up hesitantly, expecting to feel huge gashes on the side of my head where the jaguar had batted me. Instead, I found nothing but my hair and three thin lines of puckered skin, as if I'd already healed and formed scars. "No, there's no pain," I finally responded, my voice soft and disbelieving. "What *is* she?"

"Borracio wouldn't say, but I heard someone else whispering about her being a sorceress."

A sorceress who could heal? I'd never heard of anything like it. I, like all the people of Antion, had been told that sorcerers were evil, that the magic they wielded brought only death.

I pulled up the sleeve of my shirt to find the same thing — the skin on my left bicep was completely healed, with four bright pink scars to mark where the claws had bitten through my flesh, tearing my muscle.

"He said we needed to leave as soon as you were awake and feeling up to it. He acted like he couldn't wait to be rid of us." Rylan sat back on his heels, watching me as I slowly sat up.

"If he wants to be rid of us that badly, why even make the effort to have his healer help me?"

"I don't know."

"Then let's go. Prince Damian is probably going to undo all her hard work when we arrive a day late." I stood up and flexed my left hand and stretched my neck, rolling my head in wonder, not quite able to believe the pain, the horror of the night before were gone. I was scarred, but I was better. In one night. I glanced down and realized I was dressed in clean clothes and my chest was bound with a clean cloth. Whoever had taken care of me was now aware of my secret, too. The list was growing at an alarming rate.

I wanted to find this woman, to ask her how she did it, to find out how I could repay her. To make sure she wouldn't tell anyone I was a girl. Even though Borracio somehow already knew as well. But when I followed Rylan out of the room into an equally damp and dark tunnel, no one was there.

"He told me the exit was just through here." Rylan gestured to a tunnel that broke off from ours, heading to our left. He unhooked a second scabbard from around his waist and gave it to me. I recognized it as my own, the one that hadn't been by the river yesterday. My bow and arrows were still gone, but I was glad to get my sword back at least.

"Thank you," I said, strapping it on.

He nodded and I followed him down the left tunnel. I glanced over my shoulder once, hoping to see someone — anyone — but the path behind us was empty. I shivered and hurried after Rylan.

⚷

We walked out into the sunlight, even closer to the spot where we'd originally been hit with the darts than where I'd come out the first time.

"There must be a city's worth of caves and tunnels around here," I remarked.

Rylan nodded, but didn't say anything else. He took the lead this time, and I was happy to follow, although I kept checking over my shoulder, my heart beating unevenly in my chest. An uncomfortable silence weighed on the air around us, heavier even than the oppressive humidity, which coated my skin so that I was already damp with sweat. Rylan's words rang through my mind again: *I cared too much about you to risk that.* What did he mean? I felt off balance around him now, more vulnerable than I felt since the day my parents died and I was taken into the army. I couldn't believe he'd always known I was a girl. It embarrassed me for some reason.

"Rylan, I'm —" I stumbled over a tree root and my cheeks flamed. I didn't trip. I didn't stumble or blush or let someone else take the lead. I couldn't let the fact that he knew I was a girl change me. And yet, I already had. He'd never treated me any differently; I hadn't had a clue. But now I was acting like an idiot. "Can we stop for a second?"

He immediately turned around. "Are you okay? Are you in pain?" There was nothing but sincere concern in his eyes, and it made me feel even worse.

"No. I mean, yes, I'm okay. I'm not in pain. But I needed to tell you . . . I don't know. I'm sorry, I guess."

"What do you have to be sorry for?"

I couldn't meet his gaze and looked past his shoulder to the crowded trees and vines, the sudden, startling splash of rich purple

122

bougainvillea. "I'm sorry I've been angry about . . . you know what. I should probably be thanking you."

He was silent and I hazarded a glance back at his face. The intensity of his gaze made my cheeks grow hot again. The flecks of gold in his irises were prominent in the bright sunlight. "And what is it you'd like to thank me for?" he asked finally.

I cleared my throat, telling myself to calm down. He probably wasn't looking at me in any special way. The heat, the humidity, the strange and overwhelming last few days were all getting to me. That plus the fact I had no idea how to even act like a girl anymore anyway, even if I'd wanted to. "Thank you for keeping my secret." I made my voice gruff and folded my arms across my chest.

"Of course," he replied, his expression growing more guarded.

"Not even Jude knows?"

"No."

I nodded, then glanced up at the sky. The sun was almost directly overhead. "Let's get going and hope we still have positions in the guard when we get back." I brushed past him and took off down the path, making my strides as long as possible, eating up the distance between me and the palace. I didn't look back to see if Rylan had followed, but I could feel his presence behind me.

We didn't speak or stop the rest of the way except for when I spotted some bloodroot growing in a small patch at the base of a large banyan tree. Rylan watched as I gathered a bunch, but didn't ask why and I didn't volunteer an answer.

Finally, hours later, the palace walls rose in front of us. Beyond that, the city of Tubatse was visible, sprawled across the valley below the palace. Pressed up close to the outskirts of the buildings and huts of Tubatse was a whole other city of tents — the temporary stopping place for different battalions of the army on their way out to or back from fighting the Blevonese. Smoke curled up from the funeral pyres that lined the southern edge of the tent city — soldiers who had died of infection, injuries, disease, or a combination of all three, brought back from the battlefield only to die in the shadow of the palace.

We hadn't even made it to the side gate before it was thrown wide open and Jude came running out to us.

"You're alive!" he exclaimed right before grabbing his brother into a tight embrace. I watched silently.

They broke apart and Jude turned to face me. "We were sure you'd gotten lost or been killed. Prince Damian has been throwing a tantrum all day. You'd better get up there before he breaks something."

Jude headed back toward the palace gate, but Rylan paused, giving me a long, searching look first. I lifted my chin, my teeth tightly clamped together against any display of emotion or weakness. Finally, he turned and followed his brother.

Stomach churning, I stepped back into the protective wings of the palace walls, leaving the jungle and all that had happened behind me, but heading toward a different type of danger awaiting me: the fury of my prince.

⊰ EIGHTEEN ⊱

When we walked into Prince Damian's room, he didn't even turn around to acknowledge me.

"Your Highness, Alex and Rylan have returned from the mission you sent them on," Nolen said from behind where we stood in the doorway of his room.

Very slowly, the prince turned to face us, one eyebrow lifted, a sneer on his handsome face. "I believe I asked you to return before nightfall. *Yesterday.*"

I pressed my fist to my chest and bowed. "I apologize, Your Highness. We were unavoidably detained."

"Did you at least accomplish what I asked?"

"Yes, my lord."

The drapes were pulled back in his room, letting the sun pour in through the large windows. Damian's piercing blue eyes met mine from across the room and then he nodded curtly. "Fine. That is all. I will expect a full report later, but you must be hungry after your overly long journey."

I bowed again and turned to walk out, with Rylan and Nolen on my heels. I didn't know what I expected when I saw Prince Damian again, but a return to his haughty, condescending persona wasn't it. I supposed I shouldn't have been surprised. As he'd told me, he was playing a part. But he was extremely convincing — almost *too* convincing.

"Why didn't you tell him about the jaguar attack?" Rylan asked quietly as we exited the outer chamber to head down to the kitchens.

"I don't know," I replied honestly. "I wasn't sure if I should. Especially since I was healed by a sorcerer."

Rylan nodded. We both knew how King Hector felt about sorcerers or sorcery. If he found out that I'd been miraculously healed by a sorceress, he might have me burned at the stake just for having come into contact with one.

I stopped suddenly, making Rylan halt and turn to me questioningly.

"I have to find Deron." With everything that had happened, I'd forgotten about Eljin until that moment.

"Right now?"

"Yes. Immediately." I spun around and rushed back toward the prince's rooms. The first person I saw was Jerrod, standing guard at the door to Prince Damian's outer chamber.

"Jerrod, where is Deron?"

He glanced at me, irritation written plainly on his face. "He spent the night standing guard outside the prince's room since you disappeared. I think he went to his room for a couple of hours to get some rest before tonight. We assumed you'd died and that he'd have to fill your position until you were replaced."

"I'm sure you were devastated by my supposed death, weren't you, Jerrod?" I couldn't resist goading him before turning and heading toward Deron's room, back the way I'd come.

He said something under his breath that sounded suspiciously like he was telling me to go somewhere unsavory, but I ignored him. Rylan stood a little bit farther down the hallway, silently watching our exchange. I ignored him, too, and pounded on the door to Deron's room.

Within moments, it flew open, revealing our captain wearing only pants and an untucked tunic. His hair was matted to one side of his head and his dark skin was even darker beneath his eyes. When he saw it was me, his eyes opened wide and he grabbed me to him in a gruff hug. "Alex! We'd thought you'd died," he said as he released me and glanced past me to Rylan. "I can't tell you how relieved I am that you're both okay."

"Me, too," I said. "But I need to talk to you immediately."

"Of course, what is it?"

"In private."

Deron's eyebrows lifted but he stepped back and gestured for me to enter his room. Once the door was shut, I told him what had happened at the tryouts with Eljin and my suspicions. His expression grew progressively grimmer as I spoke.

"You haven't heard, have you?" he asked when I finished.

"Heard? Heard what?"

"The girl that was supposed to hang yesterday didn't die."

My heart skipped a beat. "What happened?"

"Just before the hangman sent her swinging, she was rescued. By a sorcerer."

⊰ NINETEEN ⊱

I STOOD OUTSIDE Prince Damian's door with my hand on the heel of my sword, trying to stay alert. Deron had apparently forced himself to stay awake the entire night in fear that the sorcerer would come back for Prince Damian, but nothing had happened. Now it fell to my shoulders. But the strain of the last few days was wearing on me. Even though I'd been healed — completely, miraculously — I was still exhausted and my scars ached. Perhaps my body wasn't quite sure how to handle having been mortally wounded and healed all within the space of a few hours.

I couldn't believe Tanoori was still alive, that a sorcerer had saved her. Had it been Eljin? I wondered if I should tell Prince Damian about Eljin as well. But when I tried to deliver the bloodroot to him, he was already in bed, asleep peacefully. I placed the bloodroot on the table next to him and left without waking him.

Part of me expected him to come out like he had before, to ask what had happened, to prove to me again that he was more than he seemed, even though he hadn't acted so today. But his door remained firmly shut. Silent. He was sleeping soundly while I stood guard.

A streak of lightning suddenly illuminated the dark room from the skylight above me, moments before a crash of thunder boomed overhead. Within a minute, rain began to pound on the roof, growing louder and louder as the full fury of an incoming storm rolled toward the palace. Another flash of lightning momentarily blinded me. In the heartbeat of tension-filled silence before the thunder exploded through the air, the door to the prince's outer chamber flew open, blown completely off its hinges. Through the lingering spots in my vision from the lightning, I saw Kai lying on the ground, unconscious or dead.

I pulled out my sword and crouched down, ready to fight, my heartbeat erratic beneath the cage of my ribs. Dread coiled in my stomach when the man I'd fought in the ring — the one who could have beat me but didn't — stepped over Kai's body and entered the room.

Eljin. The sorcerer.

He still wore his mask, hiding his face. I waited for him to move first, terror and adrenaline pumping through my body. In a normal fight, I was confident, unshakeable. But I had little chance of stopping Eljin. If he used the same fire against me that killed my parents, I had no hope of surviving. All I could do was try and hold him off long enough for the prince to escape. Maybe there were more secret passages I wasn't aware of nearby — that was the only way Damian would get out of this alive.

I didn't have time to think about anything other than fighting, though, as Eljin finally jumped toward me, his sword arcing down in a vicious jab. Our blades hit with a resounding crash, and we began to fight in earnest. This time, he didn't hold back, and I had to use every bit of training and skill I had to hold him off. He hadn't struck me — but I hadn't managed to hit him, either. And he hadn't even used magic yet.

I was doomed.

Then two more men rushed into the room, wielding wicked-looking scythes.

"Attack!" I yelled desperately, hoping someone nearby was still alive to help me. I hadn't had time to blow on my whistle to alert the other guards.

Despite the horrible odds, I refused to give up. I kept waiting for Eljin to send me to a fiery grave, but he never did.

I lunged at Eljin, striking faster, harder than I ever had before. My sword was a blur of silver, flashing in the lightning that still streaked through the dark night overhead. Eljin couldn't keep up with the attack, and I actually managed to nick his arm before that same invisible shield I'd hit in the practice ring blocked me from being able to push my sword farther, past his arm and into his body.

For some reason, the other two intruders just stood back and watched, making no move to help.

I clutched my sword with both hands, trying to force it through the magical barrier, but there was nothing I could do. Eljin made a movement with his hand and something hit me in the chest so hard I was knocked to the ground, hardly able to breathe from the pain. My sword lay three feet away from me. I stared up at him in horror.

And then Prince Damian's door opened, and he stood there, fully dressed and holding his own sword.

"*No!* Get back — hurry!" I called out to him, rolling over and trying to grab my sword.

"Not so fast," Eljin said, and with another movement of his hand, I was flung across the room and slammed into the wall. My head cracked against the wood panels and then I hit the ground.

"Don't kill him," I managed to croak out as I dragged myself up to my hands and knees.

"That was never my intention. Oh no, he's worth far more to us and the man I serve alive than dead."

Just then Rylan burst into the room, his sword swooping through the air and slicing into one of the men standing by the door. I wanted to cry out to him to run away, to save himself, but it was too late. The one he'd managed to hit clutched his bleeding shoulder, shouting in a language I didn't understand, while the other one charged at Rylan with his scythe raised. The sound of their blades hitting echoed through the room.

I turned in desperation to see Eljin and Damian standing across from each other, swords raised, but not fighting — yet.

"If you come willingly, this will go much better for you. I promised to bring you alive — but I never specified *how* alive you'd be."

I slowly inched my way to standing, trying not to draw attention to myself. The back of my head felt warm, which I was pretty sure meant I was bleeding. I didn't dare lift my hand to check.

So far, Rylan was holding his own against the man he was fighting. I prayed that he would somehow survive this. I couldn't bear the thought of losing him, of Jude being left behind to mourn yet another death.

I was only a couple of feet away from my cot, and the new bow and quiver of arrows I'd taken from the armory tonight. If I could somehow get close enough to grab them without drawing anyone's notice, I might be able to get off a shot before Eljin could react.

That's all I needed.

"If I come willingly, will you let my men live?"

I edged closer to my cot, holding my breath. Just another foot and the bow would be within reach. I tried to calculate whether I had time to grab it and shoot an arrow. I was fast — faster than just about any *normal* man I'd ever fought — but I didn't know if I was faster than a sorcerer.

"And leave witnesses to tell your king who took you? I think not. We'd rather he didn't know that until we decide it's time for him to find out."

Just a couple more inches. I slowly reached out. Time felt like it had slowed to a crawl. My heart beat so hard, it actually hurt. Finally, my fingers brushed the smooth wood of the bow. I breathed in once through my nose, inhaling a lungful of air, and then I grabbed the bow and an arrow, lifting it up in one swift movement, and let the arrow fly almost simultaneously to notching it.

I'd aimed true — it would have hit Eljin directly through the neck — but instead, the arrow disintegrated into a pile of ash on the ground. He turned to me, his eyes narrowed in fury.

"No! Don't hurt him —"

I heard Damian's cry a moment before I was hit once more and thrown by some invisible force against the wall. Lights popped in front of me as I slumped to the floor in a heap. I tried to climb back onto my hands and knees, but I collapsed again.

"No! Alex!" I dimly heard Rylan's voice.

There was the sound of blade hitting blade, and a cry of pain. *Please, not Rylan*, I thought as darkness spiraled in to claim me.

I'd failed my prince. I'd failed Rylan.

I fought to stay conscious, but I couldn't quite manage. As I slipped in and out of awareness, I heard the sounds of more fighting and then nothing. Only pain and darkness. Then a voice, close by.

"I'm not bringing him. That's not part of the plan."

"It is now." Another voice. They were both vaguely familiar, but I couldn't make my eyes open. I couldn't move. I couldn't do anything.

⇥ TWENTY ⇤

I WOKE UP FOR the third time in two days with an unfamiliar ceiling overhead. This time, it was made of fabric — a tent. My head ached, my body ached, my heart ached. But I was alive, which was something, I supposed. Whoever had said he wanted to bring me rather than have me killed obviously won that argument. I blinked and turned my head to see Rylan lying beside me, unconscious. An unfamiliar woman hovered over him, running her hands up and down in the air just above his torso, her eyes closed. She had dark hair, with streaks of gray running through it, pulled back into a tight bun at the nape of her neck. Her skin was olive toned, like mine.

"So, you're awake," she spoke quietly without opening her eyes, making me jump.

"Where am I? Who are you? Is he okay?" My questions tumbled out unbidden and I snapped my mouth shut in embarrassment.

She paused in her work and opened her eyes to skewer me with a baleful gaze. Without answering, she gently pressed two fingers into Rylan's sternum, cocking her head to the side. After a long moment, she nodded as if satisfied, then pushed herself off the ground and looked down at me. "He'll wake up in a moment."

And with that, she turned and left me alone in the tent with Rylan.

I sat up, my body stiff as though I hadn't moved in a long time. I stared at Rylan, who looked so peaceful in sleep. I couldn't see any wounds, and hope surged that he'd somehow remained unharmed. My heart beat unevenly in my chest as I watched him breathe, as I looked at the smooth lines of his tanned jaw, the way his brown hair curled just a bit behind his ears where it was longest. His lips were parted slightly, and I couldn't help but stare at the curve of his mouth. I still couldn't believe he knew I was a girl — that he'd always known. That he'd admitted to caring about me.

He stirred and I blushed and looked away, glancing around at the otherwise empty tent. Where were we? Was Prince Damian somewhere nearby? My stomach turned to lead as memories of the night before washed over me. I reached up to touch the back of my head, expecting crusted blood, or at least a bump, but there was nothing. I distinctly remembered my head hitting the wall; the crack of my skull against the wood; the hot, sticky warmth of my own blood spilling down my neck.

"Alex?" Rylan's voice was groggy and I turned back to see him trying to sit up. He looked unsteady, so I reached out and grasped his arm, helping pull him up. "You're okay." He exhaled, covering my hand on his arm with one of his. "I thought they were going to kill you. I thought I'd lost you again."

"No, you're still stuck with me." I attempted to joke, even though my heart raced at the gentle pressure of his hand on mine.

"I didn't only promise Marcel to keep your secret, you know," he said.

I couldn't tear my eyes from his. I felt myself getting lost in the heat of his gaze.

"I promised to help him protect you, to keep you from getting hurt."

"I don't need protecting," I said softly.

"Not until the last two days."

He had me there. If he hadn't come to my aid that night in the jungle, I would have been dead, dragged off to be that jaguar's meal. But last night, though he'd tried valiantly, I didn't think he was the one who'd saved me. Someone else had decided to keep us both alive.

I pulled my hand out from his and leaned back a bit, trying to calm my heart. "What happened?"

"I don't know," he answered. "The last thing I remember is being hit from behind. I was sure they were going to kill us both."

"Like Kai," I said, my heart constricting as I thought of him lying on the ground in the doorway.

Rylan looked down, his expression grim. "Maybe he survived somehow — like us."

"You're right. Let's assume you're right." I also thought of Jude. I hadn't seen him, but did that mean he'd been safe in bed, or something worse? From the bleak look in Rylan's eyes, I wondered if he was thinking about his brother, too. "I'm glad you're alive," I said, trying to force the unbearable questions away. "I thought I heard you get hurt before I lost consciousness."

"I did — one of those scythes got a piece of me. But it doesn't even hurt." He lifted his tunic and, sure enough, there was a taut, pink scar across his ribs, diving into his well-muscled abdomen.

"It looks the same as the scars I got from the healer after the jaguar attack."

Rylan nodded and pulled his tunic back down. "But why?"

I shook my head. It didn't make any sense. "Why attack and threaten to kill us, only to abduct us and have us healed instead?"

"An excellent question," a voice responded from outside the tent, right before the woman who'd been in the tent with us earlier opened the flap and walked in. Next came Prince Damian, his hands bound behind his back, and Eljin after him, with a sword pressed into the prince's spine. I jumped up, ready to fight, but one look from Eljin froze me in place.

"Don't even think about doing anything, or I'll knock you out again. Now sit." He commanded, pushing Damian forward.

I forced myself to sit back down, even though my whole body thrummed with tension, with the need to *do* something. I'd been trained to fight, to defend and protect. Not sit idly by while the prince was manhandled. He met my alarmed gaze and shook his head infinitesimally as he sat down next to me. He wore only a white, open-throated tunic; pants; and boots that came to his knees. His hair was windswept, unlike its usual pomaded style. He looked different — but not injured, thankfully. If anything, he was more handsome than ever.

"You may release his bonds," Eljin said to the woman, and she did as he said, bending over and untying Prince Damian's hands.

"We make camp here tonight, but we're leaving at first light. So you'd better rest while you can. My men are sick of carrying you. From now on, you'll all walk." Eljin glared at us, then swept out of the tent.

"Are you hurt? Have they given you any idea of where we are, or where we're going?" I burst out the moment Eljin was gone.

"Don't pester him with your questions," the woman chided me.

I glared at her. "You'll take part in abducting him, but you don't want me to bother him with questions about his well-being?"

"You would be wise not to attempt to judge me, child."

I lifted my eyebrows at her, irritation surging through me. "You honestly expect me to —"

"Alex, that's enough. She healed you. You owe her your gratitude," Prince Damian cut me off, his tone sharp.

I recoiled as if he'd struck me. "Excuse me, Your Highness. I didn't realize you had such high esteem for your *captors*." I couldn't keep the disbelief and anger from my voice.

"Ah, so we're back to that again, are we, Alex? And here I'd hoped that we were friends." He sighed, and began to rub his temples.

I wanted to snap back at him, but instead I clamped my mouth shut. Rylan watched the entire exchange silently, his expression guarded.

"Could someone please tell me what is going on here?" I asked when I'd reined in my temper enough to control the tone of my voice.

"Eljin and Lisbet here have been keeping you and Rylan in a controlled state of unconsciousness while she healed you both," Prince Damian responded before the woman had a chance.

"For how long?" Rylan finally spoke up.

"Four days."

My jaw fell open. Before I could recover from the shock of realizing I'd lost four days with no recollection of their passing —

not to mention how far we could have traveled in that amount of time — Prince Damian continued speaking.

"Eljin says he's taking us to a very powerful man who wishes to use me as leverage to try and put a stop to this war."

"And you're just going to let him do it?" I glanced at Lisbet, then back at Prince Damian.

"I have no choice. None of us has the ability to stop a sorcerer, it would seem."

I looked away from his penetrating gaze in shame. Guilt pounded through me, pulsing with my blood. It was a dig at me, and it hit true. I'd failed him. At least this sorcerer hadn't wanted him dead, unlike the last one who had attacked a prince of Antion.

Lisbet took a seat on the ground next to Rylan. "What Damian says is true. And if you wish to make it there in one piece, I recommend that you don't anger Eljin again. Although you did choose wisely," she continued, turning to look at Damian. "She may not have stopped Eljin, but she did put up an excellent fight. With the right training —"

"That's enough." Prince Damian held up a hand, having gone pale.

I stared at Lisbet in horror, my blood suddenly cold in my veins.

"What's wrong? I assumed you were aware that the best fighter on your guard is a girl." She had a peculiar look on her face, and despite her attempt to act surprised, I was pretty sure she had purposely revealed my secret. "You did know, didn't you?"

My heart pounded as I forced myself to look at Damian. He stared back, his blue eyes piercing through me. I felt strangely light-headed and my pulse raced, sending my blood surging through my body.

"Did you — did you —" My voice was unsteady; I couldn't force the question out.

"Alex," he said very quietly. I expected him to be shocked, to get angry. Instead, he just looked at me, regret on his handsome face. Somehow, he already knew. *He knew.*

My heart constricted; I was hardly able to draw breath. Finding out that Rylan knew was one thing — but now Prince Damian, too? Sudden panic threatened to strangle me, and I scrambled to my feet.

In one lithe movement, Damian stood up as well. I'd never felt so small before — so unmasked. I stared up at him with my stomach clenched into knots.

"How long?" I finally breathed, barely able to speak over the pounding of my heart. He stepped toward me but I stiffened and he halted.

"A while," he said softly. We stared at each other for a long, breathless moment. Suddenly, the last few nights took on new meaning. He'd known I was a girl the whole time. I didn't know whether I should get mad or cry or both.

Damian glanced down at Lisbet, then his eyes narrowed when he turned to Rylan. "You don't seem very surprised by this announcement."

I looked over at Rylan to see him grimace slightly. "No, sir."

"You knew that Alex was — is — a girl?"

"Yes, Your Highness. But she didn't know I knew. Well, until this week, after she was attacked by the jaguar."

"A *jaguar*?" Damian sounded truly incredulous now as he spun around to face me again. "How could you keep a jaguar attack from me?"

140

Heat rose in my cheeks. "*You* didn't tell me you knew I was a girl!" I forced myself to meet his accusing gaze.

Gone was any pretense of the petulant brat I'd come home to after our disastrous trip to the Heart of the Rivers. Here was the Damian I'd caught a glimpse of that night in his outer chamber, when he'd told me about his brother. Well, a much *angrier* version of that Damian, but at least the persona he adopted for everyone else to see was gone. He stared at me with disbelief on his handsome face.

"You were attacked by a jaguar, and you didn't think to tell me? Are you all right?"

"You knew I was a girl and you still came out to talk to me in the middle of the night without a shirt on?" I shot right back.

"You did *what*?" Rylan cut in, his eyes wide.

"It's none of your business," the prince snapped and then stepped closer. "Alex — if that's even your real name — would you *really* have wanted me to tell you I knew? It would have put you in danger. It would have changed everything."

I stared at him, my heart flopping like a wounded animal in my chest. "Alexa," I whispered.

"What?"

"My name is Alexa."

"Alexa," he repeated quietly. Hearing Damian say my real name sent a warm shiver sliding down my spine, straight into my belly. "And now that the truth is out in the open, I've been curious for quite some time. How did a girl come to be the best swordsman and shot in my personal guard? And what is this about a jaguar attack?"

"I believe I should go see if there is any food left from supper," Lisbet said suddenly, standing up. "I suppose I can trust the three of you to stay in here? I don't have to warn you that Eljin can do as much damage from across a campground as he can from five feet away, do I?"

We all looked at her silently, until Damian nodded once curtly. She curtsied to him, which was odd, considering she was one of our captors, and then left without another word.

Damian immediately turned to me. "I'd like answers to my questions now." It wasn't a request.

I cleared my throat nervously. "Could you at least sit down first?"

My heart skipped a beat when he didn't move, afraid I'd pushed him too far. He was still the prince. But finally he folded his long legs and sat down beside Rylan, both of them facing me. Piercing blue eyes and warm brown ones, both intent, waiting for me.

I haltingly began trying to explain myself. "My parents were afraid of your father's war. I used to hear them talking about it at night. My mother was worried that they wouldn't be able to protect me in particular, since I was a girl."

"Because they thought you might be forced into the breeding house?" Damian's eyes darkened, and his voice sent another shiver down my spine.

"Yes."

A muscle in his jaw tightened. "Go on."

I told him how I'd asked to train with my brother, and how I grew to be a better fighter than he was. Better than anyone else in the village, even though I was only a girl of fourteen when our parents were killed. I told them how Marcel and I made the desperate decision to lie about our ages and to cut off my hair and

142

pretend I was his twin brother to save me from being taken to the king's breeding house. To save me from the fate that awaited girls there — being raped repeatedly until they got pregnant, only to have the babies taken from them and raised to populate the king's army, as soon as the boys were old enough to hold swords, or to expand his breeding house, as soon as the girls got their monthly courses. I tried not to think about Kalen, or Horace, or the girl lying on the bed, or anything else I'd seen that horrible night as I spoke, but nausea still rose in my belly.

"When I am king, I want you to know that I will set those poor girls free and burn that building to the ground." The cold fury in his voice made me hope he was serious — and that he became king sooner rather than later. But what hope was there of that? King Hector wasn't old, certainly not close to dying anytime soon. Not unless something happened to him.

Shaking my head to clear the treasonous thoughts, I told Damian how no one had questioned me when Marcel and I volunteered to join the army, especially once they saw me fight, and then there had been no going back.

"So you're actually only seventeen?" he asked. "You lied about your age as well?"

I nodded.

"A seventeen-year-old girl." Prince Damian shook his head. "And how did you find out?" He turned to Rylan.

"The day she and Marcel joined the army, he accidentally called her Alexa in front of me. He realized that I'd overheard and later swore me to secrecy."

"But you didn't know that he knew?" Damian asked me.

I shook my head. "No."

"And you've been pretending to be a boy ever since."

"I'm sorry for deceiving you." I lifted my chin and met his searching gaze. "When my parents died, we didn't know what else to do. But I don't regret it. As you know, I'm very good at what I do."

"Unless faced with a sorcerer," he commented and that shut me right up. His expression was almost calculating as he looked at me. I couldn't imagine what he was thinking.

"I know of no ordinary human fighter who could beat a sorcerer," Rylan supplied, belatedly adding, "Your Highness."

"You don't need to keep addressing me like that. We're sitting in a tent in the middle of the jungle with a sorcerer ready to knock us flat on our backs if we look at him sideways. I think it would be safe for you to just call me Damian right now." But as he spoke, his eyes were on mine, making my stomach tighten. "However, I must disagree with you. There are *few* who could beat a sorcerer, but they do exist."

"You're saying that I should have been able to stop Eljin — to beat him?" I asked defensively.

"As you are now? No. As you said, you're very good, some might even say remarkable. But you wouldn't be able to stop Eljin — as we saw the other night."

Rylan glanced between Damian and me uncertainly.

"But you expect me to believe that it *is* possible to beat him, without magic?" I bit out through clenched teeth. He just *had* to keep reminding me of my failure. "And what if he'd attacked me with fire? You expect me to believe I could have defended myself against that?" I challenged him, daring him to tell me that my father shouldn't have died. If he couldn't stop a sorcerer's fire, no one could.

Damian lifted one eyebrow, giving me a scrutinizing look. "Eljin isn't a black sorcerer. He can't summon fire." He paused. "Why did you think he could?"

I glanced at Rylan, who was watching the entire exchange with his eyebrows raised, then back at the prince. "The sorcerer who killed my parents used fire. My father was the best fighter I ever knew, but he never stood a chance. The sorcerer burned him and my mother to death in a matter of seconds." I glared at Damian. "And you expect me to believe that my father should have been able to stop him?"

"A *black* sorcerer killed your parents?" Damian's eyebrows lifted in what looked like surprise. "Was he alone?"

"No," I responded through gritted teeth. "He was with the Blevonese army. And what do you mean, a *black* sorcerer?" I hadn't realized there were different types — or that not all of them could use fire as a weapon.

"A black sorcerer with the Blevonese army," Damian repeated, ignoring my question, making me even more irritated. He wasn't looking at me anymore; instead, he stared past me unseeingly. After a long stretch of silence, he shook his head slightly, his expression grim. "Black sorcerers are . . . rare. And they are the only ones who can wield fire."

So our enemy had multiple types of sorcerers fighting against us. That was unwelcome news. "And yet, you think I should be able to beat a sorcerer in a fight?" I asked Damian, my voice tight. "Even a black sorcerer?"

"Well, obviously, it would be even more difficult against a black sorcerer. But it's been done before." Damian stared directly at me, his eyes piercing. "That level of skill is extremely rare to find, but it *is* possible. It also requires extensive and brutal training — something that isn't offered in Antion, since my father despises sorcery so much." A strangely derisive tone colored his words. I felt there was more to what he was saying than I understood.

"Well, I'm very sorry that I was unable to reach that level of skill on my own. It's unfortunate that your father doesn't believe in that type of training. It might have saved us from getting into this mess." My already bad mood was rapidly deteriorating into something even darker.

"Yes, unfortunate indeed." Damian's gaze was unwavering on mine.

Rylan broke in suddenly. "As long as we're all alone in here, don't you think we should be making a plan to escape and return to the palace? Have you had any clues about which direction we're headed while Alex and I were unconscious?"

"We will not be attempting to escape," Damian responded.

"But, my lord — I mean, Damian," Rylan corrected himself. "I don't understand. . . ."

"They've kept me ignorant of the route we've taken, but I'm fairly certain we're heading toward Blevon. My decision is to wait and see what happens. We will continue to do as they tell us until we find out who is behind all of this, and then we can make a plan."

I stared at him. "You don't seem very upset for a prince who has just been abducted from the palace and dragged halfway across his country, possibly to his death."

"That's my decision, and it's final." Gone was the pretense of being friendly with us. He was our prince suddenly, giving us an order, and we recognized it.

146

"Of course, Your Highness," I said. "We will do as you wish."

He lifted an eyebrow at the use of his title again but didn't tell me to call him Damian this time. Instead, he stood up and strode out of the tent without another word.

"Didn't that woman tell us to all stay here if we didn't want to be knocked out again?" Rylan asked.

"Apparently, he didn't think that threat applied to him."

There was no sound of fighting, no impact from his body hitting the ground unconscious, so he'd obviously assumed correctly.

"Do you get the feeling that something strange is going on here?" I asked Rylan.

"Yes. I just have no clue what it could be."

I sighed. "Neither do I."

⚔ TWENTY-ONE ⚔

$\mathcal{T}$HAT NIGHT, I lay on my back, staring up at the canvas above me, willing myself to fall asleep in the muggy humidity, which lingered even though the sun had gone down hours ago, when the entrance to our tent rustled. Alarmed and instantly alert, I sat straight up on the hard ground, straining to see in the dark. Beside me, Rylan's breathing was steady and deep.

It wasn't Eljin, or even Lisbet. Instead, I stared up at the tall, shadowed form of Prince Damian in the darkness. A wave of heat cascaded over my body when he met my startled gaze and silently motioned for me to follow him out of the tent. Before, when he'd come to speak to me at night, I'd believed that he thought I was a boy. He was right — having the truth out in the open changed everything. My blood pulsed through my body as I rose and crept out after him.

The camp appeared to be asleep, except for two men who stood watch by a campfire across from us. The flames undulating in the black shadows of the jungle reminded me of the jaguar attack and I shuddered. Damian passed one finger across his lips and silently walked between a few tents and then out toward the line of trees beyond the small clearing in which our captors had made camp.

Had he changed his mind? We couldn't leave Rylan. I refused to. And there was no way I was heading into the dark jungle completely unarmed.

Finally, Damian stopped and glanced back at the camp. No one was coming after us; we'd managed to slip away unnoticed. Above us in the trees, a bird screeched, making me jump.

The scent of plants and earth and even a hint of something floral surrounded us. My skin was sticky from the humidity and I reached up to push my damp hair off my forehead.

"What is it — what do you want?" I asked, at last, when Damian didn't speak. I never would have dared be so bold before, but I was exhausted, embarrassed, and frustrated. With him in particular. He hadn't returned the rest of the night, leaving me to vacillate between being worried about him and angry with him for not getting sent back to our tent with his tail between his legs. So much for Lisbet's threat.

"I needed to talk to you," he said, his voice low. "To apologize, first of all. I *am* sorry if I made you upset. But how was I supposed to tell you that I knew my best guard — the undefeated Alex — was a *girl*?" He looked down at me with those piercing eyes of his, and an unfamiliar heat blossomed deep in my belly.

"How long have you known?" My body thrummed with tension.

He lifted one hand slowly and I froze. He took a lock of my short hair and rubbed it gently between his fingers. "I've always known."

"Always?" I repeated dumbly. His gaze was so intense, I was having a hard time concentrating.

"I know you believed me to be spoiled. Arrogant. But that didn't mean I wasn't observant — more so than most. I watched all of you. I had to. As I told you before, I've been trained not to trust anyone." He paused, searching my face. My mind flew back to the night when he told me how he'd been raised, when he said he wanted to trust me. When he asked me if I had any friends to confide in. "From the moment you joined my guard, I knew something was different about you. Just because I seemed oblivious didn't mean that I actually was that callous and uncaring. That I didn't see *you*."

I stared at Damian, my mouth suddenly dry. "I . . . I don't . . ."

"Tell me about the jaguar attack," he said abruptly, dropping his hand and taking a step back. "What happened — why were you gone for almost two days?"

Relieved to be on safer footing, I quickly told him everything that had happened, including Borracio's cryptic message for him. He listened intently, his expression pensive. When I was done, he sighed.

"If they hadn't found you in time . . ." A shadow crossed his face, and he continued, his voice lower, "I'm so relieved they were able to heal you. I . . . I need you, Alex — *Alexa*."

Hearing him speak my true name sent another jolt through me. My heart thudded in my chest at his words. The prince — *Damian* — needed me? I felt my mouth part, but no words would come. Finally, I managed to force out just one. "Why?"

He hesitantly stepped closer to me. His fingers brushed mine in the darkness, sending a bolt of heat up my arm. I couldn't have moved if I wanted to. "Because you understand. More than anyone. Because you know what it's like never to trust anyone — to be completely alone, lost in a disguise of your own making. Because . . . because for quite some time I've —"

"Don't move!" a woman shouted suddenly.

150

We jumped apart and I spun around to see someone aiming an arrow directly at my chest. At first, I couldn't quite believe it, but as the figure walked closer, there was no denying who it was. What was she doing? My heart raced, and I wished there were some way to go back in time, to stop her from interrupting us. Damian had been so close to admitting something —

"I found them," Tanoori shouted over her shoulder, then she met my disbelieving gaze directly. "Hello again, *Alex*."

"Tanoori?"

"You know her?" Damian looked at me in shock.

"We grew up in the same village," I admitted.

"Funny how quickly the tables can turn, isn't it? One minute, you're threatening me and waiting for me to hang. The next, I'm the one who might shoot you." Tanoori glared at me in the darkness. Gone was the trembling girl tied to a chair. *This* Tanoori seemed very capable of murder.

"I never wanted you to die," I said softly.

Tanoori pulled her bowstring back even farther and I tensed, waiting for the hit.

"You will not shoot her," Damian commanded.

Tanoori lifted an eyebrow at him. "Should I finish the job I started last week instead?" She turned her aim on him, making my heart leap into my throat. "I'm still not convinced that keeping you alive is the right thing to do."

"You won't be shooting anyone tonight." Another voice came from behind me, and for the first time since I'd met him, hearing Eljin was actually a relief. "You may go."

Tanoori stared at us for a moment longer, hatred clearly visible on her face.

"Now," Eljin said.

With a sneer, she lowered the bow and walked away.

It seemed that now I had to watch my back to make sure Tanoori didn't put an arrow through my heart when I wasn't looking.

"I suggest you return to your tents," Eljin said. "I'd hate to regret my decision not to keep you tied up at all times."

"I *am* rather tired," Prince Damian said. "By the by, Eljin, you may want to keep better control of your little band of rebels here." And with that, he sauntered away, without looking back at Eljin. Or me.

I gaped at Damian for a moment, then snapped my mouth shut. Eljin stood stiffly next to me, and rather than waiting for him to remember I was there and decide to punish me, I hurried back to my own tent. The arrogant, insufferable, maddening . . . I didn't care how handsome he was or how he made my heart race, the next time he came to drag me out of my tent in the middle of the night, I was rolling over and ignoring him.

Though I was exhausted, it was a long, sleepless night. When I finally did manage to doze off, I had horrible nightmares. A jaguar lashed out at me, its eyes glowing in the dark as it swiped at my head, my throat, my heart, tearing through my flesh and bones. And then it wasn't a jaguar anymore. It was Eljin driving a sword through my gut, but he had Damian's crystal clear blue eyes as he stood over me in triumph. Clutching my belly, I turned and saw Marcel lying next to me, staring unseeingly. Past him lay Rylan and Jude, also dead. I tried to scream but the blood filled my throat, my mouth, my nose —

I sat up straight on my bedroll in the gray light of dawn, gasping for air. I couldn't remember where I was or why. I twisted around, expecting to see my brother sleeping across from me, but when I saw Rylan instead, reality came crashing down on me.

Rather than trying to go back to sleep, I stood up and crept toward the opening to our tent, willing my heart to calm down, for the vestiges of the nightmare to go away. When I parted the flaps, I was surprised to see Damian standing by the long since dead fire. His arms were folded across his chest and he stared out at the jungle. Mist wound through the camp, silent and eerie, shrouding the ground. It wrapped around his boots, making him look almost like a specter. Without his usual pomade, his hair was thick and wavy in the humidity. Despite myself, my heart picked up speed again.

I thought about how he'd left me the night before at the mercy of Eljin and nearly let the flap fall shut. But the last few years of training were too well ingrained. That's all that drove me to leave my tent and wind my way silently across the camp toward him. Or at least, that's what I tried to convince myself to believe.

I stopped a few feet away.

"It's beautiful, isn't it?" he spoke softly, without turning to face me.

"The jungle?"

"My country — this nation of Antion. It's beautiful and deadly. But the people here are strong. *My* people are strong. They survive — you could even say many of them *thrive*, despite the dangers."

I studied his profile as he spoke, the strong outline of his jaw and the curve of his lips. "Yes, the people of Antion are strong. We refuse to give up — even when our own king is causing us as much suffering as our enemy." I snapped my mouth shut, horrified I'd spoken treason to the king's son.

But rather than reprimanding me, he nodded slightly. "How long can it last, though? As you say, the king is driving my people to their deaths with this never-ending war." He finally looked at me, and with the gentle light of dawn caressing his face, I couldn't help thinking that the most beautiful thing in Antion right now was him. "If there was a way for me to stop the war, to put an end to the suffering, would you condone me doing it?"

"Of course," I replied without hesitation. I'd never heard him speak like this before; it was thrilling and a bit unnerving to realize how much he really did love his kingdom.

"No matter what it was?"

His eyes searched mine, making me acutely conscious of the fact that he knew I was a girl, and that only a couple of feet separated us.

"Without knowing what the cost was, I couldn't say," I finally replied, falling back into my habit of making my voice gruff to cover how flustered I was. My heart beat fast and unsteadily. Why did he make me feel this way? This was the *prince*.

"Have you ever heard the theory that it is better for one man to die than an entire nation to suffer? Do you believe that to be true? Is it ever okay to take a life in hopes of saving others?" He took a step closer to me, so that I had to tip my head back farther to keep looking up into his eyes. I'd never felt so aware of just how tall he was before.

"I think so." I didn't know what to do with him standing so close — close enough that I could feel the heat from his body. My

154

heart beat erratically and my fingers tingled for some reason. I forced my face to remain impassive. I drew on all of my training, all of the practice I'd had over the years pretending to be a boy to maintain my composure. With a much steadier, lower voice, I said, "Whose life are you thinking of taking?"

"Don't do that with me," he replied, staring down at me with a look of almost hunger on his face. "We're too much alike to pretend with each other. At least when we're alone, let's be who we truly are." The intensity of his gaze nearly made me tremble.

No one knew me as I truly was, except for Marcel, and he was gone.

But here was Damian, the strikingly handsome, sometimes capricious, sometimes gentle prince of Antion, asking me to allow him past the guise I'd been holding up to the world since my parents died. How could I do that when all I had done for so long was train to guard him — and make sure he never realized that deep down inside, buried where no one could see, his best fighter was actually just a frightened girl?

He hesitantly lifted his hand, as though he were going to stroke my face. His fingers hovered near my skin. I held my breath, waiting for his touch, longing for it, frightened of what it would mean —

A shout from across the camp startled us, and I jumped back, my heart in my throat. Damian still stared into my eyes, unmoving. This time, I was the one who turned and fled.

⊰ TWENTY-TWO ⊱

THE SUN HADN'T even risen above the trees yet, but the heat was already starting to swell around us as Rylan and I shouldered our packs and fell into line. Lisbet and a young boy, who I guessed was her son, were in front of us, and one of the men carrying a scythe marched behind us. The boy darted in and out of line, up and back, with seemingly boundless energy. From what I could tell, he thought this was a grand adventure, not a miserable march across the jungle.

It was a fairly big group, large enough that I couldn't see the beginning or the end of the line of people under Eljin's command. I didn't see the prince again for the rest of the morning, except from a distance when we stopped for lunch. Nor did I see Tanoori, though I tried to keep an eye out, wary of the burning hatred I'd seen on her face the night before.

I couldn't stop thinking about Prince Damian. The way he'd looked at me, the things he'd said — even before we were abducted. How he'd claimed we were alike. I was terrified that I was letting my guard down too far with him — it didn't matter if he knew I was a girl. Or that, if I was being truly honest with myself, I was growing ever more attracted to him. It was forbidden. I was his *guard*.

Rylan walked beside me, but we didn't speak much, conscious of the ears all around us. We continued for hours, with no breaks, over the moist dirt and ground cover, skirting tree roots and branches, ducking when monkeys screeched overhead. At one point, a bush rustled beside me and I jumped back, my encounters with both snake and jaguar haunting my every step.

"Are you okay?" Rylan asked, reaching out to touch my elbow.

"I'm *fine*," I responded, yanking my arm away. "Just because you admitted you know I'm a girl doesn't mean you need to treat me like one."

The concern on his face immediately disappeared, replaced with a mask of indifference. He nodded and turned away without another word. He didn't speak to me again for the rest of the afternoon. I wasn't even sure why I'd snapped at him. I was confused and frustrated with myself. After so many years of never letting myself slip up, was I now expected to act like the girl everyone suddenly knew I was? With each painful, silent step, I felt worse and worse. It didn't help that I was hot and sweaty and tired.

As the sun began to arc back down toward the earth, the boy's earlier enthusiasm began to wane. He started whining and Lisbet had to keep calling after him, telling him to hurry up when he began to lag farther and farther behind.

"Jax, come on," she said for the tenth time in an hour.

"But I'm *tired*," he moaned, and plopped down on the ground. Lisbet reached down for his arm, trying to pull him up, but he slipped out of her grip. "No. I'm not getting up. I don't want to walk anymore."

Rylan and I both stopped, causing the men who were marching at our backs to run into us.

"Keep moving!" one shouted, but I didn't obey, concerned about Lisbet and her son.

I was about to say something to the boy, see if I could coax him to get up, when Prince Damian's familiar voice came from behind, startling me.

"Jax, hop up off the ground. If you're that tired, I'll carry you on my shoulders, all right?"

"You don't have to do that," Lisbet said, but her eyes were full of gratitude as Jax jumped to his feet, his face eager.

"Really? You will?" He bounded over to Damian, who stood a few feet behind us.

I turned to stare at the prince in shock, unable to believe he was serious.

"Of course I mean it," Damian said. "I don't offer to do things I don't intend to follow through on." He smiled at the boy, a smile I'd never seen before — gentle and affectionate. Then he knelt down on the ground and helped Jax clamber up his back, until he sat atop Prince Damian's shoulders.

"You're so *tall*," Jax said in wonder when Damian stood back up. "I can see forever!"

"What's the holdup?" I heard a shout from ahead just before Eljin stormed into view.

"Nothing. Everything's fine now," Damian said as he began to stride forward, with Jax on his shoulders.

Eljin stared at them in open amazement — amazement that I was sure was mirrored on my own face. Lisbet hurried to walk next to Damian, visibly relieved now that Jax was taken care of.

Rylan and I followed as well, a few steps behind them. I could hear snippets of conversation between Jax and Damian every once in a while, and even laughter. I wasn't sure if I'd ever heard Damian laugh before. Watching him with Jax, hearing him laugh with the boy made my chest ache beneath my breastbone. It made me miss Marcel. And for some reason, it made me think of this morning, of the moment Damian reached up to touch my face.

Finally, when the sun had fallen below the tree line, the line halted and Damian helped Jax climb back down.

"Can you carry me again tomorrow?" he asked eagerly.

I didn't hear Damian's answer over the shouts of the guards next to us, telling us where to set up our tent. This time, there was no clearing in which to make camp. Instead, we had to pitch our tents in whatever space we could find. The jungle felt impossibly close, almost suffocating, as darkness descended. I sat in our tent alone, after Rylan had been summoned to help find dry wood for a fire.

When the flap opened, I didn't even look up, expecting Rylan to return.

"I'd never guess you would be the type to sit around and mope." Tanoori's voice took me by surprise.

I jumped to my feet, ready to fight if she had come to take her revenge on me. But she stood by the entrance to the tent with her hands held up, empty. When I was sure she wasn't armed, I relaxed slightly. "I don't mope," I said.

"Oh please." Without asking, she sat down on the end of my bedroll. "We might not have been friends before, but I did know you for years, Alexa. And even though you've cut off your hair and you dress like a boy, I can still tell when you're moping. You might as well sit down and tell me about it."

I glared at her, but finally my exhaustion won out over my pride, and I plopped on the ground as far away from her as I could get. "Why would I tell you about it? You threatened to kill me last night."

"Oh, that." She waved her hand with a nervous laugh. "I wouldn't really have shot you. I was still mad at you for that rather *unpleasant* interrogation. And allowing me to be sentenced to death."

"And now you're not?"

"Well, I suppose I am still, but I didn't die, so . . . And I realize you were only doing your duty." She glanced down at her hands in her lap. "None of this has worked out the way I thought it would. Besides, there aren't too many people our age in the Insurgi."

"Is that the name of the group you're working for — the one that hides near the Heart of the Rivers?"

Tanoori looked up at me, her brown eyes bleak. "I never thought they'd ask me to try and kill anyone. But if I thought it would end the war, I'd try to do it again."

"I'll never let you kill him," I said. "Whether you think it'll stop the war or not."

"You like him, don't you?" Tanoori's expression was innocent, curious. But I could feel an underlying urgency to her question. Was it her own desire to know or had she been sent by someone else?

"Until recently, I couldn't stand him."

"But now things have changed?"

"I . . . I don't know. He isn't the man I thought he was. I'm not sure what I think anymore. But whether I respect him or despise him doesn't matter; I'm a member of his guard. I won't let you hurt him." I wasn't about to tell her about my conflicted feelings toward the prince. I trusted her as much as I trusted the jungle at night.

"You're not the only one. The sorcerer seems pretty intent on keeping the prince alive now, too."

"So Eljin doesn't work with you — with the Insurgi?"

She shook her head. "The first time I ever saw him in my life was when he saved it."

I'd been sure that she and Eljin were working together. If not, then why had he rescued her?

We were silent a moment and I took the opportunity to study her. Her hair was thinner than it used to be. She was obviously undernourished: I could see the outline of her ribs beneath her shirt, and her elbows jutted out when she crossed her arms. I wondered what had happened to her, what had driven her to join a rebel group and become this strange, unpredictable girl.

"So, you joined the Insurgi, and now you're here with this group — whoever they are. But *you* were trying to kill Prince Damian, and these people are trying to keep him alive. Why are you here? And what do they want from him?" I watched her intently.

"I don't know what they want. When Eljin saved me, he took me to Lisbet and she brought me to this group. I wasn't given a choice to return to the Insurgi. And no one will tell me what they're up to."

She didn't seem to be lying, but she kept looking down at her hands, instead of meeting my gaze.

The tent flap opened again and this time, Rylan walked in. I noticed the way Tanoori nervously watched him, her eyes following his every move.

161

"I got a fire going and Lisbet said the food would be ready in a little bit," he said as he tossed his bedroll onto the hard ground. Then he turned to Tanoori. "What are you doing in here? Aren't you supposed to be helping make dinner or something?"

She jumped up with a nod. "Sorry, I'd better go."

I wasn't sure who she was apologizing to or for what, but then she was gone, leaving me alone with Rylan.

"Is that the girl who tried to kill Prince Damian?"

"Yes, it is."

He stared after her for a minute, then shook his head. "If they want to keep him alive, why would they rescue the girl who tried to kill him and bring her along?"

"I don't know."

Our eyes met and locked. All the tension from the long day of not speaking rose up again.

"I'm getting sick of saying *I'm sorry*," I said.

"Then quit doing things you have to say sorry for," he responded. But he looked like he was trying to contain a smile.

I stood up and began to pace the small perimeter of our tent. "I honestly don't know how to act. I don't know what to do." Rylan stood still, watching me. "So many people suddenly know I'm a girl that it seems ridiculous to keep pretending to be a boy. But it's all I've done for three years."

"Just be yourself," he said.

"I don't even know what that means anymore. Who I am is who I've had to be to survive. And if Iker and the king ever find out . . . or Deron . . ." I stopped and stared down at the ground, fear churning the bile in my stomach. Death or worse would await me if King Hector and Iker found out, we both knew that. And I had no idea what Deron would do.

Finally, Rylan moved, coming over to where I stood, and took my arms in his hands. He looked down at me with such tenderness that my heart constricted. "Everything is going to be okay, Alexa. I won't let anyone hurt you. I promise. Not even the king."

I stared up at him, my heart in my throat. What was wrong with me? A week ago, I wouldn't even let myself admit that I found any man attractive. And now my heart couldn't seem to remember how to beat normally whenever Rylan or Damian came near me — or when either of them touched me as Rylan was right now.

"Are you two planning on eating?"

Rylan jumped back as though he'd been burned and I whirled around to see Tanoori holding back a flap of our tent, her expression shadowed in the darkness.

"Yes, sorry. We're coming." Rylan recovered first, striding out of the tent and over to the fire, where Lisbet and Prince Damian already sat on a log someone had pulled up.

When I started to walk past Tanoori, she leaned toward my ear. "For just barely admitting you're a girl, you sure do get around fast," she said, her voice so low, no one else could have heard her.

I stopped and stared at her, but she looked at me in perfect innocence, smiling cordially.

"Hungry?" she asked brightly. "I believe your prince saved you some food."

And with that, she turned and walked away, disappearing into the darkness beyond our fire.

I looked at the fire, where Rylan, Damian, and Lisbet sat, watching me, waiting for me to join them. And it was suddenly all too much. I couldn't face them. Or maybe it was that I couldn't face myself.

Tanoori's words rang in my ears, making my cheeks grow hot. I wasn't pretty and I knew it. Maybe if I grew my hair and dressed like a girl. Maybe if I didn't have hands callused from sword practice, or well-muscled arms and shoulders from training. I wasn't soft, I wasn't feminine. I barely even knew how to talk like a girl anymore, after years of purposely lowering my voice.

And yet when Damian and Rylan looked at me, I felt like they were looking at me the way a man looked at someone he found attractive. It was thrilling — and confusing.

I turned around and went back into the tent and lay down on my bedroll, curling into a ball on my side. I stared at Rylan's empty spot next to me, and tears suddenly burned my eyes. I wanted Marcel to be here with me. I longed for my brother. Even more impossibly, I wished Mama were still alive. If my parents hadn't been killed, none of this would have happened. I would have met a boy who liked my hazel eyes or my long, dark hair. It had been so thick and shiny — the one thing about me that had truly been beautiful. I reached up to finger my short hair, then I remembered Damian doing the same thing, and I shoved my hand into my armpit instead.

When I heard someone approaching, I rolled onto my other side. The flap to the tent opened, and I felt someone standing there, looking at me. But I kept still, made my breathing even.

After a moment, whoever it was left, leaving me alone with my regrets, my impossible wishes, and my foolish heart.

⇥ TWENTY-THREE ⇤

WE TRAVELED FOR days the same way. Each morning, we had to wake at dawn, force down the little bit of tasteless, dried food our captors gave us, pack up our tents and bedrolls, and be ready to march out of camp before the sun had even risen above the trees. We had no pack animals, so we had to take the tent poles apart and roll them up in the canvas, then strap all of it to our backs. Rylan and I took turns, alternating days to carry the tent. He tried to do it every day, but when I got upset at him for treating me like I was weak, he backed off.

I mentioned to Lisbet that I should just take off the binding, since everyone knew I was a girl anyway, but she flatly refused. "You must keep up the pretense of being a boy for all of the hidden eyes watching you." I wasn't sure what she meant, but the look on her face made me shiver. I kept the binding on.

We weren't given any weapons, but I wasn't as frightened of the jungle with at least one powerful sorcerer nearby. I was *pretty* sure he'd save me if some jungle animal tried to make me its meal again.

Prince Damian alternated walking with Lisbet and Jax, and staying up front where I couldn't see him. He did eat with us once or twice, and though he was cordial to Rylan and me, and surprisingly friendly with Lisbet and Jax, he didn't try to speak to me alone again. I buried my disappointment and told myself I didn't care. But deep down, I knew I was lying. I'd actually let myself start to believe he cared about me.

Lisbet hovered close by most of the time. I often caught her watching me surreptitiously, and it made me nervous. Once, I dared ask her about her ability to heal, but she'd ignored me and dropped back to walk behind me for a while. Jax had decided he liked me, though, and would often walk next to me when Damian was gone, chatting about the different types of plants or animals we saw. I didn't have to say much to keep him going, which was a relief. He'd just talk and talk as long as I nodded and agreed every once in a while. Rylan walked next to us, piping in now and again.

The only good fortune I had was that Tanoori decided to keep her distance. It was a relief not to have her popping up, threatening me with arrows one minute, trying to gossip with me the next, and accusing me of being a harlot the minute after that.

This went on for more than a week, and every day I grew more tired, more worn down, and more worried. We pressed on through rain, heat, mud, and humidity. We were definitely heading toward Blevon. We'd been traveling for so long, I couldn't imagine it would be more than another day or two before we crossed down into the lowlands, then reached the border and left our nation behind.

On the eighth day of traveling since I'd woken up, the sky above us grew cloudy once again, threatening rain. I'd actually come to enjoy the rainstorms. The deluge of water was at least a relief from the constant, cloying heat of the sunny days, and it washed away the sweat and grime of the long trek through the rain forest.

Rylan and Jax were both next to me as we trudged down a hill toward a small stream, talking about different types of monkeys. From our vantage point at the top of the incline, I could see Prince Damian a little ways ahead of us, almost to the stream. As I watched, he adjusted his bedroll on his back so that he could stretch his arms high overhead. For some reason, my heart beat a bit faster as I watched him. It was difficult to believe that only two weeks ago, I'd practically hated him. And now . . . I didn't know what I felt. I thought something had started to happen between us, but now I was afraid I was wrong. I remembered the way he'd smiled at Jax, how they'd laughed together when Damian carried him on his shoulders, and my stomach tightened. Would he ever smile like that at me?

"Are you going to stand there all day?"

I shook myself from my thoughts to realize Rylan and Jax both stood a little way below me, waiting. I fought to keep myself from blushing and moved forward to follow them when something grabbed my attention. I froze and squinted, trying to make sure I wasn't seeing things. And then I broke into a dead run.

"Damian!" I screamed as I rocketed down the hill toward the prince.

Everything seemed to happen in slow motion. He turned to look at me, his eyes widening. I screamed his name again, pointing behind him, at the trees on the other side of the stream. The archers hidden in the shadows loaded their bows as I frantically shouted at everyone to take cover. But I wasn't fast enough. I had almost reached the bottom when a volley of arrows flew out of the trees.

I screamed Damian's name once more and jumped toward him with every ounce of strength in me. I collided with him a split second before the arrow would have hit him, crashing so hard, we both tumbled to the ground. He landed flat on his back, and I was on top of him, our faces only inches apart. Almost every part of our bodies touched as he stared up at me in shock. And then Damian pushed me off him and, rolling with unbelievable grace, rose to a crouch, grabbing the sword out of the scabbard of a man who wasn't as lucky as he was. An arrow protruded from the man's throat, leaving a pool of blood beneath his head.

There wasn't time to be surprised at his agility or the comfort with which he held the sword. The men who'd shot at us were now rushing toward us through the stream, swords lifted. They wore the tattered uniforms of the Antionese army, attacking their own prince unknowingly. We were at the far reaches of the kingdom, too far for them to have received word of Damian's abduction. And few outside the palace knew what he looked like. There was no hope they'd recognize him and retreat. We would have to fight our own people if we wanted to live.

"Aim to injure, not kill!" Damian shouted as I leaped to my feet, desperately searching for a weapon to use. Bodies littered the ground, but I didn't have time to make it to another one to grab a weapon. I was defenseless.

Where was Eljin? Where was his power when we needed it?

Those with weapons raced forward to meet the soldiers, and the sounds of blades crashing together rang through the forest.

A man rushed directly at me, sword raised. I turned to run for my life, only to collide with someone — a tall, handsome prince who shouldn't have been in the middle of this battle.

"Alex, get behind me. *Now!*" Damian barked when my eyes widened in panic. Why hadn't he run for cover?

"Give me your sword!" I shouted back over the sounds of fighting.

Instead of listening, he shoved me behind him, blocking the soldier's attack just as his blade would have cut me through.

I stumbled back, and watched first in horror, then in growing amazement as Damian not only held off the man's attack, but fought back with surprising skill.

"Alex!"

I turned at the sound of my name just in time to lift my hand and catch the sword Rylan had tossed to me. Armed at last, my fear dissolved. As I gripped the hilt of the sword, my mind calmed and my body filled with purpose. *This* was who I was — *this* was what I knew how to do. I was a fighter.

Damian had disarmed the soldier who'd rushed at me, swiped his sword arm so that he couldn't pick up his weapon again, then moved on into the thick of the fight. I plunged in after him, my sword arcing through the air, carving a path through the army that obviously had no idea it was attacking its own prince. I did as Damian had asked, and struck only to injure. These were our own people. It made me sick to have to fight them, but our lives depended on it. They obviously believed we were rebels or part of the Blevonese army, and they *were* striking to kill.

I stayed as close to Damian as I could, in case he needed help. But as the fighting continued, it became very apparent that my help was not needed. He was an incredible swordsman.

He twisted and lunged, spun and parried as though he'd been born with a sword in his hand. It was all I could do to keep fighting and not stop to watch him.

And then Eljin finally showed up.

"Enough!" he shouted and swung his fist through the air, as though he was trying to smash something in front of him. A huge boom reverberated through the forest and the ground began to shake. "If you wish to live, you will retreat this instant!" His voice carried over the horrible sound of the earth threatening to tear apart beneath our feet.

We all froze, Antion's army and Eljin's own men alike.

"Sorcerer!" someone from the army shouted in fear.

"Retreat!"

The cry was repeated, and all the soldiers who remained uninjured rushed back across the stream and melted into the forest they'd emerged from only minutes before.

Eljin released his fist and the shaking stopped.

Breathing hard, my heart still beating rapidly, I gazed at the bodies on the ground in dismay. There were casualties from Eljin's group and the Antionese army. Most of the men from the army were only injured, not dead, just as Damian had ordered. I marveled that Eljin's men had followed his command, even though he was their prisoner.

Damian stood a few feet away from me, holding his sword loosely in his hand. I stared at him, half in astonishment and half in anger.

"You can fight," I finally said.

He remained silent, watching me. I couldn't tear my eyes away from his. Why had he kept this from his guard — from *me*? I remembered seeing him in his room, how I'd wondered at the sheen of sweat on his well-muscled body. I clenched my jaw to hold back everything I wanted to say to him in that moment. I was mad at him. Mad and confused and amazed. *He'd* saved *my* life.

"Alex! You'd better come here!"

I spun around to find Rylan crouching next to a body on the ground. I could only see the person's legs, those of a smaller body, definitely not one of Eljin's men. My heart stopped as I rushed to his side, praying it wasn't Jax.

When I reached Rylan, he moved aside to show me my prayer was answered. It wasn't Jax.

It was Tanoori, lying in a puddle of blood, an arrow protruding from her chest.

❧ TWENTY-FOUR ❧

I**S SHE DEAD?**" I dropped to my knees beside Rylan.

"Not yet. She's breathing, but just barely." He had his hand pressed around the wound, trying to stop the bleeding. "We've got to get this arrow out."

It was embedded on the right side of her chest, closer to her shoulder than her belly. All we could hope was that it hadn't punctured her lung. At least it was far away from her heart.

"Move out of the way." Suddenly, Lisbet was there, pushing Rylan and me aside. She held her hand above the wound and closed her eyes, concentrating. Finally, she looked up at us. "After we remove the arrow, I will need some time to work on her. But she should live."

Relief poured through me. Though I wasn't sure how I felt about Tanoori anymore, I didn't want her to die.

"Here, take this to stop the bleeding once we pull it out." Rylan yanked his tunic over his head, and handed it to Lisbet.

He knelt back down beside us and I forced myself to look away from his lean, muscular torso. I helped Lisbet roll Tanoori onto her side, to make sure the arrow hadn't passed all the way through her body.

"We can't pull it out here; she'll bleed to death. We'll have to break the shaft and then remove the arrow when I have time to work on her," Lisbet said.

We held her while Rylan got a grip on the arrow shaft. He exhaled and then snapped it off as close to her body as he could.

Lisbet immediately took the shirt Rylan had given her and pressed it around the wound.

The storm that had been hanging over us all day finally broke. Raindrops made little dots of darker soil all around us. Slowly at first, then it began to pick up speed as Lisbet hunched over Tanoori, one hand pressing the shirt into her chest and the other hovering above her body, shaking.

"We have to leave now, before they come back with reinforcements. There isn't time to do anything for her."

I looked up to see Eljin standing above us, staring down at Tanoori, his expression inscrutable.

"If she can't walk, she gets left behind." Eljin turned on his heel and walked away, leaving us crouched around Tanoori, staring at him in disbelief.

"We can't leave her here to die." I looked at Rylan, but his expression was grim.

"He's right. We do need to leave, or else we might *all* die."

"They were terrified of Eljin. They won't dare come back," I argued.

"He's obviously not willing to take that chance."

"How quickly can you heal her?" I turned to Lisbet.

"Not fast enough. The wound is bad — and we haven't even removed the arrow yet."

My chest ached with anger and desperation. Was that it, then? She escaped the hangman's noose, only to be shot down in the jungle by her own country's arrow?

"I'm not leaving her here. I'll carry her on my back if I have to." I bent down and began to tear the bottom edge of her tunic off.

"Alex, what are you doing?" I heard Damian's voice but ignored him, continuing to tear the fabric until I had a long strip to bind her wound with. "What is she doing?"

"She's apparently going to single-handedly save the girl who tried to kill you, my lord," Rylan responded.

"She also tried to kill Alex the other night, if I'm not mistaken."

One of them sighed, but I didn't look up to see who. Instead, I took the strip of cloth and tied it over her shoulder and across the wound, with Rylan's ruined tunic underneath it, pressed against her chest. Lisbet watched me silently, her expression indecipherable.

When I finished the makeshift bandage, I gently pulled Tanoori up off the ground. She was dead weight, and I grunted with the effort of holding her up. The rain fell harder and harder, making everything that much more difficult.

"We can't carry her on our backs," Rylan said as he crouched down to help me prop her up.

"Then what should we do?" I cried. "Leave her here to die? To be eaten by an animal?"

"If we could make some sort of sling or stretcher, then we could all carry her together," Damian said.

I looked up at him in surprise. His expression was guarded. I couldn't imagine what he thought as he stared down at us, trying to help the girl who'd attempted to murder him.

"If you want her to live, she needs to be kept as still as possible, so she doesn't lose more blood than she has to. Even if you are able to transport her to the next stopping place, she may not make it long enough for me to heal her." Lisbet looked at me as she spoke.

"We have to at least try," I responded.

Lisbet nodded and then stood up. "Give me one of your bedrolls. If we use the poles from a tent, we could make a stretcher to transport her."

Damian shrugged the pack that held his bedroll off his shoulders and handed the bedroll to her. Rylan found his pack, which held our rolled-up tent and the broken-down poles in it. The poles were lightweight and made to pull apart into pieces for traveling. I hoped they'd be able to sustain Tanoori's weight.

"What are you *doing*?" someone shouted. I glanced up to see Eljin storming back over to us, his eyes furious above his ever-present mask. "I told you we had to leave! If you don't come right now, I will kill you all and leave you with her."

Lisbet ignored him and kept working, deftly tying the bedroll to the poles we'd laid out in a rectangle.

"No one else will be dying today," Damian said, his voice cold. "Either help us, or go. We'll catch up if we have to."

"You expect me to leave you here?" Eljin's eyebrows lifted above his mask. "To assume you'll come find us, rather than turn around and head back?"

"We have no supplies, no map. We would most likely die if we tried to return to the palace on our own." Damian stood up and folded his arms across his chest.

While they argued, we finished attaching the bedroll to the tent poles, and Rylan and I moved over to Tanoori.

"Move her on three," he said.

I nodded.

"One. Two. *Three*."

We both heaved, and lifted her onto the stretcher.

"There, you see? It's done." Damian gestured to where she now lay on the bedroll, deadly pale and soaked. The rain running off her body was crimson from her blood.

"If she slows you down, I will have no choice but to make you leave her."

"She won't," I replied, meeting Eljin's gaze from where I crouched on the ground.

He shook his head and turned away.

We each took a side of the stretcher and hefted her up into the air. Rylan was across from me and Damian was in front. Lisbet tried to help across from Damian, but she wasn't nearly as strong as me, let alone the two men. I was afraid she'd tire soon, leaving Damian to shoulder half the stretcher alone.

Sheets of water poured down from the roiling black clouds above as we moved forward, across the stream and into the trees where the army had come from. No one was there anymore, other than Eljin and his men and us.

"You'd better appreciate this," I muttered under my breath as thunder cracked overhead.

When we finally stopped for the night, the storm had quit, but the clouds remained, murky and startlingly close to the earth, encasing the tops of the trees in their dark, swirling depths.

My whole body hurt when we set Tanoori on the ground. My back was one huge knot of pain and my right arm cramped from moving out of the same position after hours of holding up the stretcher. Jax had been farther ahead in line, and he and some of the other men had already set up Lisbet's tent. We moved Tanoori inside, and Lisbet immediately began to hover over her.

Damian, Rylan, and I all stood in a row, watching her work, until she paused and looked up at us. "This is going to take a long time, especially since the bloodroot isn't entirely out of my system. You'd best go find some food and somewhere to sleep. We'll know by morning if she's going to make it."

I stared at her in confusion. "What do you mean the bloodroot's not out of *your* system? What does that have to do with healing her?"

Lisbet ignored me and kept tending to Tanoori.

I turned to Damian. "Do you know what she's talking about?"

He shrugged. His expression was inscrutable in the dim light as he gazed back at me. "We should go so she can work," he said.

I glanced down at Tanoori. Her face was so peaceful, she looked like she could be sleeping, except for the ghostly pallor her skin had taken.

"Come on, he's right. Let's go." Rylan pressed his hand gently to my lower back, steering me out of the tent. I could feel the heat of his fingers through my wet tunic.

"Where will you sleep?" Damian asked, glancing down to where Rylan's hand still rested on me, then back up at my face. "I believe we used your tent poles for the stretcher?"

Rylan dropped his hand and sighed. "I've been trying to figure that out. I'm sorry, Alex, but I think we're going to be sleeping out in the open from now on."

"You can share my tent," Damian said quickly, looking at

Rylan, then at me. "It'll be a bit tight, but better than nothing, I suppose."

Without waiting for a response, he turned and strode away.

"That was unexpectedly kind of him," Rylan observed. "It's like he's a completely different person now. I don't get it."

I shrugged. "I guess we all have our secrets."

Rylan gave me a strange look. He was still shirtless, and he stood close enough that I felt all too aware of his proximity — and of his nakedness. He was built differently from Damian. Where the prince was lean and defined, Rylan was more solid, his arms were thicker and his chest broader. I knew from years of sparring with him exactly how strong he was. I had never let myself notice his body like *this* before — at least not for long. However, in all that time, he'd never looked at me as he was now, either.

Fighting a blush, I said, "You should go find a shirt and I'll see if I can get us some food. Then I guess we'll have to figure out where Damian's tent is."

Rylan didn't say anything; he just stood there, looking at me. "Do you like him, Alex?" he finally asked, his voice unnaturally strained.

My heart skipped a beat. "The prince? Well, I don't hate him anymore, I guess. He's different now, like you said. It's easier to guard a prince I can respect rather than a useless, spoiled brat, like before." I smiled, attempting to be lighthearted, but Rylan frowned back.

"That's not what I meant."

The smile slipped from my face and I shifted uncomfortably.

"I've noticed the way you look at him. I don't want you to get hurt. He might be acting friendly at the moment, telling us to call him by his first name, offering to let us sleep in his tent, but he's a *prince*, Alex. That will never change."

"You think I don't know that? I'm not stupid, Rylan."

"I didn't mean that —"

"And it doesn't matter, because I don't look at him any differently than anyone else. I know he's our prince. I'm in his guard, remember? Just because you both know I'm a girl now doesn't change anything."

"I promised your brother I'd watch out for you." Rylan lifted his hand to brush a stray lock of hair from my cheek. Ignoring the rush of warmth from his touch, I stepped back.

"You aren't my brother, so stop trying to act like you are."

Rylan's jaw tightened. "I'm not trying to act like your *brother*, Alexa. Has it ever occurred to you that I might care about you? That maybe I've been fighting an attraction to you that I couldn't let anyone know about, least of all you, for *years*? I had to make sure I never looked at you too long or reached out to touch you, even though I wanted to. So many times, I can't even count."

The artery in my neck pounded beneath my skin, and I felt light-headed with shock. Rylan's eyes were bright, almost fevered in the darkness as he spoke.

"Do you have any idea how hard it was to keep pretending, to bury how I really felt, knowing I'd never be able to do anything about it without endangering you? And now I finally have a chance to treat you the way you deserve — to cherish you the way a woman should be when a man loves her. And all you can do is stare at the prince."

"Rylan . . ." I looked at him, stricken. My eyes burned and my throat felt suddenly dry. He was wrong, I didn't *only* think of

179

Damian. Before I'd found out about this other side to the prince, there had only been Rylan. But I wasn't sure how I felt anymore. Everything was changing so fast, I couldn't find solid ground. I felt like I was sliding down a slope, hurtling toward an abyss.

"Forget I said anything," he said, taking a step back. "I shouldn't have told you. It's just been building up inside of me for so long, and when you nearly got killed today . . . I couldn't keep it in anymore."

"I nearly got killed?"

"*Prince* Damian saved you, remember? I couldn't get there fast enough. Good thing he's been hiding the fact that he's an expert swordsman from all of us until now."

"Oh. Yes," I replied lamely. I actually *had* forgotten, with everything else that had happened. But now the memory of that moment surged up, the shock of Damian's agility and skill with a sword.

"I'd better go find a shirt," Rylan said and he turned to leave.

"Rylan, wait!"

But he ignored me and strode away.

⊰ TWENTY-FIVE ⊱

I WAITED AS LONG as I could to go to bed, even though I was almost falling over with exhaustion. The thought of facing either Rylan or *Prince* Damian — let alone sleeping by both of them — right now was enough to make me contemplate taking my chances curled up underneath a tree. I went to check on Lisbet and Tanoori again, but Lisbet shooed me away without giving me an update, leaving me with no other option except to slowly make my way to Prince Damian's tent, near the front of the line.

Mist curled along the ground in the darkness, winding between tree trunks and bushes, stretching diaphanous fingers up the sides of the tent as I stood before it, trying to gather my courage. Damian was correct when he said Antion was beautiful. Beautiful and deadly. But the jungle seemed like the safer option compared to what awaited me inside that tent.

Stop it. You're not going to stand out here all night, hyperventilating, I told myself firmly. *Pull it together and go inside so you can get some rest.*

It was completely silent; maybe they were both asleep already. I took a deep breath and opened the flap.

Prince Damian and Rylan sat on opposite sides of the tent, wide awake. The space in between them, which I presumed was for me, was big enough for someone Jax's size. I almost turned around and walked out again to take my chances with the snakes and jaguars, but then Damian stood up.

"Would you like some help with your bedroll?"

"No, I'm fine. Thank you, *my lord*," I said, with a pointed glance in Rylan's direction.

He wouldn't meet my gaze, and my stomach clenched. But Damian looked straight at me, and his expression was one of confusion, even hurt.

This was a disaster.

I hurried to spread out my bedroll and lay down, trying to make myself as small as possible. Rylan stretched out on his side next to me, making an obvious effort to stay on the far edge of his bedroll, pressing his body right up into the fabric of the tent. But it didn't matter; the space was so small, we were still only separated by a foot at most. I scooted away from him a bit, trying to give him more space. But then Damian lay down on the extra bedroll he'd managed to find, and the entire lengths of our bodies were suddenly touching. Something deep inside of me responded to the feel of him against me and though I knew I should move away, I didn't. My stomach tightened with awareness of every part of us that connected — his arm against my arm, his leg against my leg. If I turned my face, would our lips touch?

My heart racing, I shifted my body away, to the direct center of my mat, lying flat on my back with my arms folded across my chest, staring up at the top of the tent.

"Alex," Damian spoke, his voice low.

Hesitantly, I turned my head toward him. Even though I'd moved, his face was still so close to mine that my breath caught in my throat. He stared into my eyes for a moment, looking troubled. He glanced past me to where Rylan lay with his back turned to us, then his gaze returned to me. Finally, Damian said, "Thank you for saving my life today."

I swallowed once, trying not to get lost in the depths of his blue eyes. "You saved me, as well."

Damian's gaze didn't waver from mine. "Yes. I did."

I could feel his warm breath on my lips, and my whole body hummed with a strange kind of energy. Of . . . of . . . *something*. I didn't know what. But I was also very aware of Rylan lying behind me, listening to every word. I felt like a bowstring pulled so taut, I might break with any more pressure. "Why didn't you tell me you knew how to fight?" I couldn't keep the hurt from my voice.

Damian hesitantly lifted his hand; his fingers trailed across my jaw. "It was necessary to keep it a secret. I wasn't planning on revealing myself, but when I saw that soldier rushing toward you . . ." His thumb brushed my parted lips and his gaze dropped to my mouth.

I couldn't breathe. I wanted him to keep touching me; I wanted to feel his whole body against mine again. But Rylan was here. Rylan was listening. Rylan, who had cared for me all along.

"Thank you," I said, my voice unsteady, and somehow I made myself move and turn away from his touch to stare at the tent again, my heart hammering. Rylan's back was still turned to me, but I could see how stiff he was, as if every muscle in his body was clenched.

"I hope you are able to rest well, Alex," Damian said.

"You, too," I said, making myself close my eyes, to pretend I was going to sleep. But inside, I thought, *Rest well? Is he serious?*

It was going to be a long night.

I was shocked when the sound of a bird somewhere close by woke me up, just before dawn. Somehow, I'd managed to drift off after hours of hardly daring to breathe, let alone move. I'd ended up on my side, facing Rylan. He'd also rolled over in his sleep, and his arm rested against mine. His mouth was slightly parted in sleep, his face relaxed. His jaw was obscured by the ever-thickening stubble on his face.

I could feel Damian on the other side of me as well. I turned to look and saw that he was on his stomach, his arm and leg only inches from me, his head turned toward me. He, too, had over a week's worth of stubble. His face was completely relaxed; the tightness that nearly always lingered around the corners of his mouth and eyes was gone. He looked much younger when he was asleep. Watching him made my heart pick up speed. I found myself blushing when, just for a moment, I imagined what it would feel like to have his lips touch mine. Before I remembered what Rylan had said to me the night before.

Why was I even letting myself think about touching — or kissing — the prince? I could never be his queen. It was foolish and stupid to even let myself dream of kissing him. It wasn't like I could suddenly throw on a dress and hope he would court me. My life depended on continuing to maintain the pretense of being a boy, if we ever made it back to the palace.

But maybe you won't, another voice inside me responded. *Maybe you won't ever make it back, and this will be your only chance to feel like a girl. To kiss a boy. And not just any boy. To kiss a prince.*

And then I wanted to smack myself. Tanoori was right. I *was* a harlot.

Moving as slowly as possible, trying to be completely silent, I inched my way over to the flaps. I had to get out of the tent before either of them woke up.

When I finally made it out into the muggy morning air and the gray light of yet another dawn in the jungle, I felt like I could breathe for the first time in hours. I headed for Lisbet's tent, nodding at the few men who were already up, preparing our meager breakfast before we broke camp and moved out. I noticed Eljin standing by a larger tent, in deep discussion with two other men, and I picked up my pace, not wanting to have another encounter with him.

Jax was already digging in the dirt outside his mother's tent with a stick as I approached, but when he saw me, he jumped up and ran to give me a hug.

I awkwardly hugged him back, surprised by the gesture.

"I'm glad you didn't die yesterday," he said, as he pulled away and looked up at me. He had beautiful blue eyes, nothing like Lisbet's. I wondered where his father was — *who* his father was. I wondered why Lisbet was with us at all. So many unanswered questions. It made my head hurt.

"I wasn't going to die. Who told you that?"

"No one. I was watching from the trees where Mama told me to hide." He scuffed his foot against the dirt. "I saw Damian save you. Mama said he exposed his secret because he cared too much about you to let you die. She said love can either make a person stronger or weaker, and she hasn't decided if he's getting stronger or weaker yet."

I stared down at Jax with my heart in my throat. There was something familiar about the way he looked at me in that moment, in the way his eyes pierced mine even though he was only a child.

"I . . . I . . . ah . . ."

"Jax." Lisbet parted the opening to the tent, saving me from having to answer. "Run along and find us some breakfast before we have to pack up to go again."

"Yes, Mama." He lifted his eyebrows at me, then turned on his heel and dashed off.

Lisbet's arms were folded across her chest as she gazed at me, her dark eyes guarded in the growing light as the sun slowly woke up behind us.

"You knew about Prince Damian's secret?" I finally asked. "You knew he could fight?"

She didn't respond.

"How? How do you know him? Why are you here with us and what do they want with him?"

Her eyes narrowed. I felt like she was trying to search me with the intensity of her gaze. "Did you come to see how Tanoori is?" she responded at last, parting the tent flaps again.

Frustrated, I followed her in to see Tanoori lying on the ground, still pale, with a sheen of sweat on her face and chest.

"Why does she still look so . . . sick?"

Lisbet knelt down and wiped a damp cloth across Tanoori's forehead. "Healing is a very difficult and draining type of sorcery. I used up much of my strength healing you and Rylan, and I'm weary from this journey. And as I said, the bloodroot still isn't completely out of my system. I'm doing all that I can for her, but I don't know if it will be enough."

"Isn't bloodroot used to treat wounds? Why would it have anything to do with your ability to heal her?"

186

Lisbet shook her head sadly. "The people of Antion are regretfully ignorant of many things."

I glared at her in consternation, about to demand she give me a real answer when she continued, "Yes, it can be used to help staunch the flow of blood in a wound. But when bloodroot is ingested by a sorcerer, it suppresses their magical abilities. I took it for quite some time to protect myself while in Antion."

"So you *are* a sorceress. I knew it." Was the bloodroot Damian had me gather meant for her? They certainly seemed to know each other — and yet, I wondered how.

Lisbet gave me a sharp look. "There are all sorts of magic in this world. You would do well to learn that."

"I don't agree with the king," I said quickly. "I don't think *all* sorcery is evil." Most of it, yes. But not all. How could it be, when the only reason I was still alive was because of a sorceress just like Lisbet?

"Then maybe you're smarter than he is. But don't underestimate him — and don't believe everything you hear. No matter the source."

"Do you always talk in riddles?" I sat down on the other side of Tanoori, across from Lisbet, and took the rag so I could wipe it across Tanoori's feverish brow.

Lisbet laughed once, a mirthless sound. "No. I didn't use to. But I've had to learn some tricks over the years to keep myself safe."

I paused to look up at her again. "How do you know Damian?"

She gave me a sharp look. "I believe you are discovering a new side to him, are you not?"

I rolled my eyes at her nonanswer but nodded.

"He looks at you differently, Alexa. He risked himself — *exposed* himself — for you. He is a powerful man, with the weight of a nation on his shoulders. He can't afford to make mistakes because of his feelings for a pretty face."

"Are you saying saving me was a mistake?"

Lisbet remained silent.

"Well, then you have nothing to worry about, because I don't have a pretty face. Nearly everyone, except Damian, thinks I am a *boy*." I dunked the rag in a bowl of tepid water and squeezed it out with unnecessary force.

Lisbet watched me shrewdly. "We all see what we want to. People believe you are a boy, because that's what they've been told. They reason away why you look so much more feminine than your brother did. You are an expert swordsman and practically unstoppable with a bow —"

"How do you know about my brother?" I cut her off. I could feel my temper rising, and I struggled to keep it in check. I hated unanswered questions, and she was refusing to explain anything.

"Your time to keep your secret is growing short." Lisbet ignored me. "No hair will ever mar the skin of your face. Your body has changed, has become that of a woman's. What will you do when you are unable to keep up your pretense any longer?"

I glared at her, angry at her astute observations. "I'm not answering your questions unless you answer mine."

"What's going on here?"

We both whirled around to face Damian, standing above us.

"I was explaining that I am not strong enough to completely heal this girl right now, and so we will either have to leave her or carry her all day again," Lisbet said, smoothly rising to her feet.

My chest ached from the anger and frustration building up inside. Why did she know about my brother? How did she know the prince? And why did her words — her warnings — burn like acid, reminding me of how uncertain my future was?

"How much longer before the effects of the bloodroot wear off entirely?" Damian asked, looking past me to Lisbet.

"Not much longer, but it is frustrating when she needs my help *now*."

"You're doing all you can." Damian smiled at her, the same gentle smile he had given Jax when he'd carried him. Seeing him give Lisbet such a tender look, hearing him speak to her with such respect after her refusal to explain anything to me, to answer my questions, was too much. The anger I'd been trying to subdue overtook me. She was working with our captors, and yet Damian seemed to trust her — more than me. And I had been his guard, risking my life for him on a daily basis.

I jumped to my feet and pushed past Damian, out of the tent, only to see Rylan standing ten feet away, his arms crossed, staring at me, a silent accusation in his eyes.

The pressure was coming from all sides. Lisbet's warnings; my impossible attraction to a prince I should never have let myself care about; Rylan's feelings, which only confused me even more. I wanted to get away — I *needed* to get away.

"Alex, are you okay?" Damian followed me.

I turned on my heel and ran. I didn't care where, I didn't care what happened to me, I didn't care if Eljin tied me up after this, I just had to escape. I couldn't take it anymore. I plunged into the forest, pushing the huge leaves out of my way as I ran from Lisbet, from what she'd said, from Rylan and Damian, from everything.

⊰ TWENTY-SIX ⊱

I STARTLED A FLOCK of macaws when I rushed through the foliage into a small clearing. They took to flight in a whirl of colors, reds and blues and yellows, bursting through the air. My eyes burned, and I scrubbed my hands across my face, brushing the stupid, useless tears away.

I barely had time to catch my breath when I heard someone crashing through the underbrush behind me, and spun around to see Damian standing there, his chest heaving from the effort of running after me.

"What's wrong? What happened?"

"You shouldn't have come after me," I said. "Now we'll both get in trouble."

"I don't care about that." He closed the distance between us, so that I had to tilt my head back to look up into his eyes. His eyes, which were every bit as beautiful as the macaws that had just flown into the depths of the jungle. *His* jungle. "Why did you run away?"

"You made a mistake by saving me. You revealed your secret to save my life," I said, my voice strained. "You kept that secret your whole life for some reason, and now everyone here knows and I don't know why you did that for me. You should have let me die if it was so important for no one to know."

"Is that what Lisbet told you?" The look on his face made my heart pound.

"Yes, *Lisbet* told me that," I bit out. Still upset — hurt — by the trust he seemed to place in her.

He moved even closer. I couldn't breathe as I stared up at him. He lifted both of his hands to brush the hair back from my face. "And you believed her?"

I clenched my jaw, refusing to answer, afraid all the emotion I was desperately trying to quell would bleed into my voice.

"It wasn't a mistake to save your life," he said, his voice low. He took one last step so that our bodies touched. I could feel him everywhere — our legs, our hips, our stomachs. "I've made mistakes. So many I can't even count. But saving you was *not* one of them." His thumbs rubbed across my jaw. I stared into his eyes, my heart in my throat. For that breathless moment, there was no sound, no time, nothing beyond his body against mine and his hands on my face. I wanted him to kiss me, I wanted it more than I wanted air, but the tiny part of my brain that was still functioning knew this was wrong. Impossible.

I tried to pull back, but he dropped one of his hands to wrap his arm around my body, pressing me to him, refusing to let me break away.

"But I'm not —"

"You're *perfect*," he said roughly, cutting off my protest. "And if I had to do it over again, I would save you every time." His mouth closed over mine and there was no more thought. No more worry. No more pain or loss or fear. There was only Damian. His arm tightened around me, crushing me to him, his other hand threaded through my hair. I clung to him as his lips moved on mine with a need and hunger that nearly overwhelmed me.

My whole body burned with a fire that I'd never imagined possible. I was the one who was supposed to protect him, but I'd never felt as protected as I did in that moment, encircled by his strong arms, our bodies pressed together. I dug my fingers into the muscles of his back, his shoulders, clinging to him with every ounce of strength I had in me.

His lips moved to my jaw, then down my throat, leaving a trail of fire on my skin as he worked his way toward my collarbone. I gasped for air, clutching at his tunic as he kissed me. I cursed Lisbet for convincing me to keep the binding on my breasts.

"Alexa," he whispered against my skin. "Do you have any idea what you're doing to me? I've never needed anyone the way I need you."

He pulled back slightly, his gaze heated as he stared down at me. I was weak in his arms, struggling to breathe normally. "After my mother was killed, and then my brother, I swore I'd never let myself care about anyone again. I swore I'd never give anyone the power to hurt me like that again. But when I saw that man rushing at you yesterday, with his sword drawn . . . I realized it was too late."

My heart constricted at the raw pain, the fear, the *hope* in his eyes, eyes that were like jewels in the dappled sunlight.

"It was too late," he repeated, almost in a whisper, and then he bent his head down to mine again. This time, his kiss was gentler, deeper somehow. I could feel his desperation in the way he held me, in the way his lips moved with mine, making my heart ache and burn all at once.

"Alex!"

I froze at the sound of my name being shouted from the trees behind us, and we broke apart. I took a step back, lifting one of my hands up to my swollen lips.

"Alex!"

It was Rylan. About to find me — about to find *us*. He'd know. He'd know and there would be no going back. He'd never forgive me.

"Alexa." Damian looked concerned. "What's wrong?"

I couldn't answer; I just shook my head. And then Rylan was there. He burst out of the trees and ground to a halt when he saw us both standing there, only a couple of feet apart. I had no idea what I looked like, what expression was on my face. But whatever he saw was enough. The concern on his face hardened into something else, something foreign.

"I was worried about you since you're afr — hate the jungle so much, but obviously you're just fine." I'd never heard his voice so cold, and it turned the heat in my body to ice. But even in his anger, he kept his promise not to reveal my fear of snakes. "We're leaving. Lisbet is preparing Tanoori for us to carry her again. Assuming you still wish to try and save her?"

"Of course," I said, my voice shaky.

Anger rolled off him in waves. "That's great. Carry on, then. Sorry for interrupting." He turned on his heel and plunged back into the jungle the way he'd come, leaving me alone with Damian again, my stomach twisted into knots and my whole body trembling.

"Alexa, are you all right? What's wrong?" Damian stepped toward me again, took my hand in his. I stared down at his fingers, laced through mine, and I almost cried again. I could no longer deny that I was falling for him — so fast and so hard, it scared me. But I had feelings for Rylan, too — he was the closest friend I'd had at the palace, next to my brother. And now he hated me.

I clenched my jaw to keep my emotions in check. I looked up at Damian, at the concern on his face, the worry in his eyes.

"Was I wrong to kiss you?"

I swallowed past the lump in my throat. "No," I whispered. "I just don't know what to do. You're the *prince*."

"We'll figure it out. I won't let anyone hurt you — not even my father. I promise." He squeezed my hand and I tried to smile back as I let go.

"We'd better get back before Eljin threatens to kill me again and makes you break your promise," I said, trying to keep my voice from trembling. I turned to walk away, but Damian grabbed my arm, pulling me gently back to him.

"Thank you," he said softly as I stared up at him once more.

"For what?"

"For saving me — and I don't just mean from that arrow." He smiled, a soft, wistful smile. "It's always been you, you know that, right? From the first moment I realized you were a girl — it was always you."

My heart constricted as he pressed his lips to mine. Once. Twice. Just enough to make my pulse start to race again, and then he broke away. "All right, let's go." He sighed.

I turned to follow him with tears in my eyes.

✥ TWENTY-SEVEN ✥

A FTER THE LONGEST day of my life, trudging through the final stretch of jungle, carrying Tanoori on the same makeshift stretcher with Damian in front of me and Rylan across from me, we finally stopped for the night, near the border of Antion and Blevon. It was torture to be so close to Damian after our kiss, but unable to touch him, or even to talk to him. And the trip hadn't improved Tanoori's condition at all. I began to wonder if she really would make it. She thrashed several times during the day, making it even harder to carry her. I was so sore, I could barely move after we set her down on the ground next to where Lisbet was setting up her tent.

Eljin made us pitch our tents as close together as possible, and we weren't allowed to light a fire. He stood with his back to us as we hurried to eat our cold dinner. What had once been a group of near fifty was closer to thirty-five after the attack. So many lives lost in the attempt to abduct the prince into enemy territory. I wondered again what Eljin and his followers hoped to accomplish. Were they going to demand King Hector pay ransom for his son?

"What's he doing?" I heard Jax ask his mother, nodding toward Eljin. I leaned forward to listen for her answer as they finished tying their tent down for the night.

"He's going to stand guard all night, and protect us if necessary."

"In case another group from the army finds us?" Jax sounded scared.

"Yes. But you don't need to worry. Eljin will make it so that they can't see us."

"But what if he falls asleep?"

"He won't."

I glanced back at Eljin, wondering what other powers he possessed. How could he keep an entire battalion from seeing us?

Then I noticed Rylan standing apart from the grouping of tents, near a copse of trees. It was strange to be out of the jungle, to see rolling fields of grass spreading gently downward, into the valley below. Although I hated the jungle, I was used to it; I felt exposed out here.

I glanced around but didn't see Damian anywhere. Now was as good a time to approach Rylan as any, I supposed. We would be crossing into Blevon tomorrow and I had no idea what awaited us there. I figured I'd better talk to him in case I didn't get another chance. Steeling my courage, I stood up and walked toward him.

He felt me coming — I could tell by the way he tensed up. But he didn't turn to look at me. I stopped a few feet away, my little bit of bravery failing at the scowl on his face.

"What do you want, Alex?"

"Rylan, please don't do this." I moved so that I stood in front of him, forcing him to look at me.

"Do what? I'm not *doing* anything. I guess that's my problem."

"So that's it? You're not going to talk to me anymore?" I hesitantly reached for his arm, but he pulled away from my grasp.

"Oh, would you like me to jump into the fray? Do you want to turn it into a game? See who can catch you first? Me against a prince. I'm pretty certain I know how that would turn out."

"No! That's not what I meant," I stammered, heat rising in my cheeks. "Rylan, I'm sorry I made you so mad. I'm sorry that I made you hate me. Apart from Marcel, you've been my closest friend for the last three years, and since he died, you've been my *only* friend. I don't want to lose you."

For the first time since his confession, Rylan's expression softened a little. "I don't *hate* you, Alex. And I'm not mad at you. I'm *worried* about you. And I'm suspicious of the prince."

"Why?"

Rylan looked down at me silently for a moment, debating. "I'm not sure what his . . . intentions are," he said slowly, his voice careful. "I'm afraid he's using you for some reason, and I don't want you to get hurt. But mostly, I'm mad at myself," he rushed on when I tried to break in. "I was a fool not to tell you how I felt the moment you discovered I knew. I waited and I lost my chance."

My heart skipped a beat. "Please don't say that."

He shook his head and turned away, looking out across the land toward Blevon. "I don't know what's going to happen to all of us. I feel like more is going on than we understand, but I can't figure out what. Prince Damian doesn't act like someone who's worried for his life. But apparently, he is a very good actor, so who knows."

"I don't know, either."

We were silent for a moment.

"I *am* sorry, Rylan. I'm sorry about *all* of this. If I'd been better, faster, maybe none of this would have happened. I would have stopped Eljin and we'd still be safe at the palace." I moved to stand beside him, gazing at the lush, green beauty of the lowlands.

"It's not your fault. No one could have stopped him — no natural man. Or woman," he added, glancing sideways at me.

"Not if what Damian said is true."

Rylan sighed and we fell silent again, both lost in thought as the sun slowly descended, shooting fiery fingers of red, orange, and yellow across the sky in one last salute before sinking out of sight.

Finally, I turned to face Rylan. "You don't have to worry about me getting hurt — I promise. I know it can't go anywhere. I know —"

He looked down at me, his expression inscrutable in the falling darkness. He took a step closer; I could have touched him if I moved even an inch. I felt off balance, strangely light-headed as I looked at him. If nothing had happened with Damian, falling for Rylan would have been as easy as breathing. I almost reached for him — to do what, I had no idea — but then he abruptly turned away.

"We should get some rest. It's going to be another long day." Without another glance at me, he strode off toward the grouping of tents.

I watched him walk away, but I didn't move. My heart still beat unevenly and my hands felt strangely clammy. I could see Damian standing near Eljin. They appeared to be in a heated discussion but I was too far away to be certain. As I watched, Damian shook his head, then turned and walked away. Before he reached the tents, he glanced up to where I stood and paused, looking first at me, then at Rylan, who was marching back to camp.

With a heavy sigh, I made myself follow him.

That night, long after Rylan's breathing had grown deep and even, I lay awake, staring up at the ceiling of the tent. I was almost positive Damian was still awake, too, but I didn't dare turn and look.

When he took my hand in his, I breathed in sharply. He wove his fingers between mine, and rubbed his thumb across the palm of my hand, sending spirals of need up my arm, which spread throughout my body, making my heart thud in my chest.

"Damian," I whispered unsteadily, attempting to take my mind off my sudden, urgent desire to turn and let him kiss me into oblivion, "was the bloodroot you had me gather for Lisbet? How do you know her?" I'd told Rylan that I wasn't going to let myself get hurt, but I wasn't sure if it was a promise I could keep.

"You don't want to talk about Lisbet right now, do you?" His thumb moved up to brush across the sensitive skin on the inside of my wrist.

"I want to understand what's going on. I want to know what they intend to do to you." My words came out breathy, and a blush rose in my cheeks. I was grateful it was dark.

"Eljin and his men?" Damian responded, his voice low and close to my ear.

I nodded. His thumb had moved back to stroke the palm of my hand and I found it hard to breathe normally.

"They're taking me to someone who wishes to use me to put an end to the war."

"How? Are they going to ask for ransom?"

"Not if they know my father at all. He'd never pay it. He's probably quite glad to be rid of me, truth be told."

I finally turned my head to look at him. He lay on his side, watching me, his face so close, I could feel his breath on my lips. In the darkness, it was hard to read his expression. "What is it you think they're going to do, then?"

"I suppose we'll find out soon enough." His gaze dropped to my mouth and my stomach tightened, remembering the way he'd kissed me in the jungle, the feel of his mouth on mine, of his teeth grazing my collarbone. I couldn't move, I couldn't breathe as he looked back up into my eyes. "But I won't let any harm come to you, I promise."

"Shouldn't I be the one saying that to you?" I asked, my voice shaky. Damian laughed quietly, a low sound that thrummed through my body. He let go of my hand, and trailed his fingers up my arm, my shoulder, my neck. I trembled beneath his touch, aching to feel his mouth against mine again. He gently pushed his hand into my hair, pulling me toward him, closing the gap until finally, *finally* our lips met, brushing in the darkness. Fire rushed over my skin, urging me closer to him.

Rylan muttered something unintelligible in his sleep and Damian jerked back, leaving me suddenly cold and shocked to realize I'd completely forgotten we weren't alone.

"We'd better try to get some sleep," he said.

One minute, he was making me burn from his touch and the next, he wanted me to go to sleep? Then I realized he was smirking at me. "Thanks a lot," I replied, trying to glare at him but not quite succeeding.

"Sweet dreams," he said and then closed his eyes, appearing to be completely relaxed.

I was almost positive he was teasing me, but couldn't quite

believe it. The Damian I'd known didn't tease. He didn't laugh and carry young boys on his shoulders and kiss me and tell me he needed me — that it had always been me.

But this Damian did. And I realized that despite my promise to Rylan, I was in danger of getting my heart broken by this Damian.

❧ TWENTY-EIGHT ❧

THERE WAS NO definitive sign that we'd left our nation behind the first day that our journey took us out of Antion. But as the days passed, the lush green of Antion began to subtly merge with a more arid landscape. On the horizon, I could see sharp cliffs rising out of the increasingly barren land.

We still carried Tanoori, as her condition hadn't improved. Lisbet had dark circles under her eyes, and her cheeks were sunken. In the past three days, the gray streaks in her hair seemed to have grown and her shoulders had begun to stoop forward. She could no longer help shoulder the stretcher, and Eljin had finally broken down and ordered another of his men to help. She walked alongside us instead, holding Jax's hand, while he continually looked up at his mother in concern.

I also noticed Damian watching her. He kept his face impassive, but I knew him well enough now to notice the worry lurking in his eyes. He cared for Lisbet for some reason. But I didn't dare ask why, afraid he wouldn't answer my question yet again, making it harder for me to trust him.

I *wanted* to trust him, but I knew he was holding pieces of himself back from me. He never did tell me what his message to the Insurgi had been, or when he'd learned to swordfight — and with whom. He hadn't even told me how he'd figured out I was a girl. We hadn't had another moment alone, though, except at night when we both tried to ignore the fact that we were lying inches away from each other, since Rylan was in the same tent with us. Maybe he was just waiting for real privacy. At least that's what I tried to convince myself.

And though Rylan no longer looked at me with the cold anger that had been so hard to bear, he didn't reach out to me the way he used to. Sometimes, when I looked at him, my heart still skipped a beat and I couldn't help but wonder what would have happened between us if circumstances had been different.

Every night, I had to lie between the two of them, feeling like I was being torn apart inside. I wondered how dark the circles under my own eyes were.

When we stopped for the night, Eljin came over to where we were setting up our tent.

"Tomorrow, we arrive. You will all be bound to keep you from making a spectacle of yourselves. I have been merciful in allowing you to travel so freely, but that time is over."

"What about Tanoori? How will we carry her if our hands are tied?" Rylan asked.

Above his mask, Eljin's eyes were unreadable in the dusky light. "I will have to use some of my men to carry her." By the tone of his voice, it was apparent that he was extremely displeased.

"Thank you," I said anyway, grateful for his offer to help, no matter how unwilling.

"You should take care to lower your voice. You sound like a girl these days," he said and then he walked away.

I stared at him with my jaw hanging open. Had I begun to

act like a girl — to talk like one? I didn't think so — I'd carried Tanoori with three other men without complaining once for days. I helped set up the tent, I took it down, I did everything every other man here did.

"Don't worry about him. He's just antsy to be done with us, I think." Rylan nudged my shoulder with his as he passed me to go start the campfire.

I shrugged but didn't respond. I hadn't realized Eljin knew I was a girl. Maybe I *was* revealing myself. Lisbet had told me to keep up the pretense, but why? So that these men wouldn't know? I didn't see why it mattered if they did or not. Death probably awaited me wherever we were going anyway. Maybe it would be nice to die as my true self.

I walked over to Lisbet's tent and quietly parted the flaps. Damian knelt next to Lisbet, holding her hand in both of his. Tanoori lay motionless and unconscious on the ground next to them. I watched for only a moment, but the tenderness with which he looked at Lisbet and held her hand made me ache. I silently let the flap fall back into place and backed away.

He looked at her with love on his face, the way a son would look at his mother.

I wanted to *know* him. I wanted him to trust me, the way he asked me to trust him. I wanted him to tell me *all* of his secrets. Not just the ones he was forced to reveal, piece by piece. But his feelings for me were obviously not enough to make him willing to trust me with the whole truth.

"Alex, can I talk to you?"

I was startled to realize I had wandered a little way away from camp, and that Rylan had followed me.

"Of course. Sorry, I was lost in thought." I stopped and waited for him to catch up to me.

Our camp was nestled in between two groves of trees — different trees from what I'd ever seen before. Lisbet had told us some were called pine trees and some were called quaking aspens because they appeared to shake when the wind blew. The grass here was thinner, almost yellowish, compared to the deep, verdant green of Antion. But the air was also a bit cooler, thinner. I wasn't coated in sweat just from walking this short distance like I would have been in the jungle.

Rylan gestured for me to follow him as he strode farther into the cover of the trees, away from camp.

"What if Eljin notices we're gone?" I asked as I followed him out of sight.

"I don't care. I don't know what's waiting for us tomorrow and I'm not going to waste what might be my last chance to really talk to you." He stopped and turned to me.

"What do you mean?" He wasn't as tall as Damian, but I still had to tilt my head up to meet his eyes when he moved closer. "Rylan?"

"I'm not going to let you go, to possibly face our deaths, without a fight," he said, reaching up to brush my cheek with the back of his hand. He looked down at me with a look of such raw longing that my heart constricted. But not in the way it did when Damian touched me. When Damian was close to me, my heart raced. And I could hardly breathe for the desire coursing through me when Damian touched me.

As Rylan stared into my eyes, waiting for me, I felt different from what I did with Damian. Rylan's touch filled me with warmth and comfort. But I didn't want him the way I wanted Damian.

I didn't move toward him but I didn't pull away, either. The moment stretched out, with his hand cupping the back of my head, his fingers threaded through my hair, his face inches from mine, while I battled with myself, wanting to pull away but afraid of hurting him. Before I could decide what to do, he bent down and softly pressed his lips to mine. His kiss felt like a sigh, a release. His mouth was so gentle on mine, moving slowly, tenderly. A spark of desire flared in my belly.

My hands rested against his chest, my fingers tangled in his tunic. If I'd never come to know Damian the way I did now, I could have fallen for Rylan. I knew it as surely as I knew that it was too late. Rylan held me in his arms, and my body responded to his touch, but all I could see in my mind was the hurt on Damian's face if he knew, if he came looking for me and saw Rylan kissing me. It didn't matter if he was a prince, if we could never truly be together. It was too late to go back to what might have been.

"No, wait," I said, breaking away.

Rylan immediately dropped his arms and backed up a step, breathing heavily.

"I . . . I'm sorry, Rylan. I just —"

"Don't say it," he said, his voice rough. "I thought I'd take a chance. I couldn't face whatever might lie ahead of us tomorrow without at least trying."

I wrapped my arms around myself against a sudden chill. The nights here were shockingly crisp. The breeze made me shiver as it brushed over me and moved on to rustle the leaves in the quaking aspens.

He looked at me for a moment longer, with unbearable longing. "I love you, Alexa. No matter what happens tomorrow, or any day after that, I will always love you."

My eyes burned. "I love you, too, Rylan."

"But it's not enough," he said. "I was too late."

I shook my head, unable to answer, not knowing what my answer even *was*. I did love him; I hadn't lied. But I knew it wasn't the love he wanted me to feel. Tears filled my eyes, blurring him. He reached out and touched my cheek, wiping away a single tear with his thumb, and bent to press his lips to my forehead. Then he took a step back.

"I want you to know that I'll always be here for you." He paused and then rushed on. "When the day comes that Prince Damian breaks your heart and you need a friend to turn to, I'll be right here for you, just like I always have been."

His words hit me like ice and I stared at him in shock as he strode past me out of the clearing, leaving me alone with the trees, the stars, and the cold breeze that sent a chill deep into my heart.

⊰ TWENTY-NINE ⊱

W E'D BEEN CARRYING Tanoori for about four hours when I saw the buildings of a town in the distance. Above the dwellings, nestled into the rising breast of a hill, was a huge castle encased by an immense stone wall. I knew we weren't near King Osgand's castle — it was deeper inside Blevon, from what I'd heard.

I remembered Papa's stories about the land where his parents had grown up and I wondered if it was this town or one like it somewhere else. The irony of being here, in the country where half of my family had hailed from, as a prisoner of war, struck me to the core. If Hector hadn't taken over Antion, and if his wife hadn't been murdered, would I have come here freely to visit family rather than being dragged here, likely to my death?

"Is that it, Mama?" Jax asked Lisbet, who trudged along next to us, looking paler than ever.

"Yes, son. We're almost there." The relief in her voice was audible.

I stared at the massive fortress with growing foreboding. What — or who — awaited us there?

"Halt!" The shout was repeated until we all came to a stop.

Careful not to jostle her, Rylan, Damian, the man Eljin had assigned to help us, and I laboriously set Tanoori down on the ground. Her lips were bloodless, and nasty-looking red streaks spread across her chest from the partially healed wound. I was afraid infection had set in and that we'd suffered all this time only for her to die once we reached our destination.

"She'll make it," Lisbet said from beside me. "There will be help where we're going."

Eljin marched over to where we stood, and began handing out rope to his men. "Tie up the prisoners; I want their hands behind their backs. Make sure there's no slack."

The man who tied me up yanked my arms back with unnecessary force, making my already sore muscles scream in protest. I clenched my teeth to keep from crying out. Rylan and Damian stood on either side of me, both being tied up just as roughly. When Eljin's men were done, one of them shouted something at us in the strange, flowing language of Blevon.

"You're going to have to use our language; they can't understand you," Damian responded, looking completely composed, despite the fact that his hands were bound behind him.

The man hit Damian across the mouth with the back of his hand with a resounding crack. "I will decide what language I speak, and if they can't understand me, then they will suffer the punishment. You aren't in charge here anymore, little *prince*."

Damian spat blood onto the dirt, his expression murderous.

"No, *I* am the one in charge, and you will never strike one of the prisoners without my permission again." Eljin thrust his hand toward the man who'd hit Damian. He dropped to his knees, clutching his throat. The skin of his face turned red, then began to deepen to purple before Eljin dropped his hand, and the man fell forward onto his palms, gasping and sputtering for air.

"Have I made myself clear?" Eljin turned to face the rest of his men, who were crowded around us.

They nodded and murmured their assent, glancing warily at the one who still knelt on the ground.

"Let's go," Eljin shouted. "No more stops."

Everyone quickly filed into line, we prisoners sequestered in the middle. Before marching away, Eljin looked directly at Damian with a strange look in his eyes. Some sort of silent communication seemed to pass between the two, and then Eljin turned and moved to the front of the line.

I sped up a bit to walk next to Damian. "Are you okay?" I asked quietly.

"I'm fine" was his gruff response. He didn't look down at me, and I couldn't help feeling like I'd been rebuffed for some reason. He picked up the pace a bit, leaving me to either hurry to keep up or to fall behind. I was afraid that he was trying to keep his distance from me.

He and Rylan had both been very quiet all morning, tension rolling off them in waves. But I was probably the same. I felt utterly miserable.

I'd gone into the tent as soon as I came back from the grove of trees the night before, avoiding the log where Rylan sat and the pit in front of Lisbet's tent, where I could see Damian's dark silhouette in the firelight. I couldn't bear to talk to either of them, so I'd taken the spineless route and crawled onto my bedroll, pretending to go to sleep.

Was he mad at me for that? Or did he somehow know what had happened with Rylan?

Rylan didn't come to walk beside me, either, leaving me to go in silence, alone with my thoughts as we drew closer and closer to the fortress on the hill. We skirted the town, keeping our distance from the homes and people I caught glimpses of in the streets. Many of them had dark hair and olive skin. Like me. Like Damian.

Walking with our hands tied behind our backs, after hefting Tanoori around for so long, was simultaneously a relief and pain. I just wanted it to be over with.

Finally, we began to make our way up the hill, to the front gate of the wall surrounding the citadel. It was heavily guarded, but when they saw Eljin, the sentinels parted, raising their spears and signaling for the gate to open. With a loud grinding sound, the metal bars slowly lifted into the air and we walked through the archway and entered a dusty courtyard, surrounded by at least twenty men with swords and spears.

Eljin shouted something in the foreign sounds of Blevonese, and a murmur went through the gathered men, until every one of them turned to stare at Prince Damian. The sun was hot on our backs as we stood there, but it was a different kind of heat than I was used to. It was dry and relentless.

Across from the courtyard was a massive wooden door, what I assumed was the main entrance to the castle, which soared into the air above us. It opened after a moment and a tall man, dressed in military uniform, walked out, flanked by a contingent of armed guards.

The men in the courtyard saluted him until he raised an arm in acknowledgment. Silence fell upon the courtyard the moment he began to speak in their language. Then he switched so we could understand as well.

"I am General Tinso, the supreme general of the Blevonese army. I declare you, Prince Damian of Antion, our prisoner. You are now at our mercy, and as such, must acquiesce to our demands or suffer the consequences. Three cheers for my son and his victory over our enemy!"

His *son*? Eljin was the general's son?

The men around us raised their voices in three loud shouts of celebration. Then Lisbet stepped forward. General Tinso's eyes widened and he rushed to meet her, enveloping her in his arms. With one arm still around her shoulders, he turned to face us again.

"Now that we have captured the king's son and only heir, let us pray that victory is soon at hand!"

The men went wild, cheering and stomping. Some even spit in Damian's direction, making me wish my hands were free to access a bow and arrows.

Through it all, Damian stood ramrod straight in front of me, his shoulders thrown back and his chin lifted in defiance. Pride filled my heart in that moment, even though I realized that it was a futile gesture. We were doomed.

We were ushered into the castle at spear point, Damian first, then Rylan and me right behind him. Lisbet had already disappeared into the depths of the fortress with Jax and the men who still carried Tanoori on her heels. I wondered what her relationship to General Tinso was.

The great hall was sparsely decorated, but still luxurious. Thick tapestries hung from the walls, depicting barren cliffs with a wild, stark kind of beauty, and fields of green and gold, rolling on as if they never ended. A blade bit into the skin on my back, forcing me to keep moving forward before I could take in anything else.

If only I could loosen these ropes, get a hand free. I could swipe a sword and try to fight our way out. But the Blevonese soldiers had done their job well; I could do no more than rub my wrists together, chafing the rope against my skin. And even if I succeeded, Eljin would just use his sorcery to stop me. There was nothing I could do to save us.

I glanced sideways at Rylan as the guards pushed us down a corridor and then up a winding staircase. He met my gaze with a bleak look of his own. We were most likely going to die — if not today, then soon — when the general was done with us.

I was going to lose them both.

Despite his hands being tied and the spear digging into his back, Damian climbed the stairs ahead of me as if he were on his way to a royal coronation, rather than to his inevitable demise. I wanted to reach out to him, to touch his face one more time, to feel his mouth on mine again. To tell him that I feared I was falling in love with him. But there was nothing I could do except stare at him with my eyes burning as we crested the last stair. Sunlight filtered in through sporadic windows, shining in bright patches in the otherwise dim hallway. Ahead of us, I could see the dark head of General Tinso. He had silver sprinkled liberally through his hair, and his olive-toned skin was darkened from hours spent in the sun. Was he a sorcerer, too?

Eljin was behind us somewhere, making sure we didn't attempt to escape, I supposed.

Finally, the general stopped before another door. He said something in his language, and Damian was pushed forward with a sharp shove to his back. I watched helplessly as he crossed the hallway to stand next to General Tinso. Everything in me screamed to do something, anything, but we were trapped. I could do nothing but watch.

With Damian beside him, the general said something else, and the guards stepped back, bowed, and walked away. Next, he gestured at Rylan and me, and we were brought forward the same way. Our guards were also dismissed. Eljin moved to stand on his father's other side. Up close I could see the resemblance, the slant of their eyes, the color of their skin and hair, but the general didn't wear a mask.

General Tinso said something else, and all the remaining guards bowed and turned to go. Before I knew it, we were alone with the general and his son. My heart picked up speed when he opened the door and entered the room.

"Follow him," Eljin said, gesturing for us to precede him.

Damian went first, with Rylan and me right on his heels. The room was large and rectangular, with all sorts of weapons hanging on the walls. A huge torture chamber of some sort?

My stomach coiled in dread when Eljin came in after us and shut the door with a resounding thud and then slammed the bolt in place, locking us in.

"I assume that you brought them for a reason?" General Tinso nodded at Rylan and me. But instead of Eljin answering, Damian nodded.

"Yes, it would have been a risk to leave them at the mercy of my father, and they are loyal to me."

"Then we may speak freely in front of them?"

"Yes."

General Tinso nodded at Eljin. "What are you waiting for? Cut those ropes off already."

I stared at them in utter shock as Eljin stepped forward and sliced the ropes off Damian's wrists. And then my jaw literally fell open when General Tinso walked up to Damian and embraced him.

"Welcome at last to my home, Prince Damian."

⇥ THIRTY ⇤

DAMIAN EMBRACED HIM back as Rylan and I watched in total bewilderment. While we stood there, gaping like fish, Eljin came over and cut the ropes off our hands as well. I rubbed my wrists as the blood rushed back into my hands.

"I'm sorry for all of this," General Tinso said when he released Damian and stepped back.

"It was necessary," Damian said. "I knew what I was agreeing to."

"Did you run into any problems? Besides deciding to bring two extras along with you?" General Tinso's dark eyes lingered on me for some reason.

"Alex and Rylan were in the room when Eljin came. He and his men had to fight to make it look real, and if I had left them there, King Hector would have had them killed for failing to protect me. I didn't want to lose two loyal guards to such a fate." His eyes met mine across the short distance.

"*You* saved me?" Rylan asked in shock.

Damian didn't respond; he was looking at me.

"You planned this," I said quietly. His betrayal cut deeper than I could have imagined. He'd said he needed me. He had asked me to *trust* him, to open up to him and bare my secrets, and all along he'd been keeping this enormous secret from me. He'd let me think for *weeks* that we'd been abducted, that our lives were in danger. We'd been tied up, manhandled, forced into this very room at spear point.

"Why?" I asked, my voice low with barely suppressed fury.

"Alex, just let me —"

"Why?" I screamed. I'd let myself fall for him. I'd let myself believe that he cared about me, that there might be hope for us somehow. He was a *prince* — he could choose to be with me if he wanted.

But he had lied to me. Manipulated me. I'd thought he was opening up to me, revealing who he really was bit by bit. But I didn't know him at all.

He looked momentarily stunned by my outburst, but then his expression closed and his eyes grew glitteringly cold. "I did what I had to do. I've told you that before." Then he turned to General Tinso. "There wasn't time to send a message to you, since the plan was already in action, but there was more to my decision than just saving their lives."

I clenched my jaw shut, desperately trying to regain my composure, to pull on the mask that I'd worn for years as General Tinso looked at Damian questioningly.

Calm, cool, collected, no matter what — that's what I needed to be. I drew on that mask when my parents died; I did it when Marcel died. I could do it now. I didn't dare glance at Rylan. He'd been right. He'd warned me and I hadn't listened and now I'd let the prince hurt me. I was afraid that looking at him would be my undoing.

"Rylan, the taller one, is an excellent fighter and may benefit from your specialized training. But Eljin and I believe that Alexa, who just regaled us with an unusual show of temper, might be gifted."

"Alex*a*?" General Tinso repeated, stroking his chin. "I did think she was a bit too pretty to be a boy. But you never know." He paused, looking me over. "Her parents?"

"Dead, unfortunately." Damian also looked at me, and I suddenly felt as though I were a specimen that they were studying. I hated the way he talked about me as if I weren't standing ten feet from him. As if he'd never held me in his arms and told me that he'd broken his promise to himself to never care about someone again. "But her coloring and her skill might suggest that our suspicions are correct."

"She is quite good, I take it?"

"The best fighter I have. If she weren't so young, she would have been captain of my guard, because she bested everyone else. And that was a year ago."

"Excuse me, I'm standing right here." I clenched my hands into fists at my side. "What does my coloring have to do with my ability to fight?"

"You look as though one of your parents was from Blevon, am I right?" General Tinso asked as he walked over to the wall and picked up two swords. He tossed one to me, which I automatically reached for and snatched from the air. I instantly felt calmer with a blade in my hand again.

"My father's parents were from Blevon. What does that have to do with anything?"

He circled me, and I turned in place, warily watching him. "Eljin, you agree with Damian?" he asked his son, rather than responding to me. "You believe she might be gifted?"

"It seems very likely. She's had no training defending herself against sorcerers, and yet she held me off for nearly six minutes when I challenged her in the ring at the palace."

"You fought in a ring? You revealed yourself?" General Tinso paused and gave his son a sharp look.

"No one realized I was a sorcerer, Father. Damian asked me to do it, to see if anyone showed potential to be trained."

"No one realized it except for me," I said through clenched teeth. Was he going to attack or not?

Eljin looked at me in surprise. "You knew?"

"You blocked me with magic — of course I knew." I didn't dare look away from his father again to try to read the expression on his masked face.

"You realized he used magic?" General Tinso began to circle closer to me and I tightened my grip on my sword. "Interesting."

And then he lunged at me. I parried quickly, and spinning, swung my sword back around at him, which he blocked deftly. It felt so good to fight again. All the anger, the hurt and pain and confusion inside of me flowed through my arms and hands into my sword as I attacked as fast as I could. I was a dervish of movement, of speed and agility and fury. The sounds of our swords rang through the room, while Damian, Rylan, and Eljin watched in silence. Finally, General Tinso lifted his sword to his face as he bowed and stepped back, a signal that he was conceding defeat.

"Excellent, indeed," he mused out loud, his dark eyes alight with what looked like excitement.

I held my sword loosely at my side, my chest heaving as I tried to catch my breath.

"Alexa, how would you like to train with my son and learn how to defeat a sorcerer? I presume that's why you wanted her to come?" General Tinso looked to Damian, who nodded.

"Is it really possible?" I asked, my anger at the prince warring with my curiosity.

"It's very difficult, but, yes, it's possible. However, from what they say and what I've seen here today, I believe you have the ability necessary to be successful."

So this was why Damian had me "brought along." He wanted a guard who could defeat a sorcerer. But why? How did he know General Tinso — and why were we here? Especially under the guise of having been abducted? These people were responsible for his mother's death — how could he trust them?

"I'll do it, but only if you start answering my questions. All of them. *Honestly.*" I stared at Damian as I said this.

His jaw tightened. "I'll answer as many as I can," he said.

"That's not good enough."

"It has to be. It's all I can offer. Don't make me regret saving you, Alexa."

I blinked, feeling like he'd struck me. Was I no more than a tool to do his bidding? I finally looked to Rylan for the first time since we'd entered this room. He met my questioning gaze gravely, but then he nodded once.

Damian watched me, his expression inscrutable, waiting.

"Alexa?" General Tinso prompted me. "I'm a very busy man. I have a very bloody, vicious war I'm trying to manage and even end, if possible. But my son and I will dedicate ourselves to your training if you agree to it, because your ability could play an integral role in overthrowing King Hector."

"Is that what you're hoping to do?" I forced myself to turn to Damian again, even though it hurt just to look at him. "Overthrow your father?"

He nodded curtly.

I glanced around at the four men watching me, waiting for me. How could Damian trust the Blevonese? One of their own had murdered our queen, driving King Hector to start this infernal war.

But what else did I have to lose? My family was all dead, gone forever. Antion was shriveling and dying under King Hector's rule and the price his war was exacting on us. The only person who truly cared about *me* — not just my ability — was Rylan, and his nod said to go ahead. And if I was honest with myself, part of me was curious. About this side to my heritage that I knew so little of, and about what I needed to learn to be able to defeat a sorcerer. Once before I'd asked myself, if there was any way to stop this war, would I have the courage to try?

"All right," I finally said. "I'll do it."

⊰ THIRTY-ONE ⊱

$\mathcal{E}$XCELLENT." GENERAL TINSO smiled. "I assume you are exhausted from your journey here, so we will start tomorrow. But there is no time to waste, so rest well tonight."

He turned to Rylan and Damian. "Because we have to maintain the guise that you're our prisoners, we'll be keeping you in the back of the castle where there are many empty rooms and Eljin will be your personal 'guard.' My men won't question you not being tied up if Eljin is nearby."

"Why did you pretend to abduct the prince?" I asked. "Why do we have to continue to pretend? And would someone tell me why you believe I'm 'gifted'? What does that even mean?"

General Tinso and Damian shared a meaningful look. "I'll let you answer her questions," the general said. "Eljin, show them to their rooms and I'll have a servant bring you some food. I apologize if it isn't food fit for royalty, but again, we have to keep up the guise."

"After what we've been eating for the last few weeks, anything fresh will taste like a delicacy," Damian said.

"I apologize again, but I must go. I have some top advisors from King Osgand waiting for me." He paused, though, gazing at Damian for a long moment. "You look so much like your mother. She would be proud of you, Prince Damian. I hope you know that."

A muscle in Damian's jaw tightened, and he nodded once, tersely, almost as if he couldn't speak. I stared at the general in what was probably ill-concealed shock. I couldn't believe he dared speak of Damian's mother — and that Damian hadn't lashed out at him for it.

General Tinso reached out and squeezed his shoulder once, then with a nod at us, turned and walked out of the room.

We followed Eljin to a dark, dusty stairwell at the back of the castle, and then down a flight of stairs to another hallway that was equally dark and dusty. He passed a few doors, and stopped.

"You'll be kept here, except when you're training. The less anyone sees you, the better." He took a key out of his pocket and opened the door with it.

Inside was a medium-sized room. A dresser with a wash basin rested in one corner next to a fireplace, a chamber pot sat in another, and three cots lined the wall.

"We're *all* staying here? Together?" I asked, my voice embarrassingly high-pitched.

"It'll be much more spacious than the tent, at least." It was hard to tell with the mask on, but I was pretty sure Eljin was mocking me. "You're meant to appear to be prisoners. So this is it, I'm afraid."

He was definitely smiling beneath that infernal scrap of fabric.

"I'm glad you find it so funny," I said crossly as I pushed him out of the way to enter my new quarters.

This time, I refused to sleep between Damian and Rylan. I took one cot and dragged it as far away from the other two as possible, then sat on it, and watched them both walk in. Eljin gave us a little, mocking salute. "Have a good night." And he slammed the door behind him.

We sat in silence for a long time. The tension that filled the room made the air heavy enough that I could almost feel as if I were back in the jungle. Damian sat on his cot with his head in his hands, his fingers clenched in his hair. Rylan kept looking at me, then at the floor. Finally, I couldn't stand it anymore, and I didn't care if Rylan was in the room.

"You *lied* to me." I'd intended my voice to be harsh, angry. But instead I sounded betrayed, hurt. The two things I didn't want him to realize he'd made me feel.

Damian jerked up to meet my accusing gaze, but the pain in his eyes softened my anger slightly. *Very* slightly. I tried to remind myself of what Rylan said about him being an exceptional actor. "Alex, you have to believe me when I tell you I didn't want to deceive you. But we decided long before you became involved that as few people as possible could know the truth. We had to make it believable."

"Well, you did a great job, because you had me convinced, too," I bit out.

"That was the point." Damian stood up and began to pace. "You had to believe it so you would act like you'd been abducted. We needed word to get back to my father and it had to be convincing. He's already suspicious of me and my ties to Blevon."

"What ties *do* you have to Blevon? And why did you think I couldn't act? What do you think I've been doing for the last three years of my life?" I rose, too, hating the way he towered over me when I was seated. I was halfway tempted to stand up on the cot so I would be taller than him.

"Eljin and I decided it wasn't worth the risk. It gave you plausible deniability, in case something went wrong. If you'd been taken back to Antion knowing it was a setup, Iker could have tortured the truth out of you."

"You underestimate her," Rylan cut in.

Damian spun to face Rylan in surprise. "Excuse me?"

"You told me to trust you," I accused, pulling his attention back to me. "How am I supposed to do that when you keep lying to me? When you keep secrets from me? And you didn't answer my question. What ties do you have to Blevon?"

"I thought that was fairly common knowledge," he said tersely. "Excuse me for not answering right away. My mother was from Blevon. She was King Osgand's niece. My father thinks that I might not be entirely loyal to Antion because I was so attached to her."

"Wasn't she murdered by a sorcerer from Blevon?" Rylan asked.

"No. That is the rumor my father started to justify his declaration of war, and to make our people hate sorcerers and all magic."

"Then what happened to her?" I pressed, even though I could tell he was upset.

"I don't want to talk about it."

Rylan jumped to his feet now, too. "Why won't you just answer her questions? Can't you see how much you're hurting her?"

"You think I *want* to hurt her? Do you think it makes me happy to see the little bit of trust she had in me die today?" Damian's eyes flashed as he turned on Rylan, his hands clenched into fists.

"Then just tell her the truth. Hasn't she done enough to prove herself to you?"

"Rylan —" I tried to break in.

"She doesn't need to prove anything to me." Damian's voice was harsh.

"Then why won't you answer her? Do you care about her at all? Or are you just using her in every way possible, until she's served her purpose and you can cast her aside?"

"Don't forget who you are speaking to, *guard*," Damian warned Rylan, his voice cold with barely contained fury.

My heart jumped around in my chest like a frightened rabbit. What did Rylan think he was doing?

"Are you threatening me? What are you going to do? Have me hanged? Run me through with a sword? Go right ahead, Your *Royal Highness*," Rylan sneered back, spreading his arms out wide, as if waiting for the prince to shove a sword through him then and there. I was suddenly very glad we hadn't been given any weapons.

"I'm standing right here," I tried to cut in again, but it was as if they couldn't hear me.

"Of course I'm not going to have you killed. I'm the only reason you're still *alive* — I'm the one who convinced Eljin to bring you along."

Rylan had the decency to look slightly ashamed.

"What do I have to do to prove to you that I care about her? You want me to answer her questions?" Damian turned to face me, his blue eyes fevered. "You want to know what happened to my mother?"

I stared up at him with my heart in my throat, wondering if it would have been better if they'd continued to leave me out of their argument after all. Damian was a thundercloud, ready to burst open at any moment.

"I didn't answer your question because I didn't want to talk about it, not because I don't trust you or care about you." He glowered down at me. But behind the fierceness of the expression on his face, I could sense a terrible agony. When his eyes finally met mine, the torment I saw there took my breath away. I realized I didn't want him to answer the question — not like this.

But it was too late.

"You want to know what happened to her? My *father* murdered her in front of my brother and me to teach us a lesson when I was eight. He poisoned her tea for months to weaken her and then he cut her down in cold blood five feet from me. *That's* what happened to my mother."

An awful silence fell on the room.

"Satisfied now?"

My throat constricted, and my stomach twisted in horror. Rylan stood as if frozen, staring at the prince.

"Damian, I'm . . . I'm so —"

"Don't say it," he cut me off. "You wanted an answer, you got one. Now if you'll excuse me." He strode over to the door and pounded on it. "Eljin, you let me out of here right now unless you want my knife in your gut."

The lock slid back and the door swung open. Eljin seemed about to make a joke, his eyes crinkled at the corners, but when he saw the thunderous look on Damian's face, his eyes grew serious. "Of course. Come out. There's no one out here right now."

And with that, Damian left, slamming the door behind him.

⊰ THIRTY-TWO ⊱

$\mathcal{D}$AMIAN DIDN'T COME back the rest of the night, and Eljin wouldn't tell me where he'd gone when he brought us dinner.

"But I thought we all had to stay in here to keep up the guise?"

"No one will see him; they assume he *is* in here."

"But where is he?" I pressed.

Eljin gave me a piercing look. "You'd better eat your food before it gets cold. You'll need your strength for tomorrow."

And then he shut the door in my face.

"Alex, I'm really sorry. I only meant to defend you. I had no idea —"

I held up my hand. "The damage is done. I don't want to talk about it."

Rylan nodded miserably, and started to eat. All I wanted to do was force the food down and go to sleep, so I could try and forget this day had ever happened.

But sleep wouldn't come. Long after I heard the rhythmic breathing indicating Rylan had drifted off, I was still awake, staring at the wall, with tears leaking out of my eyes.

⊹⟞═⟞

I woke up bleary-eyed and aching all over. I felt almost worse than before I'd gone to sleep. But then I rolled over to see Damian lying on his cot. Relief flooded through me. I don't know what I'd been afraid of, but seeing him there released a knot of tension I hadn't even realized was beneath my sternum until it was gone.

He'd shaved before coming back, and the smooth line of his jaw held only a hint of a shadow now. I watched him sleep with a deep ache in my chest. What kind of life had he had? I'd seen my parents killed in front of me. We'd only been spared because we were so young. But to have watched his own father kill his mother in front of him? It was unfathomable.

I stood up silently and moved across the room toward him, the stone floor cold on my toes. I shivered in the brisk air of morning. I still wasn't used to waking up to a chill.

When I reached the cot Damian was stretched out on, I knelt down. Glancing at Rylan to make sure he was still asleep first, I lifted my hand to Damian's hair and smoothed it back from his face. It was thick and so soft, I wanted to keep running my fingers through it.

He stirred in his sleep and then he startled awake. He reached up in one quick movement and snatched my arm, his eyes wild. When he saw it was me, his grip relaxed slightly, but his brow furrowed as he looked up into my face, watching me. My hand was still in his hair, his fingers encircling my wrist. The moment drew out, filling the space between us with tension.

"I'm sorry," I whispered at last.

Our gazes met and locked. I felt myself getting lost in his startlingly blue eyes. In the early morning light, they reminded me of the sky on a clear day. Such a shocking contrast to his dark hair and lashes, his olive skin.

"I'm sorry, as well." His voice was low, sending a tremor through me. He let go of my arm to reach out and hesitantly stroke the skin of my cheek. "Neither of us has had an easy life, have we?" When I didn't pull away, he ran his fingers through my hair and then cupped the nape of my neck, his thumb rubbing along the line of my jaw near my ear.

"No, we haven't," I breathed. My heart pulsed erratically beneath the cage of my ribs.

"I don't want to keep secrets from you, Alexa. But I'm the crown prince of Antion, and my kingdom has to come before my own desires."

I knew he was right, and I knew it was selfish of me to expect him to tell me everything. I knew how overwhelming the burden was that he carried. The last vestiges of my anger melted away.

"I never want to see you look at me the way you did yesterday ever again," Damian said.

I couldn't stop staring at his mouth. I could feel every nerve in my body yearning, reaching out for him. But I held back, waited.

"Can you understand why I had to do it? Can you forgive me?" His thumb stopped moving on my skin. I searched his face and saw only regret. Regret and something else . . . something that made my breath catch. "Could you ever trust me again?" He paused, and his fingers tightened on my neck. "Or . . . love me?"

The intensity of his gaze made me tremble. He was a man, but I also saw the little boy hidden deep inside — the one who'd watched his mother murdered in cold blood in front of him. The one who'd lost his beloved brother to a hired assassin. I looked at him and I saw a prince who wanted to save his nation.

I saw a man who was completely alone with the weight of the world on his shoulders.

"Damian, I — I already do love you," I whispered as a tear slipped down my cheek. "For better or worse."

It looked like his eyes glistened but before I could be sure, he pulled me to him and his mouth was on mine and all I could think about was the feel of his lips, his hand in my hair, the intoxicating smell of his skin, and my heart trying to burst from my chest. I wanted to lose myself in his kiss; I wanted him to take me in his arms and never let me go again. But I was all too aware that Rylan slept across the room from us. I forced myself to break away.

When Damian gave me a questioning look, I nodded over at Rylan, who was thankfully still asleep, snoring softly.

Damian sighed and pressed his lips to the groove where my jaw met my neck, just below my ear, sending a shiver of want through me. "Someday, this will all be over and we'll be truly alone," he said softly into my ear, his voice hoarse.

I nodded, unable to speak as he continued to kiss my throat, his lips soft on my skin. At last, when I could barely breathe, I took him by the shoulders and pushed him back. He smiled wickedly at me, a teasing glint in his eyes.

"Are you *sure* you want me to stop?"

I stared at his mouth, my heart still pounding. I almost said no, but then I remembered Rylan.

"Yes." I sighed.

He chuckled softly, but then his face grew serious. "Did you mean it?"

I knew immediately what he was referring to and my heart lurched in my chest. "Yes."

"Say it again."

I stared into his beautiful eyes for a long moment. "I love you, Damian," I finally whispered.

He closed his eyes, as if holding my words inside of him. "And do you trust me?"

"I . . . I'm not sure. I'm trying to," I answered honestly.

His hands tightened around my arms. I couldn't decipher the look on his face. After a pause, he said, "Then I will have to prove that you can."

Before I could respond, Rylan moaned. I stood up hastily, and backed away from Damian. He lifted an eyebrow, his eyes piercing. But I couldn't explain it to him — not then. I couldn't tell him that I didn't want Rylan to see Damian holding me in his arms. I'd admitted to him — and myself — that I loved him. But things weren't that simple.

There was a knock at the door and then it opened and Eljin walked in. Rylan's eyes opened and he slowly sat up in bed, his hair sticking out on one side.

"Sun's up," Eljin said. "Let's go. It's going to be a long day for you." He looked right at me and I nodded.

I was afraid he was right.

⊰ THIRTY-THREE ⊱

AFTER HOURS AND hours of nonstop sword fighting and hand-to-hand combat, I was hot, sweaty, sore, and exhausted. I still hadn't gotten any answers to my questions, and I still hadn't managed to get one blow past Eljin's magical shield. He'd told me that to succeed in beating a sorcerer in a fight, I had to be faster than his ability to draw up the shield, or strong enough to push through it. After an entire day of his blocking every single attempt, I didn't see how either option was possible.

Damian and Rylan had watched for part of the day, and then decided to start sparring as well. I found myself distracted, watching them fight, and Eljin landed a hard blow to my ribs, knocking the air out of me.

"Distractions often prove fatal. A good lesson to learn in a practice room," he said, his expression mocking above his mask.

I hated that mask. I hated *him*. I was better than this. I didn't make fatal mistakes. And no one defeated me. With a fresh surge of fury, I flew at him once more. I attacked so hard and fast that he couldn't keep up with me. I felt him preparing to draw up a shield, and my anger increased. I wasn't going to let him do that again. Not this time. I faked left and felt the surge of magic. With a lightning-fast move, I flicked my sword up to the right instead, grazing his cheek, and yanked the mask right off his face.

At first, it didn't dawn on me what I'd done, because all I could do was stare at his mutilated face. But then the heavy silence in the room was broken by a shout of excitement.

"She did it!" Rylan whooped. "You got past his shield!"

Damian gave me a nod of approval, smiling grimly, as Eljin reached out and grabbed the black scrap of fabric from the end of my wooden sword. If it had been a real blade, I would have cut off his ear.

"I think that's enough for today," he said angrily as he put the mask back in place, hiding the scars that lined his jaw and twisted his mouth into a grotesque mockery of lips. He tossed his sword to the ground and stormed away. "You all stay here."

The echo of the door slamming shut behind him was the only sound for a long moment.

"What happened to him?" I finally asked, unable to enjoy my victory with the memory of his scars in my mind.

Damian sighed as he walked over to the wall to set down his own sword. "General Tinso and his wife were from Blevon, but he was stationed at a border village when Eljin was a child. When my father declared war on Blevon, he announced it by raiding the border villages. General Tinso was on duty on the other side of theirs when it was attacked.

"General Tinso's wife — Lisbet's sister — was also a sorceress, and she tried to protect her son. But she wasn't strong enough to hold off so many soldiers at once. After they killed her, they tried to capture Eljin. He fought back, but he wasn't trained yet — he was too young and couldn't block all of them. What you saw on his face is just part of the scars he got that day. General Tinso and his men were eventually able to fight back and force the Antionese army to retreat, but it was too late for Eljin's mother. At least Eljin was able to keep them from killing him, too."

"Why didn't Lisbet heal him?" I stared at Damian, my stomach churning. Because of me, they'd both had to reveal their painful pasts in fewer than two days. I was really on a roll.

"She couldn't; she was at the palace in Antion."

"The palace? Why?"

"She was my mother's lady-in-waiting. She came with my mother when she married Hector."

"And Jax?" I hardly dared ask. I knew, even before he answered me. I didn't know why I hadn't put it together before now — the reason Jax's blue eyes looked familiar. They were the same as Damian's.

A dark shadow crossed his face. "He's my half brother. My father's bastard son. Lisbet should have left after my mother was killed, but she stayed. She hid for years, trying to watch out for my brother and me. Iker found her when I was eleven and took her straight to the king. My father raped Lisbet and had her thrown out with orders to kill her if she showed her face again."

A wave of nausea rolled over me, threatening to make my stomach heave. Was there no end to King Hector's atrocities? He was bloodthirsty and a rapist, a man who had forced our nation into a war that had lasted most of my life — and for what? What did he hope to gain?

"Even after that Lisbet didn't dare leave us boys at the mercy of the king. She was determined to stay and help, even though she'd have been killed if she was caught. Victor and I helped her hide in the abandoned wing of the palace and she began to take bloodroot to hide her presence from Iker. The only other person who knew was Cook, and she'd never tell because Lisbet healed her daughter years ago."

"That room you took me to . . ." I trailed off, remembering the dark hallway and the fear I'd felt, the sense of being watched.

Damian nodded. "I was going to see Lisbet. My father has been growing steadily more suspicious of me, which is partly why he assigned my guard to be with me at all times. And he was having me followed, on top of that." He sighed and shoved his hand through his hair. "I had to assume that all of you were loyal to him, not me, especially since I always acted like such a brat, to deflect suspicion that I could possibly be plotting to overthrow him. But by then I'd begun to hope that maybe I could trust you. And Lisbet had sent me a message that I needed to come see her right away. Since I'd been ordered to have a guard with me at all times, I took a risk and picked you."

"The boy that came through the secret passage — that was Jax, wasn't it?"

"Yes." Damian's expression was inscrutable. "It was a test, to see if you were truly loyal to me."

"Now do you see why we had to fake an abduction to get him away from the palace?" General Tinso asked from the doorway, startling us. "We have to stop Hector's reign of tyranny. We have to put Damian on the throne. But there was no way to do it with him stuck in the palace, being guarded day and night, with Hector's pawn constantly on his tail."

So many missing pieces were beginning to fall into place, my head was spinning.

"I told you I'd answer your questions when the time was right," Damian said, looking straight into my eyes. Just the force of his gaze was enough to make my legs feel weak. I wasn't sure if that was a good thing or not.

Rylan had remained silent the whole time, listening, until now. "But you decided to trust Alex and me for some reason."

"I once overheard her tell someone that it didn't matter if she liked me or not, her duty was to protect me and she always kept her word. That was when I started to hope I could trust her. When she was assigned to guard my door, I knew it was providence. And I even hoped that if she got to know the real me, she'd come to like me someday."

I flushed with embarrassment. "I'm sorry you heard that," I said.

"Don't be. I didn't like that version of myself, either." He turned back to Rylan. "Alex's ability to fight gave me new hope. With my father's guard dog always nearby, no one, not even a sorcerer, could get close enough to kill the king."

"Do you mean Iker?" I asked. I'd barely thought about him since we'd left the palace. Honestly, I'd rarely thought about him when we were *in* the palace unless he was in the room. "He's creepy, but how could *he* stop a sorcerer?"

Damian and General Tinso glanced at each other before Damian looked at me, his expression grim. "Iker isn't just an advisor to my father. He's his bodyguard. I would have killed the king myself long ago if I'd stood a chance of getting close to him without Iker stopping me first — and I think they know it. Why do you think my rooms are on the opposite side of the palace from his? Why do you think I was forced to spend so much time there — basically imprisoned in my own room?"

I shook my head, almost feeling the urge to laugh. They were all afraid of trying to kill King Hector because of *Iker*? "Are we talking about the same person?"

"Alexa." The seriousness of Damian's voice made the smile slide from my face. "Iker is a black sorcerer."

"A . . . a *what*?" My heart dropped. "But Iker is from Dansii, not Blevon. And — and your father *hates* sorcery. He has sorcerers killed!"

Rylan looked as shocked as I felt when I glanced at him.

"No, he only hates sorcerers who fight *against* him. He spread lies about sorcerers so that our people would be terrified of them and support his decree that all sorcerers be killed in Antion, ensuring that no one will ever be able to challenge him or stop him."

"And not all sorcerers are from Blevon," General Tinso added. "That was one of the lies Hector told his people to build more animosity toward our kingdom."

I stared at them in shock.

"It's true," Damian agreed grimly. "Iker was a gift from Hector's brother, the king of Dansii, to protect my father. No one can get past Iker and he never leaves my father's side."

"What makes a black sorcerer so much worse than other types?" Rylan asked as I tried to wrap my mind around all the lies we'd been told by our king. I'd hated him before, but as I continued to learn just how evil he was, there wasn't a word strong enough for the utter abhorrence that burned through me.

"It's a sorcerer who uses the forces of the underworld to increase his power. He draws on the strength of demons by making blood sacrifices to them. Because of it, he is even able to create and wield an unnatural fire. It makes him unbeatable, but in so doing, he forfeits his soul." General Tinso looked at me as he said this, for some reason. I shivered. The sun had gone down while we talked, leaving the room in shadow. I remembered suddenly the scent of burned blood, the stains on Iker's knife, the oppressive heat and unnatural darkness in his chambers. So that's what he'd been doing. Making an offering to the demons that fueled his power. I'd known something was wrong that night.

"All sorcerers are able to sense the power of sorcery in others," General Tinso continued, breaking into my troubled memories.

"So if another sorcerer gets near Eljin, he can *sense* it?" Rylan asked.

"Yes. If that person comes within a few feet of him, Eljin can tell whether he is a sorcerer," General Tinso confirmed.

"So I'm not a sorcerer, then?" I blurted out and then immediately snapped my mouth shut.

"What?" Rylan turned to me, his eyes wide. "You think you're a sorcerer now?"

"No." General Tinso smiled grimly, answering my question.

I tried not to flush in embarrassment. I'd been worried about it ever since he said I was "gifted" — especially since no one would tell me what that meant.

"Has no one answered your question yet?"

I shook my head, not daring to look at Damian or Rylan.

"My suspicion is that your *father* was a sorcerer, and a powerful one at that. Most likely one of the rare sorcerers whose gift was the ability to fight. And I believe he passed that on to you. You're not a true sorcerer, but you carry some of his power within you. It enhances your ability to fight. It's why you can sense magic around you. Average humans, without an ounce of sorcery in them, wouldn't have been able to feel the use of magic during a fight."

I stared at General Tinso. "My *father*? There's no way. I would have known. He would have told me if he were a *sorcerer*!"

"My dear girl, do you honestly think so? In a nation where being a sorcerer is akin to a death sentence?"

My mouth opened to continue to protest, but nothing came out. What if he was right? I thought again of how much I loved watching Papa practice — how he'd been so fast, so beautiful. How I'd longed to be like him. I thought of the hours and hours we'd spent relentlessly sparring, how he was always pushing me, driving me to be better. Faster. Stronger. But I'd never felt him use magic against me. I shook my head, my mind spinning.

"But . . . if he was a sorcerer, why did he die? Why didn't he use magic to stop the one who killed him and my mother?"

General Tinso gave me a sad, knowing look. "He must have been fighting someone who was more powerful than he was."

"Well, how can you be sure I'm *not* a sorcerer, then?" I pressed. "If you're so sure Papa was one."

"Because Eljin would have sensed it the moment he stepped into the ring with you. And Iker would have had you killed long ago. If the rumors are true, Iker's power is expanding so that he can sense another sorcerer anywhere in the same *room*."

I suppressed a shiver. He was wrong — he *had* to be wrong. Papa wasn't a sorcerer. He wouldn't have kept something like that from me.

"If Iker can sense sorcerers from that far away . . ." Rylan trailed off, glancing at Damian, whose expression was grim. He'd been watching me the whole time, his eyes guarded.

"If we were to try to storm the palace with every sorcerer in Blevon, he would sense us before we ever got close enough to see the king, let alone kill him. And he is powerful enough to destroy us all." General Tinso's voice was quiet.

The bleakness of our situation was crushing. If what they were telling us was true, there was no way we could ever stop King Hector. The last small bit of hope I had of somehow helping end this war died.

"If he can sense sorcerers like that, why didn't he recognize Eljin as one while he was there? Or Lisbet?" Rylan wondered.

"I told Eljin my father's schedule while he was in the palace, and he stayed as far away from him as possible, since we knew Iker would always be with the king. Sometimes it's beneficial to have my rooms on the opposite side of the palace from theirs. And Lisbet has been taking bloodroot for years to suppress her abilities, just in case Iker ever got anywhere near where she and Jax were hiding," Damian answered, walking toward me. I was right after all; the bloodroot had been for Lisbet.

When he stopped right in front of me, I gazed up into his face, knowing the hopelessness I felt was probably visible in my eyes. "There's nothing we can do, then," I said quietly.

Damian took my hands in his. "There *is* something. But it's a huge risk."

I could feel the tension in him; it flowed through his hands into mine. "If there's a possibility to stop the king, it would be worth the risk, right?" I said.

"I used to think so," he said, his eyes on mine.

"Damian, don't let emotion cloud your judgment," General Tinso admonished sternly.

"Emotion about what? What's the risk?"

But as he stood there, gripping my hands, staring down at me, the answer dawned on me. "I'm the risk," I said, my voice soft. "That's why you wanted me to train here. You want me to fight Iker."

"I don't know what I want anymore," Damian said, desperation lurking in his eyes.

"You can't expect her to fight him — you just said he's unbeatable," Rylan protested. "She'll be killed!" He stood a little bit away from us, staring at Damian's hands on mine, refusing to meet my gaze, his cheeks flushed.

"You once asked me if I thought it was worth losing one life in order to save everyone else's. Were you talking about *my* life?" I looked up at Damian, my heart thudding.

Before he could answer, General Tinso cut in again. "Alexa, you can do this. The plan has been put in action, and we only have two weeks before we must leave and begin our march on Tubatse and the palace. But you got past my son's defenses after only one day of training. I believe you have the ability to do this — I believe you can kill Iker."

"*If* I can do it — if I kill Iker . . ." I trailed off.

"Then I will kill my father," Damian said tonelessly.

The day my parents were killed, I'd sworn to do something to help stop this war — to keep our entire nation from being destroyed by it. If I'd known then what I knew now, would I have still made that vow to myself?

I stared up at Damian for a moment longer, my mind spinning mercilessly.

"Don't do this, Alexa. Don't agree to this," Rylan pleaded, his expression troubled.

Finally, I looked at General Tinso.

"What do I need to do?"

General Tinso gave me a grim smile. "I knew you had it in you. Let's get started."

⊰ THIRTY-FOUR ⊱

THE NEXT WEEK was a blur of constant training with Eljin. Every morning, he came at the first light of dawn and led us to the same room where we fought for hours on end. Damian and Rylan watched part of the time and sparred with each other the rest.

Lisbet even came and watched a couple of times. She looked like a different woman here. The dark circles were gone from under her eyes, and her skin almost glowed. She healed some of the more painful bruises I'd sustained over the last few days of fighting. When I asked about Tanoori, she assured me she was healing. Because the infection had taken such a strong hold on her body, it was taking longer, but there was another healer in General Tinso's castle who was helping and Lisbet hoped Tanoori would be completely recovered soon. It was a small comfort that we hadn't carried her for days for nothing after all.

Every night after the sun went down, I dragged my body back to the room where we slept and collapsed onto my cot, falling asleep almost immediately. My whole life, I'd trained ruthlessly, pushing myself to be the best. But I'd never had to work as hard as I did fighting Eljin and his sorcery. I was more certain than ever that General Tinso was wrong about Papa — and about me. I hadn't been able to get past Eljin's shield again once in the whole week, and I was growing progressively more discouraged.

"I can't do it!" I finally shouted at the end of a very long practice session, and threw my sword on the ground after Eljin had deflected me for the hundredth time that day. "You aren't even attacking me with sorcery; you're just *defending* yourself. The minute I go after Iker, he's going to kill me, isn't he? He won't just throw up a shield and let me try again. I'm going to fail and then Iker will kill all of you and this war will never end."

I sat down on the floor in the middle of the room and dropped my head into my hands. I was so exhausted, I couldn't hold back my sobs.

"Alexa —"

I heard Damian say my name, but Rylan was there first. He crouched down in front of me and took my chin in his hand, forcing me to look up at him.

"You aren't a quitter," he said gruffly.

"Then you obviously don't understand what it means to say, *I can't do this*," I pointed out.

He put both of his hands on my shoulders and stared into my face, his expression earnest. "Alex, you *can* do this. I know you can. You did it before, and you can do it again."

"No, I *can't*." I reached up and angrily wiped the tears from my cheeks. "What do you think I've been doing for the last week? Playing a game?"

"No," Rylan said gently. "But it hasn't been the same, and you know it. When you beat him last week, something was different about you. You've always had a fire inside that's driven you to be the best fighter I've ever known. But the time you beat Eljin, it was as if that fire had turned into an inferno. I've never seen you like that. All you have to do is figure out what was different about that day so you can repeat it."

I wiped my nose, which had decided to embarrass me further by running, and glared at him. "I don't know what the difference was. I was mad, but I'm mad right now, too, and I still can't do it." I shrugged Rylan's hands off me and stood back up. "I'm sorry, Damian. I'm sorry that I'm not good enough."

Damian just looked at me, his expression unreadable. Then he turned to face Eljin, who had stood watching my humiliating tantrum with his arms crossed and his eyes narrowed. "I think we should call it a night and let her get some extra rest," Damian said.

"We only have one week left until we must leave to make our rendezvous point, and as she's pointed out, she has yet to be successful again," Eljin argued.

I flinched at the honesty of his words. Even though I'd said the same about myself, it was different hearing it from someone else.

"All the more reason to let her rest and rebuild her strength. Maybe we're pushing her too hard." Damian walked toward me and brushed the sweaty hair back from my face, cupping my cheek in his hand. I was too upset and tired to care that Rylan was watching. I looked up into Damian's beautiful eyes and nearly started crying again.

"I'm so sorry," I whispered.

"Don't be sorry." He leaned down and kissed my forehead softly. "Let's go back to our room so you can rest. I'll have Eljin get you something to eat and you can just forget about all of this for the night. How does that sound?"

It sounded like a weak attempt to delay the inevitable. We didn't have time for me to need to rest, but in that moment, I didn't care. I was not picking up that sword again tonight. "All right," I said.

"I really don't think —" Eljin began, but Damian cut him off.

"Kindly escort us to our room, and then find her something good to eat," he said in a tone that made it very clear he wasn't making a request. It was one of those moments when I was reminded that he really was a prince — that, someday, if a miracle happened and we succeeded, he would be king.

"I'd like to stay here," Rylan said suddenly, not meeting my gaze. "I'd like to train some more."

"And if someone sees me taking those two back but not you?" Eljin said, sounding very irritated.

"We've only seen two people in the last week," Damian pointed out.

I wished Rylan would look at me, but he continued to stare at Eljin, waiting for an answer. I was sure he was upset about Damian taking control, and probably for kissing my forehead, too, and it made my stomach twist into a guilty knot. I hadn't had a chance to talk to Rylan since Damian had apologized to me. He probably thought I was being a fool, letting the prince have his way with me.

"Fine," Eljin finally said. "But after I bring the food, you have to go back, too."

"That's fine," Rylan agreed, and walked away to the wall where a bunch of scythes was hanging.

I watched him for a moment, a dull ache in my chest, but then Damian took my hand.

"Come on. Let's go so you can rest."

I followed him to the door, where he let go of my hand, so that if anyone was there, they wouldn't see. I glanced back at Rylan one last time, but his back was still turned to us. And then Eljin shut the door, sealing him inside, alone.

⌐≍ THIRTY-FIVE ≍⌐

THERE WAS A fire burning in the small hearth when Damian and I entered our room, sending light and shadows dancing across the walls and our empty cots, chasing away the chill. Eljin shut the door behind us with an audible huff of irritation.

I shuffled across the floor and sat down heavily on my cot. Damian took a seat across from me without a word.

"What, no sermon, no lecture? No words of inspiration?" I asked, my voice sarcastic.

"No," he said.

The firelight played across his face as he reached down into the pocket of his pants and pulled out a trinket of some sort. It looked like the one I'd seen him holding in his room all those weeks ago. He stared down at it, and I noticed a muscle in his jaw tighten.

"What is it?" I finally asked.

He glanced at me and held it up. It was small and oval shaped. "It's a locket."

That wasn't what I was expecting.

Using his thumbnail, Damian flicked it open and gazed down at what was inside. Grief crossed his face, and he closed his eyes briefly. Then he stood and came to sit next to me. He handed me the locket, and I looked down at a portrait of a beautiful woman with flawless, olive-toned skin; thick, dark hair; and vibrant, warm brown eyes. She had Damian's lips — or rather, he had hers.

"This is your mother," I said quietly.

"Yes."

We were silent as I stared at her portrait. "She was beautiful," I said, handing it back to him.

Damian nodded and ran his finger across the image tenderly. "It was an arranged marriage — to my father. My grandfather was the king of Dansii. He'd always had his eye on Antion, particularly our diamond and gold mines. When Hector and my uncle, Armando, were old enough to lead the troops, my grandfather sent them to war at the head of his massive army. Just one week after they succeeded in conquering the Antionese army, my grandfather died. Armando was crowned king of Dansii, and my father took possession of Antion."

I listened intently, watching Damian's face as he spoke, wondering why he was telling me this.

"At the coronation ceremony, King Osgand offered to arrange a marriage with his niece, in an effort to keep the alliance that had always existed between the two nations. He feared Dansii's growing power and reach. My father was smitten the moment he saw my mother, and he agreed to the marriage and to continue the alliance.

"The first few years of their marriage were uneventful, from what I've been told. She gave him two sons, and he kept his promise to maintain peace with Blevon. But then Dansii was attacked by an unknown army, led by multiple sorcerers. King Armando was nearly killed, and the Dansiian army barely managed to force the

250

army into retreat, and only by sheer number and size — not by skill.

"Afraid for his life and for his brother's, Armando hired two black sorcerers — one for him and one for Hector. Iker came to live at the palace. When my mother walked into the room to meet him, he sensed what she was right away, and revealed her secret — she was a sorceress."

I gasped. "Your *mother*?"

Damian nodded, still staring down at the locket. "She used to show Victor and me what she could do. We thought it was amazing, but she told us it was a secret game, that we couldn't tell anyone. We adored our mother, and we'd kept her secret. But Iker sensed her ability the moment she walked into the room and he told my father. Hector was furious — accused her of being a spy, a plant, waiting for the time to turn on him and kill him so she could hand Antion to her uncle. I remember the fight, because Victor and I had been playing in the room next door and we could hear him shouting. She tried to warn him about Iker, to explain that he wasn't an ordinary sorcerer, but my father wouldn't listen.

"He locked her in her room, and only let us see her every few days. And Iker was always with us when we visited her, making sure she couldn't say or do anything he didn't approve of." Damian paused, his voice thick with emotion.

"It's okay, you don't have to keep going," I said, terrified to hear what came next. I didn't want to make him relive it.

"I've never told anyone before. Not this." Damian finally looked up from the locket. "I got mad at my father. I yelled at him for hurting Mother, for making her stop using her magic. That night, he took Victor and me to her room. He sat us down in front of her and said he was going to teach us what happened if we ever betrayed him. He told us sorcery was evil and that he wouldn't allow it in Antion. And then he killed her." Damian shuddered at the memory, which I was helpless to erase. "He'd been poisoning her for weeks with bloodroot, so she couldn't stop him. I remember her eyes widening . . . the way she cried out when he lifted his sword. She begged him . . . begged him not to . . ." His voice broke, and he clenched his mouth shut.

I reached one trembling hand up to cup his jaw. He closed his eyes and turned his face into my hand, pressing his lips against my palm. "It's not your fault," I whispered.

He shook his head, his eyes still squeezed shut. "If I hadn't gotten mad at him . . . If I hadn't accused him . . ." His voice was unsteady.

I took his face in both of my hands. "Damian, look at me."

He did as I asked, his expression bleak, years of suppressed pain breaking free from the tight hold he'd kept it under.

"It was *not* your fault. Hector is evil. He probably waited until one of you broke down and got upset at him to do it, so that you would blame yourself. He was poisoning her for a reason. He didn't decide to kill her on a whim. He is evil."

Damian took a deep, shaky breath. "The worst part is that no matter how much I hate him, he's still my father."

I stroked the hair back from his face, wishing I could take away his torment, his pain and guilt.

"He declared war on Blevon within two weeks of killing her, claiming that a sorcerer from here had done it. And you know the rest." He took a deep breath and reached up to place his hand over mine. "The reason I am telling you all of this is so that you can understand something. He's still my father, but when the time comes for me to kill him, I won't let myself hesitate. I will picture my mother. My brother. Everyone I've loved, everyone he's taken from me. And I will have the power and courage to do what I must do."

My stomach clenched and I let my hands drop into my lap. "But now you'll never get that chance, because I'm not good enough. I can't stop Iker."

Damian leaned forward and this time he took my face in his hands. "Yes, you can. When you got past Eljin's defense, it was because you were completely focused. Every ounce of your mind and strength and power was aimed at one thing — to get that mask off his face, right? You didn't hit him in the ribs; you yanked off his mask with your sword."

I thought back to that day, how I'd been so furious. In that moment, I'd hated him and his mask so much, all I could think about was tearing it off his face.

"If you can hone that kind of focus and determination again, you will succeed. And my guess is that you have a lot more hatred for the king and Iker than you do for Eljin. When you are training, you have to imagine that Eljin is Iker, and that beating him is the only way you can avenge your parents' deaths. Your brother's death. He's the only person standing between us being together." He stared earnestly into my face and I had to blink back tears.

I could see them — my parents, lying in their own blood. The life leaving Marcel's eyes. And now Damian, the prince of Antion, was sitting before me, telling me . . . what? What was he telling me? "Are you saying you want to be with me?" My voice was hoarse.

The firelight made his eyes practically glow as he threaded his fingers through my hair, pulling my face closer. "So much that it hurts." His eyes searched mine, a hint of desperation in their blue depths. "Do you understand now why I've been afraid to let myself care for anyone? If Hector ever found out, he would use you to break me. We will never be able to truly be together until we defeat my father."

I knew it was impossible — even if he *wanted* to be with me, even if he were made king and able to do whatever he wished, he couldn't marry his former guard. He would have to marry for political advantage. Perhaps someone from Blevon, to rebuild the former peace that had once existed between our nations.

But then Damian leaned forward so our foreheads touched. And in that moment, I didn't care. I didn't care that it wasn't possible for us to actually have a future together. All I wanted was to be with him right now, in this moment. Blood pulsed hot through my body — part of me wanted nothing more than to lose myself in his touch, to kiss him until everything else faded away.

But another part was fighting, straining for release. I knew the wise decision was to ignore how badly I wanted to stay here with Damian. I had to focus instead on the sudden confidence surging through me.

I pulled back. "I want to try again."

"Right now?"

"Yes, now."

Damian smiled wistfully at me. "I knew you had it in you. And I know you *can* do this." He didn't move, though; his hand was still in my hair, holding me in place. "But would you mind waiting for just a few minutes, at least?"

"Why?" I asked, though I was sure I knew the answer.

"Because I don't know when we'll be alone again until this is all over," he said, making my heart race. His fingers tightened against the back of my head, pulling me toward him. When his mouth met mine, a rush of heat exploded in my body, burning through my veins, my skin, my lips as I clutched Damian's back, holding on to him — as though he were my anchor in a violent sea of uncertainty. I could feel his own desperation as he wrapped his arms around my body, holding me tightly in the circle of his embrace.

There was a light knock at the door and we sprang apart just in time for Eljin to open it, carrying a tray of food, with Rylan on his heels. Rylan gave me a hooded look, but he seemed resigned, rather than angry.

"I have the food you requested," Eljin said with a mocking twist to his voice.

"There's been a change of plans," I replied.

"Oh really? How lovely," he said.

"You'd better be prepared to lose." I pushed past him out the door and headed back to the practice room.

⊰ THIRTY-SIX ⊱

"ARE YOU SURE you want to try again tonight? Maybe it would be better if you *rested* for a bit." Eljin mocked me as he picked up his practice sword again.

"No, I don't need to rest," I bit out.

He shrugged and walked over. "Then let's begin."

As he began to circle me, watching for my attack, I thought about what Damian had told me. I thought of him as a young boy witnessing his mother's murder. I thought of my own parents, hewn down by an army made our enemy because of Hector's evilness. I thought of Marcel — how he had believed in me and how he'd been another casualty of this war. I thought of Iker and how he betrayed the queen's secret and sentenced her to death. I thought of the breeding house filled with terrified girls, who were raped over and over again. I thought of Rylan and his unending courage and of his love for his brother — I couldn't bear it if they had to face the same fate as Marcel and I did. I thought of Damian, playing a part all these years, trying to figure out some way to stop his father and save his kingdom. I thought of him kissing me, telling me he wanted to be with me.

But if we didn't stop Iker and the king, I would lose him. We would all lose everything.

All of it, all of my love and pain and anger surged up and filled me with fury — with purpose — with *power*. I felt it building in my chest, and I attacked. Eljin's eyes widened in alarm. Left, right, left, spin, and jab. My sword moved so fast, he couldn't follow me. He grunted, desperately trying to throw up a shield. I felt it — the moment Eljin reached for his power, when the magic surged to answer him. I refused to let him succeed. I refused to let Iker win. I refused to let us all fall to his power. With a scream of fury, I faked right and then spun around with all of my might and slammed my sword into Eljin's ribs, knocking him flat on his back. I stood over him, chest heaving, my sword clutched in my hands.

He stared up at me, his eyes wide. Silence filled the room until the sword fell from my hand and hit the ground with a clatter.

"You did it," I heard Rylan say, but this time, he didn't cheer. No one did.

For some reason, tears filled my eyes. Even though I tried, I couldn't hold them back. My shoulders shook with sobs. And then Damian was there. He pulled me into his arms, stroked my hair. "Shh," he whispered. "It's okay. You did it. I knew you could do it."

"I'll go tell my father," Eljin said. I turned my head to see him push himself off the ground, rubbing his rib cage. He looked right at me and nodded. A nod of approval.

Through my tears, I smiled grimly, and then he was gone.

The next week flew by as we prepared to go back to Antion and the palace to launch our attack on King Hector. Each day, I was able to recall that same power and beat Eljin, and my confidence grew. The one dark spot was that I could never find a time to talk to

Rylan alone. He grew quieter and more withdrawn every day, and I was worried about him. But whenever I tried to ask him if he was okay, he brushed me off. I knew he worried about what we'd find back at the palace — who we'd find alive. I fervently prayed Jude was okay.

But I also knew he was mad at me, and I was helpless to fix it in our current situation.

The night before we were supposed to leave, General Tinso ate dinner with us in the practice room. Lisbet arrived halfway through with Jax, and right behind them was Tanoori. I was sitting on the floor, just lifting a piece of meat to my mouth when she walked in. She looked at Damian for a long moment, then her gaze flicked to me. She gave me a curt nod and sat down next to Lisbet, who was saying something softly to Rylan.

Tanoori looked remarkably well, especially compared to the last time I'd seen her, when she'd appeared nearly dead.

"We need to finalize the details of our plan before tomorrow," General Tinso said when we'd all resumed eating. I looked at Tanoori suspiciously, and General Tinso noticed.

"It's safe to speak freely before her," he said.

"She threatened to kill me," I disagreed. "And she attempted to kill Prince Damian at the palace. She was going to be hanged for it when Eljin saved her." I looked to Damian for affirmation.

"She was only doing what the Insurgi asked her to do, not because she wanted to," Damian said. He glanced at Tanoori, who wouldn't look up from her food. "I'm the one who asked the Insurgi to plant someone to attempt an assassination on me, and I didn't want her to die for it. So, I'm also the one who asked Eljin to save her."

"You did *what?*"

"I knew she was going to try to murder me," Damian said calmly. "She was never intended to succeed — only to attempt it. If my guard hadn't been there, I would have had to stop her myself, which I was prepared to do if necessary."

I glared at him, my food forgotten on the plate in front of me. "Why would you ask them to attempt to murder you? Aren't they the ones who actually *did* murder your brother?" With everyone else listening to our conversation, I didn't dare yell at him for keeping something this important from me, but inside I was seething.

"Yes." Damian sighed. "But afterward, Lisbet discovered their hideout and went to them. She learned that their leaders were a trio of sorcerers, loyal to Blevon and General Tinso, who wished to overthrow King Hector. She explained that she was the general's sister-in-law, and that I was loyal to Blevon, not my father. She convinced the Insurgi that killing his heirs wouldn't stop Hector, and she also told them about Iker, warning them that they wouldn't be able to murder the king, either. They agreed to try to work together with General Tinso and me to overthrow him."

"But how does having the Insurgi send Tanoori to try to assassinate you help? And why did you send me to deliver a message to them? *Now* will you tell me what was in it?" With everything else that had happened and how focused I'd been on learning how to defeat a sorcerer, I'd almost completely forgotten about that nightmarish trek through the jungle, despite the scars from the jaguar attack to remind me.

"The attempted murder was to get Iker's and the king's attention, to make them think we had enemies out there who wanted me dead. When I had you take the message to the Insurgi, I had no other choice but to ask for your help. Lisbet and Jax usually delivered the messages, but Iker followed us to their rooms that night I took you with me. She felt his presence and told me to leave. She had to flee the castle before I could write the message for her to deliver to the Insurgi."

"It was Iker who followed us? I thought it was Eljin."

Damian shook his head.

I knew I hadn't been imagining things, but it was worse to think that it had been Iker and that I hadn't even suspected him. "So what did the message say?"

"It contained the details they needed for their part in our plan. They're going to help us when we attempt to break into the palace."

"The Insurgi are going to help us?" I looked at Tanoori, who had been eating quietly this whole time. She finally met my gaze, and I saw a ghost of the girl I used to know in the hesitant smile she gave me. I still couldn't believe Damian had asked her to try to murder him. Had she known she was meant to fail — was she just acting, too?

"They promised they would."

"They have some very powerful sorcerers and an impressive number of rebels, all of whom wish to overthrow the king. And we're going to need all the help we can get," General Tinso added.

"I agree," I said after I forced myself to eat a bite of meat. "I've been thinking about it, and even though I'm pretty sure I *could* beat Iker, I don't see how I'm going to be able to get close enough to him to even try unless you bring *your* black sorcerers to help me. Otherwise, he'll just burn me to a crisp before I even come close enough to get past his defenses."

"*My* black sorcerers?" General Tinso gave me a strange look. "What are you talking about?"

Before I could answer, Damian jumped in. "I've been meaning to speak with you about that. Alexa's parents were killed by a sorcerer's fire when part of the Blevonese army raided her village. Is it possible that there are black sorcerers helping your army that you aren't aware of?"

General Tinso's eyes widened as Damian spoke. "No. I would know if there were. Are there any other reports of this happening, or was it an isolated event?"

Damian shook his head. "I don't know."

"When you are king, we will need to look into this. I don't know who that sorcerer was, but I'm certain he was not with our army."

"So you *don't* have any black sorcerers who can help us?" I asked, confused and upset. If the sorcerer hadn't been part of the Blevonese army, who was he? And why had he killed my parents?

"No, we don't," the general said.

"Then how am I going to get close enough to Iker to fight him without him killing me first?" My stomach tightened into knots of anxiety.

"You wouldn't want a black sorcerer's help — trust me. And as it happens, you won't have to worry about getting close to Iker. If our plan works, you should be standing at his side when we come with the prince." General Tinso smiled at me like this was the best news I'd ever heard.

"And just how are you planning to make that happen?"

General Tinso began to explain, but Damian held up his hand to cut him off. "Alexa, I want you to remember that you agreed to do this. That you wanted to help."

"I know," I said bitterly, looking between him and the general. "What is it you want me to do?"

"To do the best acting job you've ever done."

"I don't understand." I glanced at Rylan, but he stared down at his untouched food and wouldn't meet my gaze.

"You're going to be taken back to the palace first, a day or two ahead of us by some Blevonese soldiers," Damian said.

"I'm not going with you?" My chest tightened, as if a hand were slowly squeezing the air from my lungs.

"No. You have to go first. You'll tell them you've been held captive with the prince in Blevon, and that you were sent back to deliver a message to the king. The message will announce the coming of General Tinso and his army with the prince as his captive. It'll say that the general is coming to negotiate the release of the prisoner in return for an end to the war."

"And I'm supposed to take this to the king?"

"Yes," Damian said, his expression guarded.

"Why would he believe you are their captive if he suspects you're loyal to Blevon? Wouldn't he realize it's a trap?"

"That's why we made the assassination attempt look so realistic, and why we have to act like the abduction was real. Hector has spies in the Blevonese army, and we can only hope they have reported back to him by now."

I took a shaky breath. "And if it works and he believes the message, what then? Are you just going to storm into the palace and hope I'm somewhere close by?"

"No. When you deliver the message, he'll probably say he doesn't care about bargaining for my life," Damian said matter-of-factly, as though the reality that his father didn't care whether he

262

lived or died was about as interesting as commenting on the bland-
ness of our supper.

"So how am I going to get him to agree to meet with you?
And why would he keep me anywhere near him?"

"You must suggest that this is an opportunity for him to surround and trap Blevon's most powerful general," General Tinso
said. "Tell him that you know which men in my army are sorcerers.
You have to convince him that you can point them out, so he can
have them shot before they got close enough to use any sorcery to
fight. You must make yourself indispensable to him so that he
keeps you with him and Iker."

"But I thought Iker could sense if another sorcerer was in
the room."

"He can, but with so many people around — and so many
sorcerers in one place — he won't be able to pinpoint who they are
fast enough. You have to convince them that they need you, without revealing that you know Iker is a sorcerer."

My head began to ache as they continued to explain their plan
to me. I listened and nodded, but my heart was pounding and I
was having a hard time memorizing what they said. All I could
think about was the fact that I was going to leave them behind,
that I was going to have to face the king and Iker alone — and
somehow try to convince them to let the general come with his
army and the prince.

The plan depended heavily on me. If I wasn't successful, it would
be a disaster, and King Hector really would have the chance to crush
King Osgand's most powerful general right in his own courtyard.

"I think we should call it a night and head to bed," Eljin finally
said, when the entire plan had been laid out for me.

"Yes, we all need to rest while we can," General Tinso agreed.

I stood up in a daze. Rylan wouldn't meet my gaze when he stood up and followed Eljin from the room. Lisbet and Jax slipped out the door quietly, but not before Jax gave Damian a tight hug. I watched as Damian bent over to embrace the boy, a look of tenderness on his face. His half brother. My chest tightened, and I had to force myself not to think about my own brother and how much I missed him. With a sigh, I started to follow Eljin and Rylan out of the room when someone touched my arm.

I turned to see Tanoori standing by me, her expression pained. "I'm sorry for what I did to you, Alexa. I just wanted to tell you that before you go. And . . ." She paused, as if summoning courage. "I want to thank you. For saving me even though I didn't deserve it. I will make it up to you someday, I promise."

I impulsively reached out to embrace her. She stiffened at first, but soon she softened and hugged me back tightly.

"Be safe, Tanoori."

"You, too." She looked at me for a moment longer, and then turned and followed Lisbet and Jax to the front wings of the castle.

"I wish you well," General Tinso said from behind me, making me jump.

I turned to look up at him. "Thank you."

He nodded and moved to leave the room. "General?" I hesitantly called after him.

He paused, glancing back.

"Papa used to call me something — a nickname in Blevonese. He never told me what it meant. I was wondering, before I leave, if you could . . ." I trailed off.

General Tinso nodded for me to continue.

"He called me his *zhànshì nánwū*."

The general's eyes widened. "Alexa, *zhànshì* roughly translates to 'champion fighter.'"

My heart began to pound. "And *nánwū*?"

"It means 'sorcerer.'"

I couldn't swallow past the sudden lump in my throat.

"You can do this, Alexa. I know you can." He clapped one hand on my shoulder, staring down into my eyes for a moment. And then, with one final smile, he left.

"Let's go," Damian said from behind me, startling me. He touched the small of my back with his fingertips, guiding me toward the staircase that would lead us back to our room for the last time.

≼ THIRTY-SEVEN ≽

*T*HE MEN WHO are taking you back to the palace don't know the truth," Damian said, his voice barely above a whisper as we walked. "They think they really are delivering a prisoner of war with a message to the king. And they still think you're a boy."

"Okay," I responded, too overwhelmed and too tired to care about this additional information. What was pretending to be a boy — something I'd done for years — to two soldiers compared to everything else they expected of me? I didn't want to think about that. I didn't want to think about how frustrated I was with Damian, either. Instead, I focused on the fact that Papa had been calling me "champion fighter sorcerer" my whole life. He'd been *trying* to tell me the truth after all, in the only safe way he knew how. But what had he meant — that he knew all along I'd have the ability to fight sorcerers, or was there even more to his nickname for me?

Damian touched my arm, gently grasping my elbow and pulling me to a stop. "I didn't intentionally keep my involvement with the Insurgi a secret from you, Alex."

I sighed as I looked up at him.

"With everything else going on, I didn't think to tell you about it. I'm sorry."

"Maybe if we survive all this, you'll get to a point someday where you don't have to think about telling me these little details, like asking someone to pretend to murder you." I couldn't keep the bitterness from my voice.

Damian's expression hardened. "I'm not used to telling *anyone* anything — let alone every secret I have. Not to mention that even though I *hoped* I could trust you, I had to be sure before I told you my whole plan. I said I'm sorry; what more do you want from me?"

"I don't know," I said crossly. "I don't know what I want. No more surprises, I guess." The one thing I knew I *didn't* want was to spend our last night together fighting. I might never see him again. "What I want is to be able to trust you."

It was so dark in the hallway, I couldn't tell for sure, but it looked like he grimaced. "Someday, you will."

We stared at each other for a long moment. My heart thudded dully in my chest. Then we heard the sound of other people heading our direction. My eyes widened in alarm. We couldn't be caught standing here in the hallway, unguarded.

I turned and hurried to the stairway, with Damian on my heels.

Rylan was already lying down, his back to the door, when we rushed into the room. I stared at him for a long time, hoping he would roll over and say *something* to me — anything before I left in the morning. But he stubbornly stayed facing the wall. Damian also walked over to his cot and sat down, staring into the fire.

The chill in the room didn't come from the wind battering the window. With a sigh, I crawled under the blanket in my own bed and curled into a ball. It was going to be a miserable journey back to Tubatse.

I wondered what I would find when I returned. Would Kai be alive? And what about the rest of the guard? This whole time, I had forced my thoughts away from that line of thinking, knowing it did me no good to wonder. But now, as I lay in the silence, I couldn't stop the questions from rushing through my mind.

Oh, how I hated unanswered questions.

I heard the creak of Damian's cot, but I kept my eyes shut, willing my brain to stop spinning in useless circles, wishing I could just go to sleep. It felt like hours passed with nothing but the sound of the fire slowly consuming the wood and burning itself out, and the wind howling outside, before I finally succumbed to my exhaustion and drifted off to sleep.

The morning dawned cold and clear, blue sky stretching as far as I could see outside our window. My stomach was already twisted in knots when I opened my eyes and sat up. Rylan was sitting on his bed with his head in his hands. Damian was sprawled out on his stomach, fast asleep.

I was about to say something to Rylan when the door swung open and Eljin marched in with two men behind him. Damian jerked awake and scrambled to stand up.

"Which one are we taking?" one of them asked in our language, glaring at us.

My heart raced and my hands went cold. This was it? I was going *now*? I thought I'd have a chance to say good-bye — to try and get Rylan to talk to me one last time before I left. A chance to mend the fight I'd had with Damian. But I remembered what he'd told me last night; these men didn't know the truth. I had to act like the unattached male guard of the prince — nothing more or less.

"That one. Take him. But be careful, he's the best guard the prince has. If you drop your attention for even a second, he'll have you disarmed and dead on the ground before you realize what hit you," Eljin said severely, pointing at me.

Rylan looked up at me in alarm, while the prince schooled his face into a mask of indifference. I stood up slowly, drawing on all of my training, all of the years I'd spent pretending to be something I wasn't — some*one* I wasn't. It couldn't be any harder than pretending Marcel's death hadn't affected me.

The two men came over. One grabbed my hands, roughly yanking them behind me and tying them with rope.

"You expect me to walk the entire way to Tubatse with my hands bound?" I asked disdainfully.

"Yes." The man who wasn't tying up my hands grinned, revealing stained, yellow teeth.

"Let's go." The man behind me shoved me between the shoulder blades, and I stumbled forward.

"Alex —" Rylan jumped to his feet, his face pale.

My new captors kept pushing me forward, and I had to crane my head to look at him.

"Be careful," he said, his voice strained. "And look out for Jude — if you can. If he's . . . if he's still alive."

I nodded, feeling as though my stomach were full of lead.

"How sweet. Now let's go," the man behind me snarled with another shove to my spine.

I didn't even get to look at Damian again before the door slammed shut behind me.

⊰ THIRTY-EIGHT ⊱

THE JOURNEY BACK to Antion was even worse than I'd feared. My captors kept my arms bound either in front of or behind me, alternating the position each day. Since it was just the three of us, the pace they set was grueling, and I collapsed to the ground exhausted every night when they finally stopped to make camp. When we crossed back into Antion, we nearly ran right into a battalion. We had to crouch behind some large bushes for an hour while the soldiers passed. Angry about the delay, my captors made us run the rest of the day until my legs literally gave out and I fell to the ground, unable to stop my fall with my hands tied behind me.

The muggy heat of the jungle was even more oppressive after the cooler air of Blevon. I was too tired and worried to be afraid of the jungle when we'd stop for the night, sleeping in the small tent I was forced to carry on my back during the day. But we made the entire journey in just under two weeks because of the quick pace.

When the walls of the palace rose in front of us, I nearly cried with relief. Until I remembered what came next.

My captors led me up to the wall with their swords pressed into my back.

"Halt! Who goes there?" A sentinel shouted down at us.

"Answer him," one of the men growled at me.

"It's Alex Hollen, guard to Prince Damian," I called out. "I have been brought back to deliver a message about the prince to his father, the king!"

"Throw your weapons down!" came the shout from above us, at the top of the wall.

The men behind me muttered to each other in their language, and then I heard the sound of their swords hitting the ground.

"Step away from your weapons!"

We all moved forward, closer to the gate. It ground open, and we were suddenly surrounded by a host of soldiers from the Antionese army, swords and arrows pointed at us from all sides.

"Let me through!" I heard a familiar voice. My legs almost went weak with relief when Deron shoved a sentinel out of the way and stood in front of me, his eyes wide. He had a new, vicious-looking scar on his face, stretching from his eyebrow to his jaw, barely missing his mouth. But it was him — my captain — alive and in shock at the sight of me standing before him. "Alex, it *is* you. We thought you were dead!"

"I have a message for the king about his son," I said, keeping my mind carefully walled in to the present. If I let myself think too much — *feel* too much — I'd break down right then and there.

"Take these men to the dungeons," Deron shouted at the sentinels, pointing to my captors. The Blevonese soldiers looked at me in alarm, but I had a hard time feeling bad for them after the last thirteen days. "Alex, come with me. And someone cut those ropes off his hands!"

My shoulders burned, and my hands and wrists ached when I pulled them in front of me, rubbing the raw skin.

271

"Let's get you some clean clothes and some food, then you can go see the king." Deron began to lead the way back into the palace. I stared at the familiar building with my chest tight. General Tinso's castle had been massive, but compared to the palace, it looked like a summer cottage. So much depended on me. I felt as if the weight of the entire palace hung over my head.

We'd made it halfway across the grounds when a door opened, and another familiar figure rushed toward us. But this one filled me with dread.

"Alex Hollen, the king requests your presence immediately," Iker said, his baleful gaze sending a shiver of foreboding through me.

"I'll go find some food for when you're done," Deron said after bowing to Iker.

"That won't be necessary. We'll see that he is taken care of," Iker said, and Deron gave him a sharp look.

"You may go," Iker dismissed him. Deron bowed and did as he was told, though worry shot across his face.

I watched Deron walk away, fear practically choking me. I didn't want to be alone with Iker. Now that I knew the truth about him, I was even more nervous around him. I'd always noticed something *off*, but I hadn't known what it was. There was an aura of dark power that surrounded him and sent a chill down my spine.

"Follow me, Alex. The king and I are quite interested in what has happened to our beloved Prince Damian." He began to walk back the way he'd come. I reluctantly followed, my heart in my throat.

We stopped before the thick mahogany doors that led to the king's counsel room, next to his private chambers. Iker knocked once briefly and then opened the door.

"Sire, I've brought the guard for your questioning."

"Excellent. Let him enter," the king's deep voice answered.

Iker swung the door wide, and gestured for me to precede him into the room.

King Hector sat upon his throne, one of many that he had placed throughout the palace. The signet crown encircled his head. He looked at me with his pale blue eyes — Damian's and Jax's eyes — and then beckoned me forward with a flick of his fingers. Sunlight flashed off the jewels of his many rings and the diamonds lining the collar of office draped over the silk robes he wore.

I strode forward and bowed low to the king of Antion. I had to appear confident, calm. A bearer of a message that I should assume would be good news for my king.

"You may rise," King Hector said. I stood up straight, my fist pressed to my opposite shoulder. I could feel Iker's presence behind me.

"Sire, I bring word of your son," I said.

"Yes, I assumed that was why you were brought back. We've had reports of my son's whereabouts. I believe you were being held at General Tinso's castle in Lentia. Am I correct?" Damian's eyes had always been piercing — beautiful and sharp. King Hector's eyes were more gray than blue. There was a spark of intelligence in his eyes, but also a dark hint of the cruelty our king was fond of. This was the man who had killed his wife in front of his sons. He was the man who had ordered countless girls raped to breed a bigger army. I had to take a deep breath to calm the fury that began to pulse through me.

"I don't know the name of the town we passed through, my liege, but the man whose castle we were imprisoned in was General Tinso, as you say," I replied, thankful that my voice remained steady and calm. I'd never needed my years of practice pretending to feel and be something I wasn't more than I did right then.

"You may proceed with your message."

"I've been asked to tell you that General Tinso and his army are preparing to march on Tubatse with the prince as their prisoner. He said to warn you that he has gathered together the most powerful sorcerers in the land of Blevon to rain fire upon our walls and our nation until we burn to our deaths, if you do not agree to a truce with Blevon.

"However, if you are willing to sign a treaty of peace, he will release Prince Damian back to you, unharmed, and will take his army and leave Antion without further loss of life."

As I spoke, Iker made his way over to the king, taking his place on his right side, staring at me as well. He bent and whispered something in the king's ear. The silence stretched out for a long moment as Iker straightened back up, and they both looked down at me.

And then the king began to laugh. A cruel, mocking sound that turned my blood to ice in my veins.

"Is this their big plan, then?" He stopped laughing and pointed at me, his voice thunderous. "They think to fool me into believing my son is their prisoner? Of the nation he loves so dearly?"

"Sire, I don't understand —" I began, but he cut me off.

"You and your men are ignorant of a great many things regarding my son. He has never loved Antion; his heart is with Blevon, where his mother came from. And I will not see my efforts come to an early and unsatisfactory end to save his worthless life." He stood up to glare down at me. Iker stood just behind him, his mouth twisted into a derisive smile. "He wants to end this war? So do I. We will crush General Tinso and his army of sorcerers, and Blevon will fall to my power." His gaze was wild as he shouted at me. In that moment, I wasn't sure if he was entirely sane.

I dropped to one knee before the king. "Sire, please, do not be so hasty. We *have* been imprisoned, and the prince *does* love Antion. He has told me of his love for his nation many times."

"Take him away." The king waved his hand at me.

Desperation made my stomach turn violently as I jumped to my feet. Iker walked toward me, and I backed up, blurting out, "Sire, please! I know who his sorcerers are — I can point them out to you. If you let them think you are agreeing to their treaty, they'll return your son to you. Then you can surround them and kill them all."

King Hector held up his hand and Iker paused, though his eyes flashed ominously.

"What good is having a traitor for a son?"

"He is not, my king. He is loyal to Antion," I said. It was the truth — Damian was loyal to Antion, just not to its king.

"Does he lie?" the king hissed, his voice low.

Iker gave me a look of pure disgust, and then turned to bow to Hector. "No, sire. I believe he is telling the truth."

King Hector contemplated me for a long moment, his cold gaze calculating. Finally, he waved at Iker again. "If my son *is* a

275

traitor, that would mean you are as well, Alex. And though you say he is loyal to Antion, I have my doubts. I'll think on the guard's words. Take him to the dungeons until I decide what to do."

"Sire, please." I tried to keep my voice low, gruff, but I was afraid my panic had already given me away. "They are only a day or two behind me — they could be here tomorrow!"

But King Hector was truly done with me this time. Iker grabbed my arm and yanked me away, pushing me to walk in front of him. Once we'd exited the counsel room and the door shut behind us, he faced me.

"After you, Alex. I believe you know the way." He gave me a little mocking bow, gesturing toward the courtyard surrounded by all of the palace wings, and far below us, the dungeons.

I pulled my shoulders back and lifted my chin, walking as confidently as I could, even though I was trembling inside.

I'd failed. The king had seen right through the lies, just as I'd feared he would. All of that discomfort and acting to convince the Blevonese army — and Antion's spies — we were truly prisoners was for nothing.

Now Damian, Tinso, and the others would arrive tomorrow, believing I would be there, waiting to stop Iker. Instead, they would find themselves walking straight into a bloodbath.

⇥ THIRTY-NINE ⇤

$\mathcal{T}$HE DUNGEON WAS worse than I'd remembered.

"What are you doing down here, Little Boss?" Jaerom asked when he saw me come down the stairs with Iker on my heels.

"He is to be imprisoned until the king decides what further use — if any — he has for him," Iker said, his voice as oily as his thinning hair.

"He wants to imprison *Alex*?"

The shock on Jaerom's face obviously didn't sit well with Iker, because he immediately snapped at him, "Give me those keys, keeper!"

Jaerom jumped to attention, seeming to remember who he was talking to. "Yes, sir. Here is the master key."

Iker grabbed a torch and shoved me past Jaerom's desk and into the dark, putrid depths of the dungeon.

"This is as good as any, I suppose," he said, stopping before an empty cell about halfway down. He tried to grab my arm to toss me in, but I pulled out of his grip and walked in of my own accord. "Prideful to the end, I see. They say pride goeth before the fall, Alex." Iker smirked at me.

"Tell the king that I can help him win this battle, if he'll let me," I said, making one last desperate attempt to accomplish my

277

goal. "I heard rumors when our guards thought we were sleeping. King Osgand's general is amassing sorcerers from all across the nation of Blevon. He's bringing as much of the army as he can. You will be outnumbered. At the very least, let me fight for you!"

Iker's dark gaze in the light of the flames from the torch sent ice through my body, and I had to fight not to shudder. Without another word, he turned and left, slamming the door shut and locking me into the eternal darkness and heat. I was completely alone in the very cell in which I'd come to see Tanoori almost two months ago. The same chair she'd been tied to still sat in the corner.

I slid to the ground and dropped my head into my hands. My eyes burned and I had to grit my teeth to keep from crying. They were all going to die. General Tinso, Eljin, the Insurgi . . . Rylan.

Damian.

There was nothing I could do to warn them or stop the massacre that was sure to happen, if I was locked up down here in the depths of hell.

Minutes, then hours passed, interminably slow. It was impossible to tell how long I'd been imprisoned. I was unable to sleep at all, even though I was exhausted. Jaerom brought me food, but I could barely bring myself to eat the disgusting slop. It was not fit for hogs. Instead, I paced and when my legs grew too tired to keep it up, I slid down against the wall, and sat on the stone floor, staring into the darkness.

I'd always joked about the inmates going insane down here, but now I was one of them, and I already felt like I was losing my mind.

After staring into the darkness blindly for hours since the last time Jaerom had brought me a meal, a key rattled in the door. I scrambled to my feet and backed up to the wall. When I saw Deron standing in the doorway, holding a torch and a sword, I was simultaneously overcome with relief and fear.

"Get out here, and hurry," he whispered harshly, gesturing at me. I cautiously stepped toward him, afraid it was a trap.

"What are you doing?" I asked, my voice hoarse from disuse.

"Something's wrong. The king has ordered every able-bodied man and boy to arm himself and assemble in the courtyard. He's made every army battalion in Tubatse come inside the palace walls. He's even forcing women to arm themselves and prepare to fight. The rumor is that the entire Blevonese army is marching on the palace."

I stared at Deron in the flickering light of the torch.

"Is it true? Are they coming?"

I nodded. "But it isn't what you think," I added when I saw the flash of fear in his eyes. "Deron, do you trust me?"

He gave me a sharp look. "What are you talking about?"

"Do you trust me?"

"Of course I do."

"Good." I glanced down the hallway, but it was empty. "Where is the rest of the guard?"

The skin around Deron's mouth tightened and he closed his eyes briefly before answering, sending my heart pounding in dread. "Kai and Antonio are dead; the king had them killed for failing to save the prince. The rest of us were punished — even those who were sleeping — but at least we're alive."

I stared at the scar on his face, realizing what it meant. "Jude, too?"

Deron nodded. "Scarred, but alive."

I couldn't believe Kai and Antonio were gone, but there was no time to dwell on it. "Where are they?"

"Gathering their weapons and preparing to fight. I told them I was going to find more men, but Iker will notice I'm not there soon if we don't hurry."

My heart began to pound as I thought of a plan — a very risky plan.

"I need you to find me a mask," I said.

"A mask?"

"Then I need you or someone else in the guard to help me get next to Iker when the Blevonese army arrives."

Deron's eyes widened. "Next to Iker? Why?"

"Because if we are to have any hope of surviving this day, and saving the prince and Antion, I have to kill him."

Deron's mouth dropped open.

"We have a great deal to talk about," I said.

Deron recovered himself, and nodded. "Yes . . . yes, I think we do."

≼ FORTY ≽

THERE WERE SO many people packed inside the palace walls that there was hardly room to walk, let alone fight. If the Blevonese soldiers were able to breach the wall, we'd be slaughtered just as badly as they would be. If I wasn't able to stop Iker, the king was almost assured his victory — but at what cost? Did he intend to be the king of a graveyard?

I stood near Deron and Jude. The other members of the guard were spread out around the grounds in strategic locations, helping me watch for Iker's location. He couldn't hide inside the palace and fight. He'd have to be out here somewhere, most likely somewhere with a good vantage point over the fighting, but not within range of archers. Not that a little arrow was anything he'd have to worry about, I realized.

Jude's face, which had always been so similar to his brother's, was now distinctly different. He had a long scar snaking down the length of one side of it, just like Deron did. I understood now why Damian had decided to do what he did, the necessity of the abduction. But it had come at a great cost to these men whom I cared for — loved.

Even Jerrod seemed relieved to see me alive. For all of his

animosity, he didn't want me to die any more than I wished such a fate on him.

The oppressive heat of the jungle swelled in the burning rays of the afternoon sun. The air was heavy with humidity and I was already sweating beneath the mask Deron had found for me. I felt like Eljin, with a scrap of black fabric covering my nose and mouth. Deron had also found me different clothes, an old uniform from someone in the army. I had a sword strapped to my waist as we searched the crowd for my target. If I had any hope of inching my way next to Iker in time, we had to find him soon. If all went according to plan, General Tinso and his army had left an hour after my captors and me. They would travel a bit slower than my guards and I had, but they planned on arriving only a day or two behind me. The Insurgi would also be with them.

Finally, Mateo flashed a tiny mirror to signal us that he'd spotted Iker. Mateo was standing near the stairs that went up to the top of the wall, where the archers would be waiting to shoot down the Blevonese soldiers before they got close enough to pull out their swords.

"There he is." Deron pointed and I nodded, my heart sinking. Iker was walking up the stairs to stand atop of the wall. How would I ever make it up there without him growing suspicious and cutting me down? A member of the army wearing a mask in this mass of people wasn't too noticeable right now. But one running up the stairs after him? Not good.

"How are you going to get up there without him recognizing you — even with the mask?" Jude asked, echoing my own thoughts.

"I don't know." I sighed heavily. Why did everything that could go wrong keep going wrong?

"We've got to get over there, though, so I guess I'll think about it on the way."

Deron took the lead, using his bigger body and strength to push through the mass of soldiers and palace workers. I followed in his wake, with Jude right on my heels. If there hadn't been so many people in the way, I could have crossed the grounds to where Mateo stood in less than a minute. Instead, it took us much longer — *too* long. Before we made it there, Iker stood over us on the wall walk.

"People of Antion!" he shouted, his voice echoing over the noise of thousands. A hush spread over the assembled men and women. I was dismayed to see so many girls and women, in their threadbare skirts, clutching weapons uncomfortably, fear written plainly on their faces. Most of them were painfully thin, and they jumped away from the men around them with looks of terror. They had to be women from the breeding house. My stomach turned and I looked up at Iker with hatred burning in me stronger than anything I'd ever felt in my life.

"The army of our enemy approaches! Will we let them conquer us?" He paused and then screamed, "*No!* We will fight! We will fight for our king and for Antion! Show no mercy to the dirty heathens who support the evil practice of sorcery!" A violent cheer of approval rose up from the men in the crowd. The woman were mostly silent, grasping their weapons with trembling hands.

"They have brought their sorcerers with them — but will we let them win?"

"*No!*" the crowd shouted back.

"We will fight them! We will *destroy* them! We will sacrifice our very lives if necessary to protect our nation and our freedom from the slavery of sorcery!" Iker punched his fist in the air and, all around me, men and even some of the women did the same, shouting and screaming in agreement. It sounded almost as if he'd enthralled them in a spell of bloodlust and hatred for the very power he wielded.

"If he were close enough for me to cut his throat, I would," Deron growled next to me, through the wild cheering around us.

"He'd throw up a shield and kill you before you knew what had happened," I muttered darkly.

"Are you sure you can do this?" Deron looked down at me.

Before I could answer, Iker turned and began to head back down the stairs. "Now where's he going?" Jude asked.

When Iker reached the bottom of the stairs, passing Mateo without acknowledging him, the crowd parted. Iker walked swiftly across the grounds to the ten steps leading to the massive palace doors. He walked up the stairs until he stood directly in front of the entryway, cutting off anyone who wished to flee inside the palace. He was visible above the crowd, but anyone who wanted to fight him would now have to cut their way through hundreds of men and women first and then climb a flight of stairs to reach him. He would easily be able to use his sorcery to stop anyone who tried to get to him.

"I've got to get closer to him," I said.

We began to work our way closer to him yet again when I saw one of the king's guards drag Jaerom up the steps to stand in front of Iker. It looked like his eye was swollen shut and his mouth was bleeding.

"Deron, stop!" I grabbed his arm and we froze, watching in fear as Iker bent over Jaerom, his face twisted with sudden fury.

We were too far away to hear what was said, but it was obvious Iker was asking him something because Jaerom kept shaking his head. Iker suddenly grabbed his throat, and Jaerom's eyes widened.

"Jaerom!" Deron cried out, but luckily the noise of the crowd masked his voice.

"No, Deron!" I yanked him back. "We can't help him; Iker will kill all of us!" Deron continued to fight me. Jude had to grab his other arm as Iker shouted something at Jaerom loud enough for me to catch the words *where*, *tell*, and *now*. Jaerom's whole body began to quake violently when he shook his head no again, refusing to speak. Icy-hot fingers of panic spread through me. I had a sinking feeling that someone had discovered I was missing and Iker was torturing Jaerom to find out what had happened.

Iker finally let go of Jaerom, who fell to his hands and knees on the ground in front of the smaller man. Deron fought wildly for us to let him go, and it took every ounce of our strength to hold him back, even though my eyes burned with tears. Jaerom was protecting me. I was sure of it.

Iker shouted again, his face mottled with rage. Jaerom looked up at him for a long moment, and I held my breath.

And then he spit in Iker's face.

Iker grabbed the sword from the guard's scabbard and Jaerom didn't even put up his arm to block the blade as Iker swung it around toward his neck.

"Jaerom!" Deron's howl of pain and fury tore my heart to pieces. He finally stopped fighting us when Jaerom's body fell to the ground in front of Iker, rolling down a couple of stairs before stopping, lifeless. Tears blinded me as my captain dropped to his knees, his face pale with shock.

"Deron, you have to get up," Jude said, tugging on his arm. "People are looking at us. Iker's going to notice!"

But before Deron could respond, the whistle from the watchtower high above us split the air.

An icy chill of dread ran down my spine.

The Blevonese army was here.

⊰ FORTY-ONE ⊱

ALL OF THE conversations around us stopped. A deathly silence fell over the crowd as the warning whistle was repeated.

Deron slowly climbed to his feet, still staring at the stairs, where Jaerom lay. I couldn't look and, instead, turned to the wall, where I could see lines of archers at the ready, their bows taut and arrows notched, ready to fly.

Where was Damian? Would he be at the front, expecting the gate to open and welcome Antion's prince back to the palace with the Blevonese army at his heels? And Rylan? Where would he be? My heart felt like it might explode in my chest from the panic and pain pounding through me. I couldn't let myself think about it. I had to focus on Iker — that was my job, my duty. Nothing else mattered if I didn't find a way to stop him.

When the first volley of arrows was loosed, I turned to see if Iker still stood on the stairs, but they were empty except for Jaerom's body. In the brief moments that I'd spent looking at the wall, he had disappeared.

"Deron! Where did he go?" I asked, grabbing his arm.

"He went into the palace," he replied tonelessly, his hands hanging at his side.

"They're here, Deron. The army and Damian are here. I have to find Iker!"

He looked down at me, his face and eyes empty.

"Captain, please!"

But there was nothing. He was broken.

"Alex, come on. I'll go with you," Jude said from my other side. But before we could move, the ground began to shake and a roar filled the air. All around us, people screamed and shouted in fear.

"The sorcerers! It's the sorcerers!" people began to yell. "Kill the sorcerers who murdered our queen!"

The sound of a massive explosion rocked the air and I spun around to see the giant iron and wood gate blown to pieces before my eyes. All the people who had been standing near it were knocked to the ground, shards of wood and iron piercing their bodies.

"They've breached the wall!"

"Swords at the ready!"

I could barely see the rows and rows of Blevonese soldiers outside the wall before Jude grabbed my arm. "Come on, Alex. We've got to go now before it's too late!"

I turned and followed him through the crowd toward the steps as the sounds of fighting broke out across the grounds from us. Blades hitting blades, screams as people were cut down. As people died. More booms, more screams. I couldn't look back. I had to find Iker.

I had to kill Iker.

And then he was there. Only this time, he wore robes of all black, and on one hand was a strange glove made of metal, inlaid with jewels. He gripped a sword in his other hand. He stood over the crowd, surveying the destruction. Instead of fear or sadness, his face was lit with a terrifying look of *hunger*. Of exultation.

"I'll approach him first, to distract him," Jude said from beside me. "Then you can attack from the other side, and take him by surprise."

"Jude, no!" I grabbed his arm before he dashed off. "He'll kill you!"

He turned to look at me with the same chocolate brown eyes as his brother's, and gently pulled his arm out of my grasp. "I know. But you said it yourself — you have to stop him. And if you just go running at him, he'll kill *you*, and then we'll all die."

I wanted to argue with him. I wanted to tell him he couldn't do this. But he was right, and I knew it.

"You can do this, Alex. I wouldn't try to help you if I didn't think you could."

"Alexa," I said, my voice thick with tears.

"What?"

"My name is Alexa."

He stared at me for a long moment, and then his eyes filled with understanding — with sorrow. "I know you can do this, *Alexa*."

I nodded and swiped at the wetness on my cheeks, under the mask. Jude reached out to grip my hand for just a second, then let go. He took a deep, shuddering breath. "You go left, and I'll go right. Watch for me to move first. Once he's distracted, attack."

I stared at him, at his scarred face and his familiar eyes, and nodded.

"Tell my brother that I love him," he said, his voice suddenly choked. And then he turned and was gone.

I stood there frozen, tears running down my face beneath my mask, until another huge boom sounded from behind me, followed by more screams. I glanced over my shoulder and saw a vast hole in the Antionese army. The opening in the wall where the gate had once been was like a gaping mouth spewing Blevonese soldiers and sorcerers into our midst. They were hewing the Antion soldiers down as if they were ants. I thought I caught a glimpse of Borracio's dark head. And Iker just stood there, watching. What was he waiting for?

Clenching my jaw, I forced myself to turn and push my way toward the steps to the palace. I had to stop this. I shoved soldiers out of my way, but most of them weren't paying any attention to me; they stared at the oncoming army, waiting for it to reach them.

Finally, I was only a few people back from the edge of the stairs. Iker stood far above me, surveying the massacre. As I watched, he lifted the hand that was covered in the strange glove, palm raised toward the sky. He closed his eyes, a look of almost blissful happiness on his face. I stared in horror as a ball of fire suddenly materialized above his hand, swelling and growing, until it was three times the size of his head. His eyes opened again, and with a horrifying grin of pleasure, he flung his arm and the ball of fire rushed through the air. I spun around and saw it crash into the front line of Blevonese soldiers and sorcerers, sending bodies and dirt flying as it exploded with a blinding boom of fire and smoke.

Many of our own army turned to stare at Iker in horror, but he was already summoning the fire again. And then they had no choice but to keep fighting as more Blevonese soldiers rushed forward with swords raised. I didn't see Eljin or Rylan or Damian or anyone I knew.

It was now or never.

I turned back to Iker, and noticed Jude creeping up the stairs toward him while the sorcerer's eyes were shut, creating his next fireball. I did the same, staying a few steps lower, crouched near to the ground, my hand slick with sweat on the hilt of my sword.

Iker opened his eyes and threw the fireball at the oncoming army again, and just as he did, Jude stood and hurtled up the stairs at him, sword raised.

Iker spun to face him with a look of anger at being interrupted. As soon as his back was to me, I jumped up and ran toward him as well. I knew Iker wouldn't spare Jude, but it still took everything in me not to cry out when he turned his gloved hand at my friend and shot a stream of fire into Jude. Tears of fury and anguish burned my eyes as he flew backward down the steps, landing on the bottom, his body broken and charred.

With a scream of rage, I hit the top of the steps and rushed at Iker, sword in the air.

⊰ FORTY-TWO ⊱

IKER SPUN TO face me, his eyes widening momentarily, and then a look of grim satisfaction crossed his face. I was sure he recognized me, even with the mask. He lifted his hand, but I was ready for it and twisted out of the way. The jet of fire just missed me. With another scream, I swung my sword with all of my might at him, but I felt the shield go up right before my sword would have cut through his abdomen. My arms shook from the impact, and I had to spin while ducking to the ground to avoid another jet of fire. It hit the door instead, which burst into flames behind me.

I had to be better than this — faster than this — or else he was going to kill me.

"I knew you'd come for me," he said before lifting his hand again. I threw myself to the ground, rolling as fast as I could, but I wasn't fast enough. The edge of the fire scorched the left side of my body. Pain exploded across my cheek, neck, and shoulder. The smell of my own flesh burning nearly made me throw up. But I forced myself to jump to my feet, still gripping my sword with my right hand, and barely dodged yet another stream of fire.

This time, when I swung my sword at him, he was still trying to hit me with the fire, and didn't get his shield up as fast. I managed to get a piece of his left arm with my blade before the power of his shield knocked me to the ground. My head hit the stone, and I lay there dazed for a moment, knowing I was going to burn.

But when my vision cleared, I saw Iker gripping his left forearm, his hand hanging useless at his side, blood rushing from his wrist. He howled, an almost inhuman sound. Grabbing his sword, he lunged at me.

I scrambled back and collided with the wall. Just before Iker ran me through with his blade, I threw my body's weight to the side, rolling across the ground and coming up into a crouch, ignoring the excruciating pain radiating down the left side of my body. He turned to face me, fury mottling his features.

"You think to stop me? You think you can defeat *me*? You have no idea the power I wield, little girl."

There wasn't even time for me to be shocked that he knew my secret, because he was stretching his arms out to both sides, his left hand bent at a funny angle and blood dripping to the stones below. That same horrible scent from his chamber all those weeks ago filled the air. He closed his eyes again, but this time, a cloud of darkness began to form in front of him, rising from his blood on the ground, crackling with power. I could see it, flashing like lightning within the depths of whatever black magic he was creating through the offering of his own blood.

I glanced around frantically, looking for cover. The door behind me was an inferno of fire now, and there was nowhere else to hide, nothing else to protect me. Then I noticed Jaerom's body, much larger than mine, lying on the step below me.

I jumped down two stairs and, using all my strength, pushed him up so I could curl into a ball underneath him, using him as a shield.

"I'm so sorry," I sobbed as I pressed into the body of my former friend, and squeezed my eyes shut. I was lying in a pool of his blood, the dead weight of his corpse nearly crushing me.

And then Iker threw the dark mass. I couldn't see it anymore, but I felt it — *heard* it. It exploded all around me, like the fury of a hundred claps of thunder crashing together all at once. The air crackled with electricity, and I clenched my muscles, preparing to die. A horrible, acrid smell filled my nose.

Then it was gone, and I heard Iker give a cry of triumph from above.

Did he think he'd destroyed me? Jaerom's body, lying on top of me, wasn't nearly as heavy anymore. In fact, I could barely feel it. What had that black mass done to his corpse? I didn't dare move, unsure of what had happened, if Iker would be able to see me hiding or not.

Desperation burned through me, hot and horrible. I was trapped and Iker was still free to continue to obliterate the Blevonese army.

And then I heard something that made my blood turn to ice in my veins.

"Iker! Stop this insanity right now! You're letting your own people die!" Prince Damian's voice rose above the sounds of battle below me.

No, no, *no*! What was he doing? It took everything in me to hold still, to keep from jumping up and rushing to his side, revealing myself.

"Do *you* think to stop me?" Iker began to laugh, a cruel sound that bordered on maniacal. "You — who did nothing but sit and watch while his precious mama was slaughtered?"

"I'm not as helpless as you think." Damian's voice sent a chill down my spine. Suddenly, the stones beneath me began to tremble and quake with a horrible, grinding sound. I had to brace myself against the stair above me to keep from being thrown down the rest of the steps.

Finally, it stopped, but I stayed tense, waiting for whatever would come next.

"So, the little prince has been keeping a secret from Iker, has he?" The malicious humor was gone from Iker's voice. Now he spoke in a cold rage.

And I realized that he hadn't made the ground move — *Damian* had.

"I don't care what tricks you have up your sleeve — you won't defeat me!" Iker shouted. "Your little pet guard couldn't do it, either — she was too weak. Do you want to hear how she begged for her life before I disintegrated her into nothing?"

I couldn't hear Damian's response over the pounding of my blood. I gripped my sword more tightly. I couldn't let Iker kill Damian, too. I had to try — one last time.

I thought of everyone I loved who had suffered because of this man, and the king he served. I thought of Damian, of Rylan. Marcel, Papa, and Mama. Jude and Jaerom.

Holding all their faces in my mind, I took a deep breath, and then sprang out from under the remains of Jaerom's body. I heard Damian's cry of fear from below me, but I ignored him. I ran as fast as I could toward Iker, whose eyes widened in shock. With every ounce of fury and hatred in me, I jumped, slashing my sword down through the air from above my head toward him. I felt Iker drawing up his shield as he lifted his sword arm to block me. When

I landed right in front of him, rather than continuing to bring my sword down at his head, I spun as fast as I could, twisting my arm down and back. With all the strength and speed I possessed, I screamed and swung my sword around at his left side.

When my blade bit through his flesh and bone, embedding itself into his lungs, I almost couldn't believe it. He took a staggering step backward, taking my blade with him. He stared at me, then down at the sword impaled in his side. Blood bubbled out of his mouth, and he dropped to his knees in front of the door, which still blazed with fire.

I watched Iker collapse, his eyes open and unseeing. My chest heaved and tears ran down my cheeks. Then my own legs buckled and I fell in front of his motionless body.

❧ FORTY-THREE ❧

ALEXA!" I HEARD Damian's shout moments before he dropped to the ground in front of me, his beautiful blue eyes bright with unshed tears. He gathered me into his arms, and I could feel his body shaking with sobs. Or maybe it was me who was shaking and he was just trying to hold me together. "You did it," he whispered over and over again as he rocked my broken body.

"Damian, you need to call a cease-fire." I heard General Tinso's voice from below us.

"I'll take care of her. You take care of your kingdom. I think you still have a king to kill." Rylan's familiar voice brought fresh tears to my eyes.

Damian reluctantly pulled back, and I was passed into Rylan's arms. I stared up at his face, sobs tearing me apart. "I'm so sorry," I tried to say, my voice cracking, the effort hurting my burned throat.

"I know. Shhh . . . it's okay. I know," he said, staring down at me, his warm brown eyes wet with tears.

Then I heard Damian's shout, and I turned my head painfully to see him standing on the top of the stairs. It seemed like there was something about him that I was forgetting — something important.

"Halt!" he shouted at the top of his lungs. "As the crown prince of Antion, I order you to cease your fighting immediately!"

General Tinso stood next to him and also shouted, "Soldiers of Blevon, stand down!"

I glanced out at the crowd and saw Borracio standing back-to-back with Eljin, holding off a whole horde of Antion soldiers. But when the two leaders shouted their orders, they turned with everyone else to look at the stairs. Some in the crowd turned in relief, and some in confusion.

"My people, we have been misled and mistreated long enough!" Damian cried out over the sudden silence. I couldn't tear my eyes away from him, even though my burns were excruciating and my vision kept dimming. I fought against the darkness, fought to hear my prince's words. A few people cheered, and then a few more. "My father, the king, has *used* our people, perpetrating atrocities, which shame me and our nation. I will stand for it no longer!" he shouted. I couldn't see his eyes, but I imagined the blue fire as he looked out upon all the people — *his* people — staring up at him with cautious hope lighting their faces. "I have negotiated peace with Blevon and will call for an immediate cease-fire and end to this pointless war with a nation that desires only amity with our people!"

No one cheered anymore and I glanced out at the crowds in fear, worried that they weren't going to follow him. That they didn't want peace.

But then I realized why they weren't cheering. One by one, they were pressing their right fists to their left shoulders and dropping to one knee, bowing their heads to their prince, until everyone was on their knees, some with tears running down their cheeks.

Damian pressed his fist to his shoulder, and bowed his own head back to them.

At first, I thought the noise behind me was just the sound of the door burning. But something warned me to turn and look.

"No!" I cried, and tried to jump up in time to stop the king as he burst through the now obliterated doorway with his sword overhead.

Damian heard my cry and spun around in time for the king to swing his sword at him. I watched in horror as the blade rushed toward Damian's throat. He didn't have time to lift his own sword to deflect it —

And then the king's sword stopped, as if he'd hit an invisible wall. Or a shield.

Oh yes, Damian *had* kept yet another secret from me. He, too, was a sorcerer.

He punched the air in front of him and the king went flying back; Hector hit the wall, then fell to the ground. He moaned and tried to get up, but Damian rushed forward and pressed his sword to his father's throat.

King Hector looked at Damian with hatred burning in his eyes. "You truly are your mother's son," he spat.

Damian stood over him, gripping his sword, his chest heaving. I stared at him and saw the conflict on his beautiful face. I remembered him telling me, "He's still my father."

"He can't do it," I said under my breath.

But then his gaze hardened. "You will never speak of my mother again," he said, his voice cold.

For the first time, fear crossed King Hector's face. "Damian . . . my son . . . you don't want to do this. Have mercy on me — I'm your *father*!"

Damian stared into his father's face, but I noticed the king reaching down for his boot.

"Damian, watch out!" I cried out, just as King Hector pulled out a knife and moved to stab his son.

Before he could, Damian drove his sword through his father's heart. "I will show you the same mercy you showed her," he snarled, his voice low and hoarse.

King Hector's grip on the knife loosened, and his hands fell limp at his side. He stared up at his son for a moment longer, and then his head dropped to the ground. Damian closed his eyes briefly. I saw a muscle in his jaw tighten, and then he pulled out the blade, which was coated in his father's blood. Rylan and I were probably the only ones close enough to see the way his hand shook and the look of grief that crossed his face.

Hector had been a terrible, evil man, but he'd also been his father — Damian's last surviving parent.

We were both orphans now.

Slowly, Damian made his way back to the front of the step, his shoulders slightly stooped. The crowd was completely silent, having watched the whole thing in horrified shock. Prince Damian looked out over the mass of people for a moment. Then he clenched his jaw and raised his sword.

"My father's tyranny is at an end!" he yelled.

General Tinso bowed to him, and then shouted, "Hail, Damian, king of Antion! Long live the king!"

The crowd took up the cry, repeating, "Hail, Damian, king of Antion! Long live the king!" over and over, until Damian bowed low at the waist to them.

Then he turned and I could see the tears in his eyes when he looked straight at me and said, "We did it." His voice broke when he repeated, "Alexa, we did it."

I tried to smile at him through my tears, but my ruined face hurt too much. I wondered how badly I had been burned.

"She needs Lisbet's help," Rylan said.

Damian — *King* Damian — nodded.

Rylan stood up, with me in his arms, and the pain escalated until I couldn't bear it. But it didn't matter — I'd done it. I was finally sure that the people I loved were safe at last.

⇥ FORTY-FOUR ⇤

WHEN I WOKE, I was lying in Damian's bed, and Lisbet hovered over me. At first, I couldn't remember what had happened or why I was there. But when I moved, I felt the pull of my injured skin, and everything came rushing back, making it hard to breathe.

"Shhhh . . ." Lisbet whispered. "It's okay, Alexa. It's all okay now — thanks to you."

I shook my head, struggling for air against the panic that held my lungs in an iron-tight grasp.

"Alexa, look at me," Lisbet commanded, and I stared up into her dark eyes helplessly. "Breathe, Alexa. Nice and slow. In through your nose, out through your mouth."

I tried to do as she asked, and slowly, slowly, the panic receded, until I could breathe normally, even though my heart still raced.

"There you go. That's better. Just breathe, sweet girl."

Sweet girl? *Lisbet* was calling me sweet girl?

She must have seen the confusion on my face, because she laughed softly, a sad, wistful sound. "Don't look so surprised," she said as she wiped a cool cloth over my brow. Her hand grew still and her expression somber as she stared down into my eyes. "Thank you," she said. "Thank you for what you did. For saving all of us."

"But at what cost?" I finally managed to whisper. It hurt to talk; the skin on the left side of my face and neck pulled funny when I did. I reached up to touch my face. Where once there was smooth skin, it was now bumpy. I pulled my hand away in horror.

"I did the best I could," Lisbet said sadly. "It wasn't normal fire that burned you. I couldn't heal all of the scars it left, though I was able to heal some."

I shook my head. "I don't mean my face. I mean all the people who died in the battle. Jaerom. And Jude." Tears ran down my ruined cheek.

Lisbet wiped them away with her cloth. "It was a terrible cost. But they gave their lives in hopes that it would ensure freedom from the king's atrocities for those they loved. Don't belittle their gift by living your life dragged down by regret and guilt."

I stared up at her, my chest tight. Before I could respond, there was a knock at the door.

"That'll be one of your suitors, I'm sure. They've both been pacing holes into the ground. I wouldn't let them come in until you'd had a chance to rest and heal up a bit." Lisbet stood up. "Would you like to see them now?"

Panic clutched my chest again. How could I face either of them?

Rylan would never forgive me. After all the years he'd protected me, for Marcel, I'd failed to save Jude.

Or Damian — he'd take one look at me and retreat in horror; my scars were surely worse than Eljin's. And he was the king now. He shouldn't be bothering with me; he had a country to run — to heal.

Lisbet stepped closer to me again when there was another

knock. "You'll have to face them sometime, but if you don't feel up to it now, I'll tell them to give you another night to rest."

I nodded gratefully, not even daring to speak. When had I become such a coward? But I couldn't deny the relief when she cracked the door open and quietly said something before shutting it again.

When she walked back over and sat down next to me on the bed, I took a deep breath. "I want to see myself," I said.

She gave me a searching look, and then nodded. "Okay. That's probably a good place to start."

She rose and moved away, then returned, holding a hand mirror. I took it from her with trembling fingers. I held it down on my lap for a long time, too scared to look.

"I'll go find you some dinner," Lisbet said, "if you would like some time alone."

I nodded again, grateful for her sensitivity.

She walked across the room, and then paused by the door. "Don't hold it against him," she said suddenly.

"What?" I asked, confused.

"Against Damian. Don't hold it against him for not telling you that he was a sorcerer. I spent his whole life ingraining in him that he could never, ever tell anyone. He took bloodroot every day of his life until he left the palace to suppress it so that Iker wouldn't sense him and have him killed — or worse. I tried to train him when he came to me, but he had to work so hard to make anything happen, since he was purposefully poisoning himself." Lisbet's voice broke and my heart constricted. The bloodroot I'd gathered . . . I had been sure it was for Lisbet. But I'd been wrong — again. "His life has been nothing short of hell. He's had no one, except for me, he could talk to or trust. Until you came into his life and he started to fall for you. I thought he was using you at first — that he was trying to make you care for him so you would do what he wanted. But, now . . . please don't break his heart."

I stared at her, stricken.

"I'm sorry. Forgive me for meddling. I just . . . I care for him as if he were my own son. I loved his mother so dearly. . . ." She broke off again. After clearing her throat and dashing her fingers against her eyes, she nodded. "Right. I'll go get that food now."

She slipped out of the door, leaving me alone with her words hanging in the air and the mirror in my cold hands.

My heart pounded as I sat up in Damian's bed, staring at the back of the mirror. I tried to summon the courage to look, replaying what Lisbet had said to me over and over in my mind. I *was* upset at Damian for not telling me — for keeping what had to be the biggest secret of all. That had to be why he'd known I was a girl; just like every other sorcerer I met. He'd had the chance to tell me in the corridor on our last night in Blevon, hadn't he? Or had we heard the people coming too soon? Even if he didn't have time then, there had been other opportunities.

But that wasn't the true problem.

It was the same realization I'd come to in General Tinso's castle, when we'd been alone in the room together.

There was no future for us.

I was not the one who would become his queen.

I clutched the mirror tightly. Maybe it wouldn't matter anyway. Maybe I was so hideous now that he would take one look at me and decide he didn't care about me anymore. Only love —

true, unwavering love — could remain unblemished in the face of the horror I was sure to see when I lifted this mirror. And though I'd told him that I loved him, he'd never repeated it back to me. He'd told me he cared about me. That he wanted to be with me. But did he love me?

When he walked in here and saw me, I'd know.

"Let's get this over with already," I finally said out loud to myself. "You're being ridiculous. It's just a face."

I took a deep breath and held it, then brought up the mirror to see how bad it was.

My eyes widened and then filled with tears as I stared at myself. All my life, I'd seen my twin in my reflection.

The face I saw now didn't look a thing like Marcel. The right side, yes. But the left . . . My tears spilled out and ran down my cheeks, leaving wet streaks on the silvery, ridged scars that covered my left cheek, trailed across my jaw and down my neck, plunging beneath the neckline of my nightgown and out of sight. At least my mouth hadn't been affected, or my eye.

I turned the mirror around and set it down as far away from me as possible on the bed.

Lisbet had tried her hardest, I was sure. But I would always be a walking reminder of the horrors Antion had suffered under King Hector and Iker's rule.

I was a monster — made by the hand of the true monster.

When I heard Lisbet opening the door, I flung myself down on the bed and pretended to be asleep. I couldn't bear to face her, not yet. Not when I knew how bad my grief would make her feel.

I never wanted to see my face again. And I never wanted anyone else to see it, either.

306

⊰ FORTY-FIVE ⊱

I HELD RYLAN AND Damian off for three days, making Lisbet send them away again and again. But finally, I knew I couldn't put it off any longer. I had to come out sometime; I wasn't going to spend the rest of my life holed up in the prince's room. I wondered if he was using the king's rooms now, or if they held too many horrible memories for him. Maybe I was causing him to suffer by not letting him take back his old room.

With that thought in mind, I nodded when Lisbet said, "The king is here to see you . . . again," on the fourth morning.

"She will see you now, Your Majesty." Lisbet bowed and opened the door wider. I turned my face away, so that he wouldn't see the ruined side yet, but I heard him say, "Lisbet, please, you don't need to do all that."

I remembered how I used to think it was an act when he'd tell us he didn't like having us bow and use titles to address him. It made me flush with embarrassment, now that I knew how wrong I'd been about him.

"I'll give you some privacy," Lisbet said, and I heard the door shut, leaving me alone with Damian. The king of Antion.

He was silent for a long time. I could feel his gaze on me, but he didn't come closer. Was he afraid to see what I looked like?

At last, I heard him take a hesitant step forward. "Alexa . . . would you like me to leave?" He sounded so concerned, so unsure of himself.

I shook my head.

"May I . . . may I come sit by you?"

I took a deep breath, trying to calm my racing heart. I clutched my hands in my lap. They were cold and yet slick with sweat. "Of course, Your Majesty," I said, my voice shaky.

"Not from you, please, Alexa. I'm Damian to you still, aren't I?" I heard him cross the distance between us, and felt the bed dip beneath his weight when he sat down beside me. I could see him out of the corner of my eye now. He wore the signet crown over his thick, dark hair, but his collar of office was a simple gold chain, unadorned by jewels — unlike the gaudy one his father had worn.

"You're the king now," I said.

He reached out and covered my hands with one of his. "Please don't shut me out. I'm still Damian — and I still need you."

I squeezed my eyes shut and the tears I'd been trying to hold in spilled onto my cheeks. "If you wish for me to continue to serve on your guard, I would be honored to do so."

His fingers tightened over mine. "Alexa, look at me."

I shook my head, my eyes still closed.

"Look at me, please. I don't care about the scars. I care about *you*," he said, his voice achingly tender.

I'd never heard him sound so unsure of himself.

"Please look at me, so I can tell you how much I care about you. How much I *love* you."

It was hearing those words that undid me. My eyes flew open. For a moment, I forgot how ugly I was and turned to stare at him.

He didn't flinch or turn away. He looked straight into my eyes, and lifted his hand to softly cup the ruined side of my face.

"Alexa, I love you. Please forgive me for keeping so many secrets. There are no more; I promise. And I need you. I *need* you," he repeated, his voice barely above a whisper, his familiar eyes intent on mine and oh so very, very blue in the light of the morning sun.

I didn't pull away when he leaned forward and very gently touched his lips to mine, as if he were afraid of breaking me. My breath caught in my throat. I ached to melt into his arms, to believe his words, to believe I really could be with him.

But he was a king now.

And I was . . . not worthy of a king.

When I didn't respond, he pulled away, his expression guarded. The hurt in his eyes nearly shattered my already broken heart.

"Alexa?"

"You're a king, Damian. Do you intend to make me your queen? Because that's the only way we could be together. And you and I both know I am not fit to be queen of Antion." I gently pulled my hands out from his.

"Don't do this," he said.

"We both know it's the right thing to do. If you wish me to serve you as your guard, I will. Although it might be difficult for me to be so close to you. Especially once you do decide to marry someone who is worthy to be your queen."

Damian's eyes flashed and he stood up abruptly. "Yes, you're right, I *am* king of Antion. And I have the ability to decide who is worthy to be my queen."

I had to make him leave, or else I wasn't going to have the strength to say no any longer. Even if he couldn't see it, I knew I was right. No one would respect him if he made his scarred, former guard his wife. He needed someone powerful, someone who could help him rule and heal his nation.

"Damian, it isn't just that," I said. My heart constricted in my chest, but I had to do it. For his sake. "I can't trust you. I can't be with you; I can't be your queen when I can't trust you."

His jaw tightened and he stared at me. "After everything we've been through — after everything we accomplished together — this is your answer? You don't trust me?"

"I'm very sorry," I said, trying to make my voice firm, not to let him notice how I was trembling. How my eyes were stinging from the tears I couldn't let him see.

He looked at me for a moment longer, then he nodded curtly, his expression hard. "Fine. Then, as your *king*" — he spat the word as if he hated it — "I order you to continue to serve on my personal guard. And maybe someday, you will decide I am worthy of your trust after all."

Without waiting for my response, he turned on his heel and strode to the door. He yanked it open and was gone.

I rolled onto my stomach and buried my sobs in my pillow.

⇥ FORTY-SIX ⇤

$\mathcal{E}$VERYONE LEFT ME alone for the next couple of hours, and eventually I forced myself to dry my tears and draw up my courage. I wasn't going to hide in here any longer. I didn't want Rylan to come visit me while I was lying in bed, too. I would face him on my terms — on my own two feet, even though the thought of looking at him, talking to him, knowing I was responsible for his brother's death made my stomach turn.

I stood up and looked around for something to change into, instead of the long nightgown I had on. Everywhere I turned were reminders of Damian, of the night I'd come in to see him thrashing in bed from a nightmare. The time he'd stood by his desk, fidgeting with what I learned was his mother's locket. I had to clench my jaw to keep the tears from rising again. I was certain I'd made the right decision, but it nearly destroyed me to do it.

Just as Damian had said to me all those weeks ago, duty came first with me. He'd been praising me for it then. I was sure he was cursing me for it now.

There was nothing for me to wear, and I finally went to the door and cracked it open. The cot I'd slept on was still there, and I had to take a deep breath to calm my emotions yet again. Lisbet was sitting on it, and when the door opened, she jumped to her feet.

"You're up," she said.

"I need some clothes, please," I said, glancing around the room, grateful to see it was empty.

"What would you like to wear? King Damian's official coronation is in a few hours. I'm sure he'd want you to be there." She gave me a searching look.

I felt like I'd been punched in the gut. I'd rejected him on the day of his coronation. Why hadn't I been told? But then again, my answer would have still been the same.

"I've been commanded to continue my duties as guard to King Damian, so I would like to wear what the other guards are wearing," I finally responded.

Lisbet nodded and turned to walk away.

When she came back, she handed me a uniform similar to what we'd always worn, but now it had the insignia of the king on the pocket of the vest.

"Will you be continuing your position as Alex or Alexa?" Lisbet asked, giving me a look from the corner of her eye after I climbed out of the bath she'd drawn for me.

"Alexa," I said. "I'm not hiding who I am anymore."

Lisbet nodded. "Your hair is growing out. Soon you'll be able to braid it when you're on duty, if you'd like."

I reached up and was surprised to realize she was right. In the many weeks of traveling, it had grown a few inches, nearly reaching my shoulders now. Tears pricked my eyes again, and I smiled hesitantly.

"You're still beautiful," she said softly as she helped me get dressed. My left shoulder was stiff; Lisbet had told me it might take some time to get my full range of motion back.

"You don't have to lie to me." I wiped the wetness from my face in irritation before letting her help me pull on my shirt. For the first time, I wore a woman's undergarment beneath it, instead of a cloth binding to hide my breasts.

Lisbet gently took my shoulders in her hands, forcing me to look at her. "True beauty is what lies inside of us, not what the world sees. A beautiful shell that houses a vile soul becomes sullied over time. But an outer shell, imperfect as it may be, that houses a beautiful soul shines with that beauty, radiating it for all who have eyes to see."

I stared down at the floor, not meeting her eyes.

"We still see *you*, Alexa. Not your scars. Your scars are nothing to be ashamed of — they are a manifestation of your courage and determination. They are witness to the fact that you saved this nation." She reached down and picked up my vest, guided my arms through it. "Those who truly love you will only ever see you for what you really are."

I didn't reply as I buttoned up the vest and strapped a scabbard around my waist. When I was dressed, Lisbet turned me to face the full-length mirror.

"You see? You're fierce *and* lovely."

I stared at myself, and at first, all I could see were my scars. But the longer I looked, the more I noticed other things. Like my hair, thick and dark and growing longer again. My eyes, untouched by the fire. My eyes were still my brother's eyes, and our father's. I still had my arms, my hands, my legs. I wore the uniform of the guard, but I looked different, and not just because of my scars. Without the binding, I had the figure of a woman, and I wondered what everyone else would think when they found out — if they didn't already know.

But it didn't matter. I didn't care. As I stood there, becoming familiar with my new reflection, an unexpected peace flowed over me. Warmth filled my chest until it spread throughout my whole body.

I was alive. Scarred — yes. But I'd done it. I'd done what I needed to do to save Antion, to give Damian the chance to save our nation — and I'd survived.

For the first time since the day I'd had to chop off my hair and pretend to be a boy, I smiled at my reflection.

Lisbet left to prepare for the coronation, but I lingered for a few minutes, relishing the newfound peace I'd discovered — however brief it might be. There was so much ahead of me that was still going to be difficult, even heartbreaking. Guarding Damian would be torturous, but I wouldn't fail him, no matter how hard being near him would be. He still had a nation to rebuild.

And there were so many deaths to mourn.

But for this brief moment in time, I felt like I could face everything that waited for me.

When I finally walked into the outer chamber of Damian's quarters, Rylan stood across the room from me, and my tentative courage wavered. He heard the door and paused, not turning around yet. "Alex?"

"You can keep calling me that if you want, but I'm not going to hide who I am anymore," I said.

"Alexa, can I turn around?"

I walked to him, my heart pounding. "Yes," I said when I stood only a few feet away.

Slowly, he turned to face me. His eyes widened slightly, and I recoiled, thinking it was from the scars. But he shook his head. "No, it's not what you think — it's that . . . you . . . you're so beautiful."

I would have responded the same as I did to Lisbet, told him to stop lying, but I could see the truth in his eyes. He even flushed a little bit. "I'm glad you aren't hiding who you are anymore."

I nodded, and then took a deep breath. "Rylan," I began, my voice already trembling, "I'm so sorry."

A shadow crossed his face, but he reached out and took one of my hands in his, warm and reassuring. "Please don't apologize. Deron told me what happened. He told me how Jude sacrificed himself to give you the chance to attack Iker. I'm proud of him." His voice was thick with emotion.

"He wanted me to tell you that he loves you," I whispered.

Rylan nodded, and blinked hard a couple of times, his eyes glistening.

"Without his sacrifice, I wouldn't have been able to do it." My voice broke and Rylan looked away from me, trying to keep control. But then I stepped forward and wrapped my arms around him. He held me tightly as we cried together for all that we had lost.

Finally, he pulled back but kept his arms around me. He gazed into my face, and I knew he was one of those Lisbet had told me about — a person who loved me enough to see *me*, not my scars.

"Is it wrong to be grateful I'm still alive?" I asked.

"No." Rylan smiled sadly down at me. "It would make them happy to know that their deaths gave us the chance to live in peace and happiness. I think Jude and Marcel would want us to be happy."

"And Jaerom. And my parents," I agreed.

Rylan nodded and as he looked into my eyes, his expression changed. "I'm the one who needs to apologize for the way I acted in Blevon. It was the worst mistake of my life to treat you the way I did because I was jealous. When I thought I'd lost you without your knowing how I really felt . . . it tore me apart."

"Rylan, I —"

"Just let me get this out," he said, his arms tightening around me. "I told you once before, and nothing has changed. I love you, Alexa. I've loved you for years, and I will continue to love you. I know you don't feel that way about me. I know you love Damian." The pain in his eyes made me want to comfort him, but before I could respond, he kept going. "I think you made the right decision about him, though. He's going to be *king*. I don't think he realizes yet what that's going to mean."

Did everyone know I had rejected Damian? I'd hoped it would have been something private.

"What I'm trying to say is that I know you love him. But maybe with time, things will change. Maybe someday, you'll feel like you could give me a chance. I'll always be waiting and hoping for that day."

I stared up at him, my stomach in knots. "I can't do this right now, Rylan. I'm sorry. I did tell Damian no, but it was the hardest thing I've ever done."

"I know. I won't bring it up again. I just wanted you to know." He finally dropped his arms and stepped back.

I took a deep breath, trying to steady my racing nerves, my trembling hands.

"We should go," Rylan said. "You don't want to miss the coronation."

I looked at him for a moment longer and then nodded. "Okay. Let's go."

﹄ FORTY-SEVEN ﹃

T HE CORONATION WAS being held in the grand ballroom. When Rylan and I walked in, my heart skipped a beat. It was magnificent. Bowers of flowers adorned the walls and the beams high above us, cascading down in brilliant shades of purple, white, and fuchsia. The chandeliers hanging from the ceiling held thousands of candles that were already lit in preparation for the coming of night, and the afternoon sun filled the room with golden light. The ballroom was packed with noblemen and soldiers, women and children — as many as could fit in the pews that had been set up, lining both sides of the room. The bright and glittering tones of jewels and silks mingled with freshly cleaned and pressed cotton.

The aisle down the middle of the room had a thick red carpet rolled out, leading all the way up to the ornate throne where King Hector used to sit and watch his lavish parties. Standing next to the throne was a tall man with olive skin and dark hair liberally laced with gray. He wore a beautiful crown of gold, inlaid with diamonds and rubies.

Rylan and I walked forward and bowed to King Osgand of Blevon. Damian's great-uncle.

"You are the one who defeated Iker, I believe?" he asked when I had risen.

"Yes, Your Majesty," I replied.

"We all owe you a very large debt of gratitude." King Osgand's eyes were kind, but power exuded from him in a palpable wave. I wondered if he, too, was a sorcerer, or if this was just what decades of being a king — a *good* king — did to a man.

I bowed to him again, not sure of what to say. And then Rylan and I moved to join the rest of the guard, who stood in a row to the right of the throne. On the left side stood a line of men dressed in the colors of Blevon — King Osgand's guard, I assumed.

As I took my place next to Deron, I remembered that I wasn't the only one who had been left scarred by Iker and King Hector. Deron looked down at me, his eyes still full of sorrow, the scar on his face a vivid reminder of what he'd been through as well. Next to Rylan, the rest of the guard stood at attention, but when they saw me, they nodded or smiled. Every one of them — Deron, Jerrod, Asher, Mateo — bore the same scars on their faces. I couldn't believe that the six of us were all who remained of the prince's guard.

So much loss, so much death.

I stood tall, my hand on the hilt of my sword, and gazed out across the crowd. Many of them stared at me, whispering to one another. I wondered what they said — did they speak of my victory or my scars or my rejection of the king?

Then I caught sight of Kalen in the crowd, gripping her older brother's hand yet again, just as she'd done the first time I'd seen her. Only this time, she was smiling and so was he. And I realized I didn't care what the people of Antion were saying — whether they were judging me or not. This was why we had all sacrificed so much — to save innocent lives, like hers, from the horrors of King Hector's rule.

Lisbet sat in the front row, with Jax next to her. When I looked at her, she smiled at me and nodded. I knew what she was thinking, and I pulled back my shoulders and stood a little taller.

A trumpet sounded and the crowd instantly went quiet.

"All rise for Damian, king of Antion!"

Everyone stood as one and turned to face the back of the room. When I saw him standing there, wearing the rich scarlet robes of the king of Antion, the collar of office reflecting the sunlight, my heart stopped. He was overwhelmingly beautiful. He slowly walked forward, his expression composed. But his eyes were on mine the whole time. My pulse began to race.

When he stood before the throne and King Osgand, he finally looked away, turning his gaze up to his great-uncle.

"People of Antion," King Osgand spoke, his deep voice carrying across the ballroom. "This is a remarkable day — a day of celebration. Today is a day that you will speak of to your children, and your children will tell their children. It is the day that Antion rises from the dust and blood of her past and steps forward into a future of peace and prosperity!" He paused as the crowd erupted into cheers. My heart swelled as I watched Damian standing before King Osgand.

"You do not know your king yet, not as I know him. But he is a good man — just and true. He will lead Antion with a firm but gentle hand. No longer will your women and children live in fear."

There was more cheering as King Osgand reached down to the pedestal beside him, where the crown of Antion sat. He lifted it with both hands high into the air.

"Damian, former prince of Antion, kneel," he intoned.

A hush of anticipation fell upon the crowd as Damian dropped to one knee. Slowly, King Osgand lowered the crown until it hovered just above Damian's dark hair. "Do you, Damian of Antion, swear in front of these witnesses that you will do all in your power to lead, govern, and protect your people with justice and fairness?"

"I swear it," Damian responded.

"So it shall be." King Osgand placed the crown on Damian's head. "I give you Damian, king of Antion! Hail, King Damian, long live the king!"

Damian stood as the crowd repeated the cry, staring up at King Osgand for a moment, and then turned to look out over his people.

All of the guards pulled out their swords, lifting them into the air in salute to the new king.

"My people," Damian began, his voice sending a shiver through me. "Today marks the first day of a new era for Antion. An era of peace, starting with a renewed alliance with Blevon. As I have just sworn before you, I will do all in my power to lead you with fairness." He paused and turned to look straight at me. "This day would not have been possible without the help of *many* people who believed in me and aided me along the way. But above all, we owe our new freedom to one person."

My eyes widened when I realized what he was about to do.

"All hail, Alexa Hollen!" he cried out.

There were gasps from the crowd as jaws dropped and hands flew to mouths. But when he shouted it again, his people eventually joined with him.

"All hail, Alexa Hollen!"

"All hail, Alexa Hollen!"

My heart pounded. What did he think he was doing?

"We owe you our very lives," he continued when the crowd quieted again. "This is the day of my coronation, but I would not be here without you." And then he pressed his fist to his shoulder as I had done so many times, and bowed to me.

I stared at him, stunned.

Then Lisbet dropped to one knee, followed by Jax at her side. General Tinso was next, then Eljin. Slowly at first, but then with greater and greater speed, the entire crowd lowered to their knees, bowing their heads to me. Even my fellow guards dropped down to the ground, their fists pressed to their shoulders.

I was at once honored and mortified. Did Damian hope to make me rethink my decision by doing this? No matter how grand a gesture it was, it didn't change the truth of our situation. Tears burned in my eyes as I returned Damian's bow. He smiled at me, a tender smile that made my heart ache, and then he straightened up.

"My people, will you join with me in leading Antion into a future that is brighter than it ever has been before?" King Damian asked as the crowd rose to their feet again.

Many of those gathered broke into cheers and gazed up at their king with something I'd never seen before — *hope*. But there was so much pain and fear still written on the faces of the women who cradled babies in their bony arms. In the tight stance of the men and boys in tattered uniforms, not quite sure how to relax, not to always be on guard.

There was still a long way to go to reach out for that bright future Damian was promising us.

But no matter what came next, I knew that this moment would be branded on my mind and heart forever. Damian looked at me once more, and this time, when he smiled, it was with the brightness of the sun that burst through the windows, painting everything gold and white.

I nodded at him, returning his smile. But mine was tinged with bittersweet regret. There was still so much ahead of us. So much work to be done, so many wounds to be healed — inside and out. But he was right. The future had never been brighter — now that *he* was the king of Antion.

And I would be at his side, guarding him from the dangers that lay ahead. As I watched my new king take his place on the throne of Antion, my fingers tightened around the hilt of my sword.

⊰ ACKNOWLEDGMENTS ⊱

Wow, I have dreamt of writing an acknowledgments page for so long, it's hard to believe it's really happening! Over the many years it has taken me to get to this point, the list of those I need to thank has continued to change and grow. There have been so many wonderful and amazing people along this long road who deserve more than just a mention in my book, but I guess this is what you'll have to settle for!

First of all, I have to thank the incredible Lisa Sandell. I feel like I won the editor lottery — I can't imagine a more phenomenal person to work with on this book. Thank you for believing in *Defy*, for loving my characters as much as I do, and for turning a lifelong dream into a reality. Your passion for what you do and your talent in helping me shape this story into the best it could be have meant the world to me. Thank you for everything, including your friendship!

A huge cheer (and a hi-*YAH!*) for my amazing ninja agent, Josh Adams, the reason any of this is happening. I somehow lucked out to not only get an incredible agent, but also gain a trusted friend and advisor in you. Thank you for everything you've done and continue to do to bring my dreams into reality! And thank you also to Tracey and the rest of the fantastic Adams Literary team and family!

Thank you to everyone at Scholastic who has worked so hard to bring my story to life and to the shelf. Thank you all for your belief in *Defy*; for the gorgeous cover that literally took my breath away (and then caused me to commence screaming, and jumping up and down) because I was so happy when I saw it; and all of the little and big steps along the way that take a manuscript and turn it into a book.

Endless thanks go to the many readers over the years — there are too many to list them all. Every one of you, who has read my book and loved it or told me you believed in me, has helped more than you can know. But I'm going to try and list off a few:

Elisse, you have read for me from the beginning — way back when the books were handwritten. Your support has lifted me up when I was down. I'm so grateful to have such a fantastic, understanding friend and critique partner in my sister. Thank you for being willing to read endless drafts, and for always having a positive word for me no matter how low I got!

A, T, and E, way back in the beginning, your support, friendship, help, and advice meant so much to me. Thanks also to Stephanni Myers (no, not that one) whose editorial experience and advice helped shape the writer I am today and taught me that all those red marks covering the pages meant she liked it!

Thanks to Ally, for being there for me during a pivotal moment with chocolate, music, a note, and more. Just what I needed! And thank you for continuing to be a wonderful friend and support through the years.

Thank you to Natalie Whipple for your friendship, support, and critiques. You've always been there for me, and I can't thank you enough!

Thank you to Hannah Brown Gordon for believing in me first; I will always be grateful. And to Mandy for being the first to adore *Defy* — thank you.

I wish I could list every person who ever helped me, but it would be impossible. This is an attempt to acknowledge some of the people who have been pivotal to my journey: Julie Berry, Brodi Ashton, Bree Despain, Elana Johnson, Chersti Nieveen, Carolina Valdez Miller, Anne Blankman, Bethany Hudson, Michelle Argyle, Kasie West, Renee Collins, Sara Raasch, Candice Kennington, Jenn Johansson, Elle Strauss, everyone from the *best* BYU WIFYR group ever, the incredible YA Valentines, Sarah Cox, Stacey Ratliff, Dialma Jensen, and Erin Thain, and so many more. . . . Thank you for supporting me and my crazy dreams, for reading or critiquing queries or manuscripts for me, and above all for your friendships.

Kathryn Purdie — I'm so grateful for you in my life. You are the reason I dared hit send on those queries for *Defy*. Your love of this story meant the world to me, but far more important has been the gift of your friendship. Thank you!

Kerstin, Kaitlyn, and Lauren — I'm so grateful for your support and love. Thank you for reading and loving my stories over the years. All four of my sisters are the best cheerleaders and best friends a girl could hope for! (Lauren, I'm still lobbying for you to play Alexa someday. I'll let you know how that goes.)

Mom, I can't thank you enough. For being the person I want to be when I grow up. For believing in me. For always reading and giving your honest feedback. I hope I've made you proud! Dad, who is the best dad a girl could ask for! Thank you so, so much for everything. I always know I can count on you for anything, anytime. No matter what. How lucky am I?

To my in-laws, Marilyn and Robert, for being excited for me and for helping spread the word and for your support — thank you!

To Hans Zimmer, Florence and the Machine, James Horner, Sia, Imogen Heap, and so many other composers and musicians whose music has helped inspire me over and over again. I can't write without the perfect song to match my mood, and your music has been on repeat for a long, long time.

And last, but far from least, my family. To my three beautiful children, who love me despite my failings as a mom and my long hours "working on my book" on the computer. You are my angels. The gift of being your mother is one I hope to be good enough to deserve someday. To Trav — my rock, my support, my everything. You never stopped believing, you never stopped cheering me on, you never let me even talk about quitting. You are the one who kept me going no matter what, no matter how desperate things were. There aren't words adequate enough, but this will have to suffice: Thank you, I love you — now and forever.

⊰ ABOUT THE AUTHOR ⊱

Sara B. Larson can't remember a time when she didn't write books — although, she now uses a computer instead of a Little Mermaid notebook. Sara lives in Utah with her husband and their three children. She writes during nap time and the quiet hours when most people are sleeping. Her husband claims she should have a degree in "the art of multitasking." On occasion you will find her hiding in a bubble bath with a book and some Swedish Fish.